GUNPOWDER LIGHTNING

Bloodshed and bitter hatred—a hatred that bursts into flame in Texas and burns all the way north into Montana's Bear Paw Mountains—because Old Gene Stark and his eight sons refused to be pushed around by Bill Parsons, a self-appointed cattle king.

Caught in the middle is young Brock Parsons. He despises his father's utterly ruthless intention to own more cattle than any other man—and he loves Louise Stark, who is the daughter of his father's sworn enemy. It is a bitter and thrilling destiny that he works out for himself.

Bertrand W. Sinclair was born in Edinburgh, Scotland, and was raised in Canada. He spent seven years as a cowboy in Montana, riding the range and hearing first-hand about the real-life exploits of frontier outlaws. With his first marriage, to previously married Western author B.M. Bower, Sinclair struck a bargain of exchange. Sinclair would tell Bower everything he knew about cowboying in exchange for her teaching him how to write. Bower wrote stories for various Street & Smith magazines, and before long Sinclair's fiction, usually stories set in the Northwest, began appearing in the same magazines, sometimes in the same issues. This marriage, that began in 1906, ended in scandal in 1911. Sinclair wrote fifteen novels of Western and North-Western fiction, four of which were made into motion pictures. After his first marriage, he returned to Canada, settling eventually in Pender Harbour, British Columbia, and becoming a commercial fisherman. One of his most popular novels was *Poor Man's Rock* (Little, Brown, 1920), a North-Western about the salmon-fishing fleet he came to know so well. Among his most noteworthy later titles are Westerns like *Pirates of the Plains* (Hodder and Stoughton, 1928) and *Gunpowder Lightnings* (Little, Brown, 1930). He turned his boat, the Hoo Hoo, into a trawler, and in a final astonishing trip, when the Hoo Hoo was 55 and he was 83, he trolled around Vancouver Island. Although by the end of 1930s, Sinclair had quit writing, the early 1950s brought renewed popularity to his earlier work, with stories being reprinted in Zane Grey's Western Magazine and many of his novels being reprinted in paperback editions by Dell Books. *Pender Harbour Cowboy: The Many Lives Of Bertrand Sinclair* (Victoria: Horsdal & Schubart, 2000) by Betty C. Keller is the first book-length biography of this skilled author and fisherman who lived his life to the full to an advanced age.

GUNPOWDER LIGHTNING

Bertrand W Sinclair

GUNSMOKE

This hardback edition 2002
by Chivers Press
by arrangement with
Golden West Literary Agency

ISBN 0 7540 8201 6

British Library Cataloguing in Publication Data available.

X000 000 006 1522

Printed and bound in Great Britain by
BOOKCRAFT, Midsomer Norton, Somerset

Gunpowder Lightning

Chapter One

Bulls Minus

Every American schoolboy knows that upon a certain day in the '60's a certain group of men fired on Fort Sumter. Whereupon these United States embarked upon four years, more or less, of intensive warfare—which, promising to disintegrate a powerful nation, ended by welding it into an indissoluble unit. Like all great wars, the by-products of this struggle were numerous and varied.

When the echoes of Gettysburg died away, close on two million men began to scatter over the face of North America. They were inured to hardship, accustomed to bloodshed. War colors the human sense of values. A soldier is taught to turn the other cheek only for the purposes of retaliation upon the enemy. Grant's cavalry, Lee's dragoons, Quantrell's guerrillas, were men suddenly without an occupation save to seek fortune and adventure in private life with all the dash and ferocity war had taught them.

They were true men on horseback, properly contemptuous of those who toiled afoot. It followed naturally that in search of profitable activity a lot of them gravitated west of the Mississippi, to a region where the horseman was king. Buffalo blanketed the plains. Hunting them was an industry. Placer gold abounded. California, Colorado, the Black Hills in Dakota, Last Chance and Virginia City in Montana were already sending virgin gold to the mint. The Rockies and all its lesser ranges were haunted by fur-bearing animals.

The end of the Civil War, a million restless, eager souls, competent in any desperate situation, afraid of nothing but inactive monotony—this aspect of what helped to make the West wild is commended to historians.

One phase of its manifold phases is of immediate concern, that which ultimately contributed to Louise Stark finding a personable young man lying wounded and unconscious under a cottonwood tree on the bank of an unnamed fork of the Republican River in western Nebraska.

The Starks were three generations Texas born when the Civil War broke out. A Stark died in the Alamo. Another rode to its relief. One Corrigan Stark had a home and ranch and cattle on the Brazos before Texas came into the Union. He begat a son, Eugene, who eventually went off to fight in the Civil War. He was wounded and discharged from active service in '64—and the following year his only daughter, Louise, was born in Forth Worth. Prior to his war experience Eugene Stark already had six sons.

At about the time this Eugene Stark, the only son of Corrigan, was big enough to gallop a pony back and forth between his father's ranch and school, a lanky youth named Bill Parsons came out of the hot lowlands bordering the Mississippi by Memphis, Tennessee. Parsons was restless, ambitious. He followed his nose with little care where it led him. A restless, ambitious man west of the Father of Waters in those days could find plenty of scope for any sort of undertaking, lawful or otherwise. Young Parsons wandered into the cattle country, into Kansas, cut his eyeteeth in the dust of Longhorn herds. He ended up eventually on the Nueces River in southern Texas riding for a cattleman who had no sons and only one daughter. Parsons married this daughter. In ten years his father-in-law retired to Houston with ample funds to give him all he wanted for the rest of his days. Even so early the cattle business in the Southwest was a gold mine. This man left his son-in-law, Bill Parsons, in charge of a good ranch on the Nueces, nearly twenty thousand longhorns and innumerable horses.

In another decade the retired cattleman was dead. Bill Parsons and his wife inherited the entire estate. During that decade, under Parsons's management, the original brand somehow got transformed into a WP. And WP stock increased and multiplied on the Nueces until it seemed as if they would overrun the earth.

Life is curious. It is orderly, progressive. Or it is intricate, obscure, a complex pattern of which only crossed threads may be seen here and there. Who can say that certain things are a matter of choice or a matter of destiny?

Five years before the outbreak of the Civil War Eugene Stark on the Trinity River was a lesser cattleman by far than William Parsons away south on the Nueces. Each was successful to such degree as success comes to able energetic men. The chief difference lay in that Parsons married the foundation of his fortune and Eugene Stark built his up bit by bit from nothing with his own hands. Neither knew the other, at that time. Parsons had never heard of the Long S on the Trinity. The Starks knew the WP on the Nueces, as all big cow outfits are known far beyond their own range.

There would have been no affinity between them if they had known each other. That much is certain. Parsons was physically a big man, beefy, heavy-handed, determined, arrogant. He took what he wanted wherever he could, without compunction, without mercy. He was tolerably good-natured until he encountered opposition to his will or his plans, or his ambition. Then he brushed away such opposition as a housewife brushes away dust.

Bill Parsons had the acquisitive instinct powerfully developed along two lines—land and cattle. That became a passion with him. He wanted more and more. He aspired, dimly at first, definitely at last, to be the greatest individual cattle owner in North America. When he gave a dinner in Houston or San Antonio, in Kansas City, even in St. Louis, such places as he went for business or diversion, occasionally he would drink enough to make him talkative. Then he would announce his ambition.

Eugene Stark, on the other hand, was apparently a mild, open-handed man, an amiable citizen who did well enough in the cow business, who was more proud of his numerous sons than of his material possessions. His ranch house on the Trinity was comfortable to the point of luxury. He had never taken issue with a man in his life unless it was forced upon him. With experience of both actual and private war he preferred peace. Yet it was an accepted fact in the Trinity country that neither Eugene Stark nor any of his sons would step aside an inch in the face of a declared enemy. It was both their code and their nature to be considerate, kindly, easy-going until they were aware of some deliberate transgression of their rights, privileges, or possessions. In other words the Starks were easy men to get on with and bad men to stir up.

Eugene Stark married young. His oldest son was a full-grown man when his father returned from the Union-Confederate clash.

Bill Parsons also married young. His wife presented him with an heir the first year. Thereafter for a long time she was childless. Four years before the war she gave birth to a second son and straightway became a semi-invalid, ruling her house, and her husband in so far as she was able, from a couch.

Mrs. Parsons was anything but a nonentity. She had ideas about life and living which her husband tolerantly listened to but never put in practice. She had very little education, in the broad sense of the term. Neither had Bill Parsons. He had horse sense, a native shrewdness, breadth of vision as applied to certain potential phases of the cattle business. But of the niceties of living he knew little and cared less. Education to him meant ability to read, write, and reckon figures. He bred his oldest son to the saddle, a second edition of himself in physique, speech, and action.

But with the second boy, born late in life, his wife's craving for culture, her slowly accumulated dreams of something approaching gentility, focused on the younger offspring. She made an issue of his upbringing. He should be a gentleman. He must have schooling that would fit him for something more than hard riding, hard drinking, round-up camps, and cow towns. He might, she secretly hoped, be a doctor or a lawyer—something learned—something of a higher quality than the common run. He must go to such institutions as rich men's sons frequented.

"What difference is there between you and Matt and any cowpuncher on your payroll?" she demanded once of her husband, "except that you own the cattle and they don't? What's the good of our money if our children can't be somebody?"

She had her way. A half-sick woman, persistent in her clamors, can wear down the strongest man. And Bill Parsons was fond of his wife, in his own fashion. He had been proud of her once. The bloom was long gone from her, and he went his way as it suited him. So he conceded the point.

"Oh, all right," he said. "Matt's been raised the way a cowman ought to be, an' he's some punkins. See you make as good a job of the baby if you bring him up accordin' to *your* ideas. If you want somebody in the family quick on the trigger with double-barreled words an' used to boiled shirts an' a plug hat, why I expect we can stand it. It's agreeable to me for you to make a gentleman of him if you can. But watch out you don't make him just another blamed dude!"

So the youngest Parsons began life with cultural prospects that his father and brother alike regarded as of small value. And coincident with these prospects and the close of the Civil War, Bill Parsons began to outgrow the Nueces country. His herds increased. He bought out neighboring outfits. Eventually, by one means and another, he dominated all that immediate region. Unable to expand farther, he began to look abroad. And the chance meeting in Dallas with a cattleman who was shifting most of his cattle off the Trinity river and had a ranch with tremendous acreage to sell, brought the Parsons interests into direct contact with the Starks.

This purchase, made in the year of our Lord 1882, made Parsons owner of a rich area of bottomland along the Trinity thirty miles above the home ranch of the Stark family. That particular range would easily carry twenty thousand cattle. As a starter, Parsons sent three big herds up from the Nueces with a hustling, aggressive range boss named Polk Munce in charge of the new layout.

Munce was a hired man, in much the same sense that

the president of a corporation is frequently a hired man. Without actual ownership the president has the delegated power of the owners. So had Polk. Bill Parsons sent him to the Trinity with ten thousand cattle. He gave him a checking account in a Fort Worth bank, outlined a policy for him, told him to get results—which is a business synonym for profits.

Polk was a smart cowman. He looked over the Trinity and outlined his ideas. Parsons agreed that they were sound. The Nueces was stocked to the limit. So the cattle he sent to the new range were all breeding stock, dry cows, cows with calves at foot. Out of the three herds there were five thousand two-year-old heifers.

"In five years," said Polk Munce, "we'll have so damned many cattle on the Trinity some of these little fellers will have to move out."

Parsons nodded. He, himself, was already preparing to move, along far-seeing lines. The Northwest was opening up. Breed in the south, fatten his steers on northern grass. If Wyoming and Montana were half as good as reported, Parsons could see himself realizing his ambition—the biggest, wealthiest cattle owner north of the Rio Grande. He could even be a Terrazzas, pastoral emperor of the State of Sonora, with five hundred Mexican *vaqueros,* five thousand saddle stock, and three hundred thousand cattle under his brand—lord of the high justice, the middle, and the low, over the leagues upon leagues of land he owned by grace of Porfirio Diaz.

There wasn't a chance for such feudal power in the United States. But with a strangle hold on the Nueces, increasing scope on the Trinity, his beef steers shifted north year by year to fatten on buffalo grass, up there where ten thousand square miles of virgin pasture scarcely vacated by the vanishing bison could be had for the taking—well, Parsons could visualize tremendous pastoral operations with the assurance that he could carry them out.

So Polk Munce hit the Trinity river with his ten thousand cows. The first two herds arrived according to Hoyle.

But with the succeeding two composed of five thousand heifers, either Bill Parsons or Polk Munce—experienced cattlemen, both—made a curious mistake.

They neglected to send along a quota of bulls.

Chapter Two

A Taste of Their Own Medicine

IF AN ISOLATED TOWN with a normally balanced population of men, women, and children were to suffer a sudden invasion from overwhelming numbers of young and attractive women, the result may be imagined. The result of these five thousand heifers turned loose on the Long S range doesn't need to be imagined. It is a matter of record, written first in gun smoke and blood, later set down in black and white in the county court records of Oxbow.

In every land under the sun men have clashed because of slights real or fancied, over possession of desired objects, over the mere matter of disliking the shape of each other's faces. The cattle country had its collisions over range rights, over trespass by sheep, over water which is always precious in a dry land. The Trinity country beheld a ruction over a scarcity of longhorned bulls.

The WP herds arrived on the Trinity in the height of the breeding season. A week later Eugene Stark and his son Dave rode into the newly acquired Parsons ranch. Polk Munce sat sunning himself on the porch. A cowpuncher pointed him out when the Starks asked for the foreman.

They didn't immediately dismount at Polk's invitation. They sat sidewise in their saddles looking down.

"I understand," old Gene said, "that you have right lately turned loose about five thousand heifers on the edge of my range—without ary a bull among 'em."

"We overlooked the bulls," Polk drawled, "for the time bein'."

"Here's hopin' you don't overlook 'em too long," old man Stark observed politely. "It was kinda careless of you. Them young cows are wanderin' all over my range. I been to quite a lot of trouble an' expense improvin' the grade of my stock with Hereford bulls from Ioway. It ain't hardly the thing for Bill Parsons to expect me to supply him with free bulls for breedin' purposes. That's about what it amounts to, as she stands. I'd like for to have you attend to this here bull business right away."

"Oh, sure, we will," Polk declared. "We'll have a herd of bulls up here right off."

The Starks had dinner with Polk Munce and the WP riders, and parted from them affably enough.

A couple of weeks later Clay Stark with a trace of irritation said to his father, "Dad, them tarnation WP heifers is everywhere. We'll have less'n half a calf crop next spring. I'd put a bug in Bill Parsons's ear about it."

His father nodded agreement. Once more he took his son Dave and rode to the Parsons ranch, half a day's jaunt up the Trinity, on the opposite side of the river. Polk Munce had gone to Oxbow, they learned. Stark would not discuss such a matter with anyone but the boss of the WP. So he rode home. The following morning he hitched a buggy and drove into Oxbow.

Polk was still there. Polk wasn't a drinking man, but for once he happened to be well-primed, as a result of a big winning at poker. Polk had a mean, arrogant streak in him that seldom appeared when he had himself in hand. Furthermore he was on pleasure bent. He resented an elderly cattleman calling him to account in a hotel lobby over this matter of bulls.

If Polk Munce hadn't been well lubricated, he would have noted that Eugene Stark drew him aside, and though he was very peevish his complaint was couched politely. Polk simply didn't want to be bothered about bulls. In addition he may have been influenced unconsciously by a long sojourn in the atmosphere of the Nueces. There the WP was monarch of all its riders surveyed and WP bosses were never called to account for anything by lesser cattlemen. Polk was used to having the right of way both on the range and in any argument concerning the rights and privileges of the outfit he represented.

"Hell," he snarled at Stark. "Quit roarin' about that. We'll 'tend to it when we get around to it. What difference does a few bulls make?"

"Make a difference of maybe two thousand calves to me next spring," old Eugene said quietly. "You're handin' the Long S a raw deal, I want you to know, whether it's through carelessness or ignorance. I want you to get your share of bulls on that range an' get 'em there quick. The WP had no license in the first place to throw all them heifers on my side of the river. Since there's plenty of room if you all shoot square I'm not makin' an argument about that. But I'm certainly tellin' you about these bulls."

"You can't tell me nothin'," Polk replied haughtily. "The WP'll run any range it takes hold of to suit itself. Roll your hoop, old-timer. The powwow's over."

"You're drinkin' an' your tongue's run away with you, Mister Polk Munce," the old man answered tartly. "If you want to make an issue of this, it's up to you. But you can put this in your pipe to smoke: I'll take means to protect my stock—if you ain't got a matter of two-three hundred bulls loose on that range in ten days."

He turned his back on Polk, disregarding certain rumblings which made his eyes glint a little. A man with liquor in him sometimes spoke out of his turn. So old Gene walked steadily away. There was another hotel in Oxbow. He went to that.

Before he turned homeward he amplified these remarks in a letter to Bill Parsons on the Nueces River, and posted it forthwith. Then he drove home to wait out the ten days.

He got no reply to his letter. No bulls appeared, so far as his sons, daily abroad on the range, could discern.

"Darn 'em," old Gene growled at last. "They asked for it an 'they'll get it. I aim to be neighborly. But I aim to protect myself also. This high-handed outfit from the Nueces can't get away with nothin' like that."

Whereupon the Long S roundup wagon went out with a crew, began to gather and throw south of the Trinity River all those WP heifers that were illicitly engaging the attention of the Long S bulls. The Stark feelings in this matter were not soothed by gossip that went drifting around. Texas appreciated a joke along broad lines. The

WP on the Trinity regarded this bull business as something of a joke on the Starks. The WP riders said so. What they said was repeated.

But it ceased to be a joke one afternoon when old man Stark, Ed, Clay, Dave, and young Con, with three hired hands, were shoving several hundred WPs out of the shallows of the Trinity onto the south bank.

Polk Munce rode down to meet them with a dozen riders at his back. He was sober, cool, but annoyed. They faced each other, eight riders in one group, thirteen in the other, all armed.

"Stark," Polk Munce said. "You got no business punchin' WP cattle around on the range, an' you know it."

"You got no business havin' five thousand WP heifers on my range without no bulls among 'em an' *you* know it," old Gene returned calmly. "I give you plenty of time to remedy that. You didn't, so I'm goin' to remedy it m'self."

"If you throw another hoof of our stuff across the Trinity there'll be trouble," Munce warned.

"Then there'll have to be trouble, I reckon," Stark replied firmly. "Because they're all goin' south of the river an' they're goin' to stay there till Bill Parsons supplies his share of bulls."

There was nothing Polk could do in the face of that plain defiance. So he contented himself by repeating stubbornly that the Long S had no right to shove WP cattle around on a public range, on free government land—and he would see about it if they did. With that he rode away with his men.

The Starks splashed back through the river, loped to their camp, ate, mounted fresh horses, made another roundup. Ten miles farther up the Trinity, in the blaze of a Texas sunset, they shoved another three or four hundred WP heifers into the stream.

On the opposite bank a crackle of gunfire arose. Clay Stark's horse collapsed under him. A hired cowpuncher put his hand to his side, looked with curious pained wonder at the blood that stained his fingers, and slid slowly sidewise out of his saddle. Ed Stark cursed as his mount spun in a circle, stung by a bullet.

These hostile guns continued to speak with thin whip-cracking voices. Dust flew in spurts under their horses' bellies. Another Stark rider went down. Dave Stark felt a burning streak across his chest.

"Get into the brush," old Gene barked.

A post oak clump gave them cover—five men mounted, one afoot. Two others lay still in the grass back of a gravelly strip of shore. Bullets whistled over them. The Starks didn't shoot. They could see nothing to shoot at.

"The damn dirty bushwhackers!" Clay ground his teeth. He was brown-skinned, black-eyed, dark like an Indian, the only dark man among the Stark sons who ran to light brown hair and gray eyes. Clay had something like aboriginal ferocity in him. His face was pale with rage.

"Hurt bad, Dave?" he demanded.

"Nothin' to speak of," Dave grunted. "Don't cripple me none."

"Let's go for 'em, Dad," Clay pleaded. "Come on. We're not goin' to stand this, not from nobody."

Old Gene gestured for silence. He scanned the farther bank, the river, the flat bottoms that lined the opposite side.

"Over there's a draw with scrub an' chapparal," said he. "If we hit the river on the run, an' keep dodgin' through cover, we can make that draw an' get up through it to the top of the bank where they are."

They all carried .44 Winchester carbines, short-barreled saddle guns. Without having discussed it as a probability, they had half-expected trouble—but not from ambush. That stirred them to fury. To retaliate was as natural as breathing. The Texan quite literally accepted the old Hebraic dictum of an eye for an eye.

"Wait for me a minute," Clay said. He was afoot. He had run a few yards to that timber. Now he went crawling back through the grass until he reached one horse whose rider would never mount again.

He swung up and darted back and his movement

brought two or three shots. The shooting light was none too good in that river bottom. Long shadows slanted down, black bars bisecting the last of the sunglow.

"You-all ready?" Stark senior inquired. "Keep abreast of me, but spread out considerable."

They nodded. Bending forward in their saddles, they hit the river on the run, breasted it where the current rose to their knees, pounded through and up the opposite bank, where they galloped, weaving behind clumps of brush, leafy scrub oaks, until they surged into the mouth of that draw which came down like a trough from the upper levels. Polk Munce's gunmen—presumably—kept up a scattered fire with no hits on such fast-moving targets. The Starks reckoned on that. Their casualties had come as they sat still on the opposite shore watching the WP cattle take the stream. They knew how hard it was to hit a rider on the run three hundred yards away.

So they plunged up that draw without fear, spurred by anger and excitement, until they reached a point where it was an easy climb to the top. They took that slope with blood in their eye.

The plains ran away level as a floor, cut at great intervals by arroyos, by an occasional pothole. They could see cattle and horses, but WP riders, riders of any sort, there were none. They charged like cavalry to the crest whence the shots had come. Hoof marks in a little bunch where the horses had stood together. Flattened places in the grass on the rim of the valley where men had lain prone to take aim. Scattered empty cartridges bright in the grass where they had been levered out.

"They dropped into the river bottom an' streaked for home when they seen us take into that draw to get behind 'em," Clay declared. "There's their dust. See?"

They saw.

"There were five of 'em layin' here, one holdin' the horses back outa sight," Clay continued bitterly. "They didn't have the guts to stand an' make a fight for it. It's only ten miles to the WP, Dad. Let's follow up an' give 'em a taste of their own medicine!"

Chapter Three

REPRISAL

THE MOON SENT LONG SHADOWS slanting away behind each rider when Eugene Stark and his sons jogged slowly on tired horses back to the point of attack. Clay's horse lay where he fell, silver conchos on saddle and bridle gleaming against the carcass. One riderless beast stood patiently on drooping reins. And the two Stark riders who had fallen under the first shots were stiff in the grass.

They lashed both bodies across one horse and climbed out of the valley. On the rim they halted to look back. A faint glow tinged the horizon up the river, on the south side.

"I reckon that'll hold 'em for a while," Clay said harshly.

Giving the WP a taste of their own medicine had been a considerable success. Hotly determined, the Stark men had chased the other six into their own dooryard and dismounting on a rise above the ranch had fired on everything that moved until the light failed. In the dusk, Clay, unknown to the others, had stolen down and fired a haystack. The flames spread to buildings, to the dry grass, and licked out on the open range. That was the glow on the skyline, miles of WP grass turning into a black-ash waste.

They were not particularly pleased with that stroke. Yet neither his father nor brothers could criticize Clay—not in the face of two men shot from ambush, not when Dave could scarcely sit in his saddle from pain in his torn side. And they knew Clay Stark. Once started on the warpath, he was a wolf. He would have fought the WP single-handed.

"Dirty murderers," he broke the silence again. "We'd oughto hung around an' picked 'em off to the last bushwhackin' hound—all but one, an' left him to go back to the Nueces to tell Bill Parsons this is a white man's range."

"We done enough," his father said. "They'll think twice before they jump us again."

They buried the two cowpunchers. Dave went into Oxbow to have his wound attended to and report the affray to the authorities. The rest of the Starks went on gathering WP heifers and shoving them across the Trinity, and watching to see that none crossed back.

Nor did the Long S work short-handed. Certain lusty youths began to ride up to the Stark roundup shortly after Dave reached Oxbow. The dead riders had friends, eager to take their places. Old Gene told these cowpunchers there might be trouble. They merely frowned and shrugged their shoulders.

So the Long S had a full complement of riders and for over a week they put Parsons cattle by the hundred over the Trinity until their range was all but clear of these longhorns from the Nueces. And neither Polk Munce nor any WP riders ever loomed on the horizon.

Then the sheriff of Oxbow country drove out to the Stark roundup in a side-bar buggy. He was a middle-aged, rotund person well qualified for his office and he had known the Starks all his life.

"I got a warrant for you-all, Gene," said he. "You an' the boys—the whole kit an' boilin' of you. 'Tain't no more agreeable to me than it is to you, but Parsons has swore to complaints chargin' you-all with murder, arson, an' such. Most every crime on the calendar it seems like. You better appear for a preliminary hearin' an' arrange bail. Hope it don't put you out much."

"So that's how they're goin' to make the next play, is it?" old Gene smiled. "Well, seein' we're all under arrest, Walter, we won't embarrass you none by resistin'."

Oxbow beheld the spectacle next day, of a reputable citizen with six sons and five other cowpunchers like a bodyguard around Walter Doag's side-bar buggy. They made an imposing cavalcade. The cook tooled the chuck wagon far in the rear, to make camp in the outskirts of town with the *remuda* grazing on scanty grass.

Oxbow citizens walked with a wary eye that afternoon

and evening. Bill Parsons, Polk Munce, and a dozen WP riders—all Nueces men—were in town. Oxbow had seen feuds come to a climax more than once in its dusty streets. A scowl, a tart word, could easily touch off an explosion.

Yet both sides stepped softly. They kept each to their own side of the street. Parsons had appealed to the law, and the Starks were content to let it go at that. Old Gene cautioned his sons and his men.

"We got the best of it, as it stands," he declared. "Nothin' we can do will bring them two boys back to life. If the WP wants to be showed up in court let 'em have it thataway. Keep your mouths shut an' your guns in your holsters."

"I will bet you a dollar to a plugged nickel," Clay said, "that this Parsons outfit aims to have one good crack at us right here in this town before we get out of it. This bringin' us to trial is a joke—or a bluff to get us bunched here. They can't prove a thing only what we admit. They can't get away from the fact that they ambushed us, killed two of our boys, and nicked Dave."

"Just the same, you hold that temper of yours down, young feller," his father said sternly.

"I will," Clay promised. "But you'll see."

Yet it was Clay himself who started the gunpowder lightning flashing across Oxbow's sky. No one, not even his father, ever blamed him. It was inevitable, and loyalty in the Stark family had no reservations.

Clay said nothing more. He kept with his father and brothers. They walked in a body to the office of the local justice of the peace, an old 'dobe building, between a hardware store and a hotel.

The Starks lined one side of the room. The WP contingent sat or stood along the other. The J.P. humped behind a desk, a trifle annoyed because cattlemen's difficulties took him from a hardware business that required his individual attention. It was hot and stuffy in that room. Walter Doag had quietly sworn in four more deputies to reinforce his regular staff of two. As much of Oxbow's population as could crowd in was there to look and listen.

Two dozen armed men, who had already been at each other's throats, didn't help to make the atmosphere less electric.

Parsons had a Fort Worth lawyer sitting by, although the proceedings were in the hands of the Oxbow prosecuting attorney. A little buzz ran around the room when it transpired that each member of the Stark family had an individual charge against him. Old Gene and six sons—seven separate trials.

Stark's lawyer protested. "These offenses as charged," he declared, "if any, which we do not admit, could only be the result of these men acting in a body. To commit each separately for trial is an unwarranted proceeding, as well as an entirely unnecessary expense, both to my clients and the county. I object. I demand that the complaints be thrown out or amended."

"My learned friend," the county attorney admitted with a frown, "is probably correct. But objections cannot be sustained. There are the individual charges, duly sworn to by the complainant."

The Starks pleaded not guilty as a matter of form. The J.P. listened to evidence from both sides. Polk Munce and his men denied flatly the ambush from the river bank. The Starks didn't deny the raid on the WP ranch. They went outside the questioning of the J.P. and the county attorney to demand who shot at them. They cited what proof they had that the WP men fired on them. Out of it all stood the salient fact that two Stark riders and one WP man had been killed and three more Parsons men carried bullet marks. Property to the value of many thousand dollars had been destroyed by fire. Ten square miles of good grass had gone up in smoke.

It was no duty of the J.P. to determine guilt. His business was simply to decide if the evidence warranted committal for trial in the county court.

So presently Eugene Stark and his six sons were bound over in the sum of three thousand dollars each to appear for trial when the fall term of court began. Before the words were out of the court's mouth bondsmen stepped forward. Old Gene had reckoned on that necessity.

And the justice of the peace would thereupon have dismissed court. But Stark's lawyer checked the words on his lips.

"I ask for the arrest of Polk Munce on a charge of murder and of William Parsons as accessory after the fact," said he sharply. "We wish to swear to a complaint embodying these charges. I ask that these men be apprehended before they leave the jurisdiction of this court."

"Arrest *me?*" Bill Parsons rose to his feet. "Charge *me* with murder? I'd like to see you get away with that."

His lawyer pulled him down by his coat tails. They whispered together. Old Walter Doag stood by stroking his sandy mustache while the complaints were duly sworn. Then he stepped over to Polk Munce and Parsons.

"You're under arrest, both of you," said he. "As a matter of formality these here two deputies uh mine'll stand by you. You can't either of you leave this courtroom. I expect Judge Simmons'll give you a hearin' right away."

"Hell, this is ridiculous!" Parsons fumed. "Far as I'm personally concerned I was four hundred miles away on the Nueces when this fuss come off."

"Sorry. Law's law," Doag replied laconically. "I ain't no judge. I'm an officer of Oxbow county, doin' my duty."

They were duly committed for trial, the justice of the peace hurrying through the formalities. Parsons and Munce were allowed bail, which they proceeded to arrange. Everybody filed out.

A dozen steps from the door a WP man stopped to glare at Clay Stark. And Clay stopped to glare back.

"Think you'll know me again?" he inquired coldly.

"Run along with poppa," the WP man sneered, "before you git spanked."

"Try spankin' me, will you," Clay's dark eyes blazed. "You'll find it a man's job."

"Oh, I dunno," the fellow drawled. "I've spanked bigger boys 'n you."

Men stepped quickly aside from behind both of them, not so much at the words as the tone. Both stood still, like antagonists left staring at each other in a cleared circle.

The WP man was hunched forward a little. Clay stood with his feet apart, as if he were braced. Neither spoke again. Nor did any man on either side move or speak. The Starks looked on in silence and so did the Parsons men. These two would stare at each other a minute and walk away. Or they would reach for their guns.

The WP rider made a mistake. Clay Stark was thinking of his father and brothers, the promise he had made to keep his temper. He knew that if one gun cracked a dozen would be smoking before the first echo died. And the WP man thought Clay was afraid to force the issue. He smiled, a taunting lip-curling grimace, as eloquent as words. "Yellow!" he said under his breath. "Go crawl into your kennel."

"If you're thinkin' of checkers, I'm in the king row," Clay answered softly. "An' it's your move."

The WP man's right hand closed on his pistol-grip. But he miscalculated. Of all the Starks, Clay was fastest on the draw. His gun came forward and up in one motion.

With Clay's shot and the second bullet the Parsons man let aimlessly go as he slumped to the sidewalk, the battle of the missing bulls opened in the streets of Oxbow.

Chapter Four

Bloody Dust

Except for Clay and the WP man, the rest of the two groups were thirty, forty, some fifty yards apart. Bill Parsons, flanked by his lawyer, and Polk Munce had turned in one direction. Stark was marshaling his sons the opposite way. Older, more cautious, each in his own way for entirely different reasons had sought to get the match and the powder keg farther apart. But the flame had touched the powder and one man was dying on the plank sidewalk and half a dozen WP guns snapped at Clay—missing him by a miracle. A miracle that was partly due to Oxbow citizens in Clay's vicinity.

Parsons's crew were all from the Nueces. This was a Stark town, Stark country. One or two bystanders wounded and the WP would have all Oxbow to fight. They knew that. Eager as they were to clash with the Starks they did not relish shooting it out with a hundred angry citizens.

Bill Parsons shouted at his men too late. Their guns were smoking. They were firing and dodging for cover at the same time. So were the Starks and the townspeople. Clay himself had flung in behind the corner of the nearest building. Thence, going instinctively to the heart of the trouble, he tilted Bill Parsons's hat askew on his graying hair with a bullet, thus by a scant inch failing to put a full stop to the pivotal center of the feud.

And a minute after he missed Parsons so narrowly a wild shot struck through the frame corner of a saloon and hit Con Stark above one eyebrow. He collapsed, spilling his blood and brains on his father's boots. After that—a man dead on each side—nothing mattered but more killing. Make their point or die. Wipe out the enemy. Blood for blood. Both sides alike. Both cast in the same mold of fierce determination. Both groups stung to complete disregard of consequences by anger, excitement, that strange sanguinary lust that sometimes turns even rabbitlike men into something deadly while the mood lasts.

The street emptied. The townspeople took to their houses, to their cellars, anywhere to be safe from those .45 slugs that whistled like angry bees whenever a head or an arm showed. Business stood still. It had to. Twenty-four armed men intent upon destroying each other could and did suspend the normal activities of a hundred citizens who had no part in the clash. It was death to move in that street now. Stark and Parsons men alike would fire on anything that moved. They were shifting here and there, cognizant of each other's general location, stalking each other like Indians. The first general fusillade had ceased. A shot here. A burst of sharp reports there. Casualties unseen. Wisps of powder smoke drifting from this corner and that. No outcry. Silence, except where two men muttered as they stood within speaking distance of each other, straining their eyes for a living mark to aim on.

Walter Doag, his two regular deputies, his four temporary ones, were powerless to cope with that situation. Left to their own preferences, if any one of the seven had mixed in that firing it would have been to lend the Starks a hand. The Long S was their neighbor, their familiar friend. The WP was an interloper with a reputation for high-handed aggression. Still, law and order meant something in Oxbow, where both were being set at naught that still, hot afternoon. Doag kept his deputies together, gathered in the rear of a log-walled hotel, out of the firing line.

"After they've wasted some more lead an' one or two more on each side has got ventilated, they'll cool off," he said. "Then we got to step in. This sort of thing can't go on."

"I dunno," one cried. "Clay Stark killed a Parsons man first rattle outa the box. Con Stark's killed. I see him go out right at the old man's feet. Them boys'll clean up on each other, I'm afraid."

"It's got to stop somehow, sometime," Doag murmured. "I certainly wish this damned Parsons outfit had stayed on the Nueces."

"Parsons is expandin'," another deputy observed. "An'
I expect he aims to run Oxbow county to suit hisself like
he does the Nueces."

"I don't reckon he will," Doag said shortly.

Nor did Bill Parsons greatly cherish that ambition in
the next hour or so. He was fearless enough, nowise backward about a fight. But he had a great deal more at stake
than any of his men. Once embroiled, they would fight for
fun, for loyalty to their salt, out of sheer distaste for backing down an inch before anything or any man. Parsons
used his gun as well as his men. But he used his brains also.
He didn't control Oxbow county. He could beat the Starks
in a street scrimmage and still win nothing. Their home
town was no place to smoke them up. The open range
was the place to carry on a range war. He had elected to
fight them in court in preference to raids and counter-
raids, because after that first clash on the Trinity he had
shrewdly calculated that he could fight the Long S better
with writs and injunctions than with powder and lead.

Nor was the WP winning this particular fight. Three
Parsons men were down. Two or three more were nursing
slight wounds. Parsons didn't know the Stark casualties.
He didn't care. He was intent on something vastly more
important than killing a hothead or two.

So presently, between his own calculations and the advice of his Fort Worth attorney, he decided it was to his
interest to stop this futile gun-fighting. The WP he reckoned had shown the Starks and Oxbow that it had teeth
and could use them if pressed, that it could not be bluffed
over a gun barrel. Now, to get these fighting cowpunchers
out of town and begin the process of legal attrition. Bill
Parsons would hardly have comprehended that phrase.
But it was what he had in mind when he began swearing
out warrants and bringing civil suits. Trials cost money.
He had ten times the resources of the Starks.

Having arrived at this conclusion, Parsons sent his attorney forth with a white handkerchief fluttering on a
stick, knowing that the lawyer would be recognized as a

noncombatant, safe under this flag of truce. For some such sign from either side Walter Doag was waiting. He was in the street with his six deputies before a Stark head showed. He knew the Fort Worth lawyer, and he grinned sardonically at the man's first words.

"We call on you to keep the peace, sheriff," he said.

"A hell of a lot your crowd cares about the peace," Doag growled, with all the contempt the man who enforces the law at frequent physical danger to himself has for those who discuss law ponderously and profit most by its infraction. "What's Parsons's proposition?"

"No proposition, except that while his outfit intends to defend itself there is nothing to be gained for either side by any amount of bloodshed. If these hotheaded Starks will put up their guns, we'll draw off. Personally, if I were you, I'd arrest and disarm both factions."

"You try that job once," Doag flung at him. "See how far you get. You can reckon how Bill Parsons's crowd would take to bein' disarmed. An' you know blamed well Eugene Stark an' his sons would have to be shot first an' shot plenty before any man could take their guns. Talk sense, Howell. I'm not deputizin' citizens to kill men that elected me to office, just to oblige Bill Parsons."

"Well, it seems as if something ought to be done," Parsons's attorney suggested.

"It does. I'll do it," Doag replied. "If you'll guarantee your side mounts their horses an' rides back to their ranch an' stays south of the river till court sits, I'll see if I can get Gene Stark an' his boys to let it drop. I don't know that they will. I wouldn't blame 'em if they figured they might as well have it out with the WP right here an' now. If they do, I can't stop 'em. An' you can tell Bill Parsons I said so if you want."

"Well, talk to the Stark bunch if you can," Howell said. "The place to settle this dispute is in court. This sort of fighting is sheer lunacy."

Doag moved up along the street. He knew no Stark would fire on him. There would, in fact, be no shot fired on either side so long as that white flag waved from the lawyer's stick. And presently old Gene beckoned him in behind a pile of lumber in a vacant lot. His face was hard as flint. His boy lay stretched on the ground, a blood-stained hat over his face to keep off the buzzing flies. He listened in stony silence to the sheriff. Clay edged up from cover, his shirt front a red smear where a bullet had raked his flesh.

"I'd call off the boys, Gene, an' let Parsons get his outfit out of Oxbow," Doag advised. "I don't blame you for this fuss. I don't criticize you nohow. As a private citizen I'm with you both ways from the ace. But as an officer I got to stop this lawlessness as soon as I can. Parsons is willin' to quit an' draw off. I don't know how bad they're hurt but I expect they've had their bellyful. If you insist on forcin' this thing after he wants to stop it, the best you'll get'll be the worst of it, Gene. Because I'll have to call on Federal troops to restore order. I won't deputize Oxbow citizens to shoot up one another. There's been one or two town people hit already in this ruckus."

"Tell Bill Parsons to walk into the street an' shoot it out with me single-handed," Clay broke in fiercely. "I started this row today. I didn't mean to, but there's some things I won't take off anybody whether he's a cattle king or a hired hand. I started it an' I'll finish it with nobody involved but me an' Parsons himself if he's game to settle in thataway. You seen Con layin' there, Walter? I'd a heap rather it was me."

"Hush up, Clay," his father said slowly. "If it was to be settled that way, it would be my job. I'm the head of this family. But it won't be like that. Parsons hires his fightin' done. There is no sense in turnin' this town upside down, nohow. If Parsons wants to call off his hands, 'tain't right we should persist in shootin' Oxbow all to hell to satisfy our own personal grudges. Clay, you tell all the boys not to fire another shot until I say so—unless they are fired on by this Parsons crowd."

Clay turned away obediently. Eugene Stark said to his friend the sheriff, "I want to talk to this man Parsons, Walter, before he leaves town. Get him into the Oak Leaf

Hotel. I ain't got much to say but I want to say it to his face."

"Is it just a matter of sayin', Gene?" Doag said. "Or a matter of shootin'?"

"That depends on him," Stark replied. "All I aim to do is say a few words. If *he* wants to shoot I'll accommodate him."

"That's good enough," Doag replied. "Because chances are I'll have to guarantee him protection before he'll meet you personally. Will you send these boys of yours out to camp as soon as these WP men pull their freight?"

Stark nodded. Doag went back to Parsons's lawyer. The sheriff left his six deputies standing in the street. If either faction opened fire now they must fire directly upon the collective authority of Oxbow county, and Doag gambled that neither side would risk that. He himself sauntered up to where he could speak to Bill Parsons in the cover where the WP men stood on their guns.

Parsons had courage to back his arrogance. He hadn't got to be a power in Texas without that quality. He issued orders and his men obeyed. In ten minutes the WP riders were mounted and riding, taking their dead and wounded with them. When they were a quarter of a mile distant the Starks swung into their saddles and jogged out to their camp. And they too bore two dead men with them, bodies limp across the saddles they had swaggered in that morning. Old Gene stood in the street to watch them go, until with a sigh he turned to the hotel which Doag, Parsons, and the Fort Worth attorney had already entered, escorted by the six deputy sheriffs.

For a few seconds the two cattlemen eyed each other, feelings masked behind weather-beaten faces.

"Doag said you wanted to talk this over," Parsons broke the silence first.

"No. I just wanted to ask you somethin'—an' tell you somethin', too. Do you reckon bulls is worth more to you than men's lives?"

Bill Parsons flushed. He made an impatient gesture.

"No use discussin' bulls now," said he. "They were

turned loose on the range yesterday—five hundred of 'em
—grade Herefords. You started this fuss too soon, Stark,
an' you're goin' to pay for it. You an' your hotheaded
boys."

"You lie when you say we started it," Stark said calmly.
"This Polk Munce, your range boss, started it by firin' on
us from ambush to try an' stop us from doin' somethin'
we had a right to do in self-protection. Your men started it,
Parsons, an' you stand back of your men. You've set out to
walk over people on the Trinity like you've done on the
Nueces. It'll be rough goin', Parsons. You've killed three of
my hands so far, decent young fellers that just happened to
be workin' for me. You've wounded three of my sons an'
killed one, the mildest, kindest boy outa my family of
eight. If you was a white man with any sense of fair dealin'
none of this woulda happened. But you ain't. You're a
inbred hillbilly an' success has gone to your head."

Parsons's great florid face burned.

"It's safe for you to insult me with a crowd of your own
county officers to protect you," he growled. "No man can
talk to me like that, Stark. Some day I'll ram them words
down your throat."

"An' some day," Eugene Stark told him savagely, "you'll
look at one of your sons layin' dead at your feet an' your
feelin's'll choke you. I want to tell you this, Parsons. It
goes just as I say it. If the WP fires another shot on this
range at me, at my sons, at a single rider in my outfit, I'll
take a leaf outa *your* book. I'll hire me a swarm of gun-
fighters an' carry this war to the Nueces, into your own
home, where *your* sons are."

With that he turned on his heel, walked out to his
horse, mounted, and rode away to his own camp to sit and
stare at nothing over a canvas sheet that covered the dead
body of his son.

Chapter Five

UPROOTED

THE DEAD WERE BURIED. The wounded sat idle till their torn flesh healed. Oxbow went about its business, dating events from that battle in its dusty streets. The Long S attended to its affairs. The Stark riders presently verified Bill Parsons's statement that a quota of bulls was loose on the range. They spoke of it with irony. A belated gesture which, made three weeks sooner, would have saved all that useless bloodshed. But neither WP heifers nor bulls ate grass north of the Trinity. The Starks saw to that. That was their business, their firm determination, as they went forth on spring roundup with a carpet of new grass pushing up through the gray winter-bleached mat that covered the plains.

It didn't matter really whether one thousand or five thousand WP cattle strayed across the Long S range. There was plenty of room, grass, water. Only Eugene Stark knew that if WP cattle in any number moved north of the Trinity a WP roundup crew would come to gather them in season. And Parsons men trafficking there meant another fight. He couldn't hold his sons. From fourteen-year-old Eugene junior to Dave who had half-grown sons of his own they were a unit in their hatred. They seldom spoke of that ambush on the Trinity, that raid on the WP, the fight in Oxbow. But they mourned Con. If the lightning had killed one of that strangely united group of brothers the rest would have cursed the sky for its wanton bolt. So they looked south and cursed the Parsons outfit. Parsons, himself, his kin, his riders, it was immaterial. For the Stark boys everything connected with the WP was lumped in one category. A Parsons rider would fight for his outfit with the single-minded loyalty of a feudal retainer. Hence he was an enemy. And they went armed at all times, Winchesters under their stirrup leathers, six-shooters holstered on belts full of ammunition. Old Gene Stark didn't have to be told what was in their minds, what each and all would do in a pinch. He knew his own brood.

So the Long S kept its range clear of WP's. As drifting Parsons cattle crossed they shoved them back. There were no more ambuscades. Old Gene Stark knew there wouldn't be. Parsons had adopted tactics less direct—likely to be in the end more effective in the way of material injury than powder and lead. He was shooting holes into the resources of the Stark family from behind a legal barricade. It was safer, surer than gunfire. He was a shrewd and remorseless man. He moved craftily. He removed one source of friction. He took back with him to the Nueces Polk Munce and every WP man who had engaged in that Trinity war. He sent a new range boss and a new crew to the Trinity. Ostensibly he moved for peace on the range. Actually every man he sent up was a picked gun-fighter, under a foréman with a reputation that ran from the Brazos to the Panamints in Arizona. And coincident with that he launched one civil suit after another against the Starks. Suits for personal injury. Suits for property damage. Suits on behalf of the families of his slain cowpunchers. Suits in the name of every man in his outfit so much as scratched by a Stark bullet. His activities turned the sheriff of Oxbow county into a process server who wore out the road to the Stark ranch.

"Ain't there no way of stoppin' this bombardment of blue papers?" old Gene asked his lawyers.

In all his years as a cattleman he had never been involved in litigation over money or property. His Oxbow attorney, growing appalled at the number and variety of actions Bill Parsons brought as claims, insisted on Stark engaging counsel from the Capital. They sat in Mark Hohne's office in Oxbow—two lawyers and a troubled cowman. And even two lawyers could scarcely handle the job. It required a corps.

"No. All you can do is defend these suits. If you win, you can plaster him with costs in the civil cases," both Hohne and the assisting lawyer declared. "You can't stop a man bringing action against you. You can counter-claim. All this is just meant to harass you. The only real ground he has against you is that raid on the WP ranch after they ambushed you on the river. You shouldn't have admitted responsibility for that. He'll win that likely. No valid defense—in law. The rest will probably fail, or be thrown out of court."

"It's goin' to cost us a powerful lot of money, all this damned law business," old Gene said to Dave as they rode home. "No matter if we win out. Lawyers' fees, fees for this an' that an' the other thing. Hell, he can pile expense on us till we're snowed under."

"Be expense on him too," Dave replied. "Parsons loves a dollar better'n we do."

"He's got twenty to our one, that's the trouble," his father said soberly. "He can spend dollar for dollar with us an' still be a rich man when we're broke."

"If he breaks us that way, stingin' like a bloodsucker through the courts," Dave said soberly, "the Stark boys will break *him* on the open range if they have to turn outlaw to do it. But he won't, Dad. He don't own Oxbow county."

"His attorneys are movin' to have all them cases taken out of Oxbow county," old Gene cited a new angle. "Askin' a change of venue for all these trials, both civil an' criminal. Claims he can't get an unprejudiced hearin' in Oxbow. I reckon he'll get the civil suits transferred. He's got smart attorneys. They can drive a four-horse team through the law. It don't look rosy for the Long S, Dave. I don't want my family took down to poverty to satisfy a overbearin' man's grudge an' fatten lawyers' pocketbooks."

"Law ain't everythin'," Dave said curtly.

"It's what we got to live by mostly," his father answered. "Time when you could settle any argument with a gun, an' know it was settled permanent, is gone. Texas is civilized, my son. That's what the old-timers worked an' fought for, civilization an' law an' security. It's better'n fightin' Injuns an' livin' like savages. Even if it has its disadvantages, when skulduggery like this Parsons business can tie a man's hands an' bleed him to death."

"Texas may be civilized," Dave Stark cried. "But Bill Parsons ain't. Still, the Stark family has never took a whippin' yet, Dad. No use borrowin' trouble."

They didn't have to. It came to them freely, as a gift, bestowed whether they would have it or no. At various times through that summer every Stark man who had been involved in that fracas spent as much time coming and going, cooling his heels in court corridors, as he spent in legitimate range work. Bill Parsons got his change of venue to another county where Starks and Parsons alike were viewed impartially. But there as elsewhere the weight of tremendous resources used without scruple counted heavily.

Eugene Stark's funds flowed out and vanished like water spilled on parched earth, were dissipated like dust in a whirlwind. He drew on his bankers. His cattle and land were ample security. But there seemed no end to the drain. Legal fees, bonds, charges for this and that, appeals, ate up money insatiably. And the end was never in sight. From every angle that clever legal minds could devise Parsons attacked Stark, willing to spend a thousand dollars any time if it could inflict expense on the Long S.

By fall two or three salient facts stared the Starks in the face. The criminal cases on both sides brought acquittal, after floods of expensive oratory and conflicting testimony. No Texas jury would convict for killing done in an open fight. Justifiable homicide remained more than a legal phrase. A fight was still a fight.

The damage suits for personal injuries Parsons lost one by one, yet every case thrown out of court cost Eugene Stark more money than he liked to think about. But the civil suit for property destroyed in that retaliatory night raid on the WP was a different matter. The torch to haystacks and buildings, miles and miles of range grass gone up in smoke, couldn't be gainsaid. A verdict for Parsons was assured on the Starks' admission. They wouldn't perjure themselves to deny that—although Clay Stark swore truthfully that no soul in his outfit knew his intention when he stole down and put a match to the WP ranch.

He was a man grown, responsible for his own acts. Nevertheless his act was tied up with his family, with the Long S. If life is cheap, property holds a high value in the eyes of mankind. A jury gave a verdict that made the Starks gasp—fifty thousand dollars and costs. Against which the Long S could appeal to one supreme court after another if they chose—with the legal certainty that every superior court would uphold the judgment.

Lastly, by the time fall roundup was over, the last beef gone to market, the Starks knew that Bill Parsons had massed fully thirty thousand cattle from the Nueces along the south bank of the Trinity. There wasn't pasture for them there. They would cross. Nothing would stop them. By spring the Stark range would carry two WPs for every hoof bearing the Long S. And then Parsons range crews would cross in the spring to sweep the Long S range from end to end. Eugene Stark knew that under such conditions it was only a matter of time till some rider pulled a gun and the ball would open again.

Gene Stark wasn't an old man in spirit. Yet fifty-eight years had left their mark on him. He had lived all his life in Texas, as his father had done before him. He had always taken it for granted that he would end his days on the Trinity in the comfortable home he had created and leave his sons in possession to carry on.

But he cared a great deal more for his sons than he did for his own ease, his land, or his cattle. He had been a hard fighter but he knew the value of peace. To stand pat on the Trinity with seven sons and half a dozen hired riders, fight the WP tooth and toenail, meant certain bloodshed and ultimate poverty for them all. Hence he looked for a way out before disaster took its final toll. So long as Bill Parsons lived and commanded power he would harass the Long S. He had so declared himself. His acts proved his assertion. He was a big fish who had always eaten little fish. If he had blunted a few teeth on the Long S it had, Eugene Stark knew by all the signs and tokens, only made him more determined to swallow them at a gulp.

No man likes to take a whipping. The Starks didn't. Yet, except in a blind burst of fury, no man dashes his brains out against a solid wall. There was a way out. Stark and his sons discussed it pro and con. They didn't agree, but they considered.

Sixteen hundred miles northwest a virgin country was opening up. Once reckoned fit for nothing but the buffalo, the Indian, and the wolf, it was proving a cattleman's country, providing an outlet for the southwestern ranges, now filled to overflowing.

The Texas longhorn was already moving in on that northern grass, laying the foundation of a new pastoral empire. The longhorn had been king of the south and he was extending his dominion as the Romans reached out for the barbarian provinces. Gene Stark found himself lending ear to Uncle Bill Sayre of Fort Worth when that worthy banker and lifelong friend counseled him.

"It'd be the wisest move you could make, Gene. You ain't whipped. You've done your damnedest. You're just up against something that you got to sidestep for your family's sake. If another range fight starts, it'll only mean more killin' and nothing settled in the end. You'll lose more of your sons. No, you'll lose nobody's respect if you put the width of three states between you and Bill Parsons and his hired gunmen. The north's a good country. I'm sending cattle up there myself. In ten years the Trinity will be grazed to death anyway, and everything you'd run there would have to be under fence. Get in on the cream of a new grazin' territory while you got something to go on. If you stay with the Trinity, even if there's never another shot fired, Parsons will buck you till you're broke."

Stark mulled that over until he accepted it as a way out. And so did his sons. Not with too good a grace—but old Gene, for all his affection and kindliness and indulgence, still exercised a patriarchal authority over his numerous brood.

Neither the Starks nor Uncle Bill Sayre knew that already Bill Parsons, far-seeking, hewing to the line of his ambition to be the biggest individual cattle owner in North America, had that very season reached into the Northwest with three herds and taken a prime location.

It might not have made any difference. if they had known. By spring Eugene Stark knew he had little choice. When his obligations were all met his fortune had shrunk to a point that appalled him. He could take the road with one herd and just about enough cash to carry the outfit until it had beef to market again. And above that he had his ranch on the Trinity. He could sell or mortgage to raise more operating capital. And he elected to sell, cut every tie, tear up the last root, and like the Israelites march with his hoofed and horned beasts, his sons and his sons' sons, his gear and his household goods, out of a land that offered nothing now but bondage to a festering grudge.

Chapter Six

THE DUDE

BROCK PARSONS LEANED BACK IN HIS CHAIR. The forefinger of one hand traced an invisible pattern on the tablecloth. He looked out a wide window on green grass and shrubbery, plumy tufts of pampas grass, a rose garden coming to bud, beds of tulips and narcissus, lying between the ranch house and the hurrying Nueces. His invalid mother had feasted her eyes on that for years, from a couch in an upper front room.

Brock's mind was divided between recurrent pity for her and a consideration of the matter his father and Matt had been discussing and a curious sort of indignation that stirred in him. No man likes to have himself, his code, his opinions, held in contempt. He turned his head to look across at his father's heavy, scowling face and say, "You're bearing down heavy on a rotten deal. It's small—and I always thought you were a big man."

For a second Bill Parsons opened his mouth in sheer astonishment. Not so much at his youngest son's words, because Brock had said the same thing in more diplomatic terms earlier in the discussion, as at the direct challenge to himself.

"I'm not gaugin' either myself or my range policy by the opinions of a blamed dude that knows a lot about books an' less than nothin' about cows—or men," he blared finally in his big voice. "Time you've spent a few years in the cow business you'll cut your eyeteeth maybe. Meantime keep your damn criticisms till I ask for 'em. If you'd been raised the way you'd oughto been you'd know enough to keep your mouth shut. Some professor tell you that when somebody walks on your toes it's polite to step aside an' apologize for bein' in the way? Ever strike you that your expensive education wasn't paid for by lily-fingered methods of doin' business?"

Brock flushed. "I didn't ask you to educate me," he answered. "I didn't even ask to be born. Whatever I am I'm pretty much what you've made me. And a man doesn't have to have the expensive education you're all the time flinging in my face to have ideas about fair play. I'm not the only one that criticizes your tactics. Maybe it just happens that I'm the only one that's fool enough to say things to your face. This Stark business has got to be a stink in Texas. And you're still figuring how you can carry it further."

"Them Starks happen to be friends of yours?" Bill Parsons leaned back in his chair. For a moment his eyes swept over all he could see from the three-windowed sides of the dining-room. From the broad porch that faced on the Nueces, Parsons could look over a territory he controlled as absolutely as he controlled the motions of his hands. Twenty miles from his front door to the boundary of his own land. A strangle hold on every waterhole and creek within a fifty-mile radius. And this bald-faced kid telling him his methods were wrong! He glanced at Matt with a different expression. Here was a man after his own heart, he thought.

Matt rolled a cigarette, apparently unmoved at the passage between his father and younger brother. He was a Parsons. He knew the cow business inside out. He had no university degrees and rather scorned them. Matt had taken his degree on the plains, in the dust of herds, the smoke of branding-fires. He was six feet two of rough recklessness. And he had never spoken to his father in his life as Brock dared to speak now—never on any subject.

Matt knew that to speak of the Starks, the Long S, the Trinity, almost made Parsons senior foam at the mouth. That fight had already cost him a lot of money. It wasn't finished. It never would be finished as long as Bill Parsons could get any satisfaction from carrying it on. Matt would have dropped that feud himself. His father never would. That apparently was what stirred Brock. Matt sat back, interested, waiting to see how far this would go. He didn't quite share his father's opinion of Brock. This kid brother

had nerve and persistence. Matt never opposed his father
on any grounds.

"You settin' yourself up for a friend of this Stark outfit,
I say?" Parsons almost bellowed.

"I have never laid eyes on any one of the family so far as
I know," Brock answered quietly. "Only I have had this
row brought to my attention in so many different ways
that I'm sick of hearing about it. Neither the beginning of
it, nor the fighting, nor the litigation is any credit to the
WP. What's the use of hating people and piling trouble
on them just because they object to being walked on?"

"That'll be all from you," Parsons snarled. "Don't you
never talk to me again like that. You'll go up the trail an'
you'll make a hand till you get sense enough to know your
business and mind it. By the Lord, I've a mind to kick
you plumb upstairs an' down again. If I'd had the raisin'
of you, you wouldn't a been a useless, butter-fingered dude.
If your mother—"

"Leave mother out of this," Brock flashed. "I don't care
a damn what you say to me, what you think of me, but
don't blame her for anything I do or say. Mother has nothing to do with what I think of your rough-and-tumble way
of shoving everybody off the map the minute they refuse
to dance to your tune."

Parsons looked at his son. Matt knew that he was nearly
speechless with anger, as he always became when anyone
crossed or defied him. Then his hard, beefy face cracked
in a wolfish grin.

"All right, me brave buck," he grunted. "You've called
the turn. I *do* make 'em dance to my music. So will you,
or I'll shove you off the WP map."

"Until last summer," Brock said, looking steadily at his
angry father, "I never was on the WP map except as something for you to sneer at when you happened to feel that
way."

"All college has done for you is to swell you outa
shape," Parsons senior declared. "You was supposed to be
made a gentleman to humor a sick woman's whim. You
ain't nothin'. You don't know law, medicine, business.

You don't know beans. You don't know nothin' you ain't
read in a book. Except to be gabby outa your turn. You
can be as windy as a politician about things that don't
concern you, that you don't *sabe*."

"Oh, Lord." Brock laughed in his father's face. "I have
no monopoly on being windy. There are none so blind as
those who will not see. I held up my end on a trail herd
last summer. I brought back a *remuda* from Nebraska
when your trail boss wanted to take the easy way home.
You might as well quit depreciating my personal stock. I
have learned more about the cow business in twelve
months than some of your valuable employees have
learned in a lifetime."

"You got a lot to learn yet," his father assured him
grimly. "An' you'll learn it or I'll know the reason why.
You'll go up the trail again. You'll go as a hand under
Polk Munce, an' what Polk says will go for you till I say
otherwise."

Brock shifted uneasily in his chair. "If you send me
north under Polk Munce," he stated after a brief silence,
"the chances are you will be shy one of your pet foremen
or one of your sons before we cross the Platte."

Parsons thrust his head forward aggressively.

"Just what you mean by that?" he demanded.

"Just what I said," Brock replied. "I don't like Polk
Munce. He doesn't like me. I not only don't like him, but
I despise his type. If you figure it's part of my range education to work as a trail hand I don't mind. But you have
three other trail herds going north. Why should I have to
rub elbows with a man like Polk Munce when it isn't
really necessary? If you want to find out what I'm made
of, give me a trail herd to take to Montana myself."

"Polk," said his father sourly, "is a smart cowman. He's
made money for me. All you've ever done is spend it. Polk
knows his business an' you don't. You're goin' as one of
his trail crew day after tomorrow. I'll find somethin' for
you to do at that Judith ranch when you get there. A
couple of seasons in Montana'll make you or break you.
You'll learn somethin'. Polk Munce is the man to learn

you."

"He may learn something himself that'll complete his education," Brock replied tartly. "Why do I have to cut my teeth in the cattle business under a man who'll go out of his way to make it hot for me every chance he gets?"

"Because I say so," Parsons growled.

Brock's blue eyes flamed for an instant. Then he smiled with deceptive sweetness.

"All right," said he, "if Polk Munce can stand it, I reckon I can. If anything happened to Polk en route would I be supposed to take charge of the herd?"

His father and brother stared at him.

"Ain't nothin' goin' to happen to Polk," Bill Parsons said slowly.

"Something will happen to him," Brock drawled, "if he tramps on my toes more than once. You may have confidence in him and like him. But I like him just the way I like skunks and rattlesnakes."

With which Brock arose and left the room. They heard his feet pad lightly on the stairs leading to his invalid mother's room. Bill Parsons frowned blackly as he lit a cigar. Matt looked thoughtful.

"Dad," he said with the frankness of a favorite son, "do you reckon it's a good idea to send Brock up the trail under Polk? He seems to have considerable feelin' about Polk Munce for some reason."

"Do him good. Polk'll show him where to head in at," his father muttered. "Damn spoiled brat!"

"The brat," Matt observed, "stands about six feet in his socks an' weighs around a hundred an' eighty-five, an' appears to have considerable temper. Also he has plumb vigorous notions about things. If Polk should get uppity with him—well, I dunno. An' Polk *is* mean, Dad. You know it. He's meaner'n ever since that fuss on the Trinity. He pulled a bonehead play there an' he's aware that a lot of people in Texas don't think much of him for it. If the play comes up, Brock'll talk to him about this Stark business plainer than he did to you. Brock may be a dude but he don't seem to be afraid of anything much."

"He ain't got sense enough," Parsons growled. "I've said he's to go an' he's goin'. He'll never be worth a damn to me unless he changes his tune. If he'd been raised the way you was he might be some account. All he knows is to sling a lot of highfalutin' language an' criticize things that don't concern him. If that's what colleges do for young fellers, I'd turn 'em into livery stables."

Matt said nothing more. He knew his father's moods, his stubborn way of facing an issue. Matt had his own methods of coping with that. But he didn't feel called upon to make an issue of Brock. Matt was keen-witted enough to realize that Bill Parsons resented his college-bred son. Matt didn't. He could perceive certain advantages in Brock's manner, his language, his cool assurance in any sort of situation—the things that simply exasperated his father.

What he should do, Matt thought to himself, *is to give the kid a herd an' start him north as a trail boss. Give him a real chance to show what he can do. Him an' Polk Munce is liable to tangle over nothin' at all. Bullheaded as he is, the old man would feel pretty sick if his oldest range boss killed his youngest son. But, hell, it's no use talkin' to him. It ain't my funeral anyway. Maybe he won't go.*

But Brock did go. Four days later he left the Nueces punching the drag of a WP herd under Polk Munce, eating dust like any other forty-dollar trail hand.

And it never occurred to Brock that his father's last words to Polk had reference to himself.

"That boy of mine don't have to be handled with gloves, Polk. He's got a lot to learn. You don't have to be eternally recollectin' he's the owner's son."

"He'll get along all right, I reckon," Polk drawled. "All he's got to do is make a hand. If he don't, he'll go down the road talkin' to hisself, Bill. He's just a stock hand, far as I'm concerned. I don't play no favorites."

"That's the ticket," Parsons nodded. "Don't baby him none."

It might have surprised even Bill Parsons to know just how Polk Munce interpreted that conversation.

The route of the WP herd took them across the Trinity halfway between the new WP in that territory and the old Long S ranch. For a trail crew Munce had almost the same personnel that he led in the battle of the bulls—which, as Brock knew, was how Texans generally spoke of that bloody clash. They crossed the river, as a matter of fact, within gunshot of where Polk made that first ambuscade.

Polk had some hard pills in his trail crew. But they were not all of that stripe. A Kansas youngster about Brock's own age reined up beside him as they climbed in the wake of the herd up the north bank. He spoke about that trouble.

"Polk bit off a trifle more'n he could chew that time," the boy grinned. "I figured it was kinda raw, but when you're workin' for a cow outfit you don't argue with the boss about things like that."

"It was so damned unnecessary," Brock commented. "Those people were only protecting their own stock on their own range."

"Yeah, but you know how it is," Slater replied. "The WP has always had everything its own way on the Nueces. It made Polk sore to have them Starks shove our cattle off an open range. I guess nobody reckoned they was such an all-fightin' bunch. Anyway, the WP come out on top. They've got this range in their sack now. I hear the Stark outfit sold their ranch this spring an' pulled for Montana. They were sure a fightin' family, I'll say that for 'em. I reckon they figured if they fought it to a finish they'd be broke in the end. The WP is too all-fired big an outfit to monkey with."

Brock let that pass. He knew the history of that feud better than anyone surmised. It ran in his mind, filled him with an uncomfortable distaste for the hatred he knew these people must feel. Coupled with that was a touch of shame because Brock knew what a good many Texans thought of Bill Parsons for all he had heaped on the Long S.

After supper Brock was free until he went on middle

guard. He caught out another mount besides his night horse, saddled, and loped down the river. He had a curious impulse to see the home these Starks had abandoned to strangers, because of the spoke his father insisted on thrusting in their wheel at every turn.

He sat his horse before the Long S ranchhouse in the pearly translucence of a southern evening. The new owners had not yet taken possession. It ran in Brock's mind that it would be just like his father to move heaven and earth to acquire that ranch, simply to make his triumph complete. It was profoundly silent about that place. The Starks had occupied this spot thirty-odd years and they had made it beautiful, even more beautiful than the grounds his mother had striven for around the WP.

"They must have had several thousand acres of good bottom land," Brock mused, marking the long lines of fence. "And eventually I suppose he'll manage to buy it in and make it a private pasture for himself. Funny people can't get along in as big a country as this without reaching out to cut some other fellow's throat."

When he turned his sweaty mount loose and stood cinching his saddle on his night horse Polk Munce sauntered by and said to him, "Young feller, it ain't exactly the custom for a hand on a trail crew to amble off from his outfit thataway."

Brock looked at the trail boss over his shoulder for a second, then continued to do up his *latigo*. He didn't even trouble to answer.

Polk watched him stroll over to where his bed lay flattened in the grass by the wagon.

"Some of these days," he whispered with a rancor out of all proportion to the offense. "I'll make you talk outa the wrong side of your face, you swelled-up pup!"

Chapter Seven

ONE OF THESE PERSONAL MATTERS

FROM THAT CROSSING the WP herd shoved up the Trinity, keeping the river close on the left until the roofs of Fort Worth appeared. At their noon halt that day a buggy came rolling out from town to stop at the chuck wagon. Brock, on herd, saw that the driver was a woman. When he was relieved to eat and change horses he perceived further that the woman was Esther Munce, whom he hadn't seen for three years. Once, long ago, he and Esther had played together through a memorable vacation on the Nueces. Old man Munce's only girl. She knew Brock as soon as he dismounted. She left her seat on a roll of bedding beside Polk to come over and talk to Brock when he filled his plate with food.

Nature has a strange way of fashioning people of infinite variety from the same materials. Polk Munce and his younger brother Tuck were hard-looking men, indeed ugly-featured men. They had thin lips and mean, small eyes. Polk especially resembled a badly weathered gargoyle. His long nose drooped in a predatory curve. Wind and sun and bad temper had graven deep lines in his face. Tuck had better features and a more saturnine expression —if that were possible. Brock dimly recalled old man Munce as very like his sons. He had been a cattleman in a small way on the Nueces until his holdings were absorbed by the ever-spreading WP, which had likewise absorbed both his sons into its service.

Yet this Munce girl was almost beautiful. Nothing about her offended the most critical eye. Her hair was fluffy gold, her skin like that of a healthy child. Her blue eyes sparkled as if some joke eternally lurked behind them. Her voice was a low, soft drawl from between lips that parted in an enticing curve.

"It's been a long time since I saw you, Brock," she

greeted.

"It surely is," Brock smiled. Hat in hand he looked down on her five feet three with a smile to match her own.

"Sit down and eat your dinner," Esther said. She moved into the shade of the chuck wagon beside Brock when he squatted on the grass, plate in lap. "You all through school? And going up the trail with the longhorns to Montana?"

Brock nodded.

"I'd trade places with you," Esther said. "I'd sort of like to go north. I'll never be through with school, I reckon."

"Why? How's that?" Brock asked.

"Oh, I'm teaching. Schoolma'am. Fully ordained," she laughed. "Be an old maid with cats and a parrot, by and by."

"No chance," Brock grinned. "Some of these days a man will come along and good-by classrooms forever."

"Oh, I don't know," she cocked her head on one side to look at him quizzically. "I like teaching better than keeping house. Are you coming back this way in the fall?"

"That I can't say," Brock replied. "I'm subject to orders, being a mere private in the WP army. The big chief has gone on record that a course of sprouts on the northern range may make something of me. I'm liable to be up there a couple of years taking a post-graduate course in the cattle business."

"What does your mother think of that?"

Brock frowned. "Like myself, she hasn't much say. W. J. Parsons runs this show to suit himself."

Brock finished his dinner, rolled a cigarette to smoke with his coffee. He liked Esther Munce. It was a pity, he reflected, that some of this girl's kindness and sunny nature hadn't been bestowed on Polk. He could see Polk scowling, his eyes on them. And presently he walked over past their seat by a wagon wheel.

"You're due on herd," he grunted.

"You deal in the obvious," Brock answered.

"What's that?" Polk growled, unable to interpret the unfamiliar phrase. His tone was just a trifle more ill-natured than usual—and it was never genial when he addressed Brock.

"I know I am," Brock translated. He wouldn't have troubled to make his meaning clear if he had been alone. The hardest task he found on trail was being civil to Polk Munce.

"Oh, forget being a trail boss for a little while and try being a human being, Polk," Esther admonished with a smile. "I haven't seen Brock for ages. I want to talk to him a minute."

Polk walked on. Brock rose.

"You shouldn't be a trail hand under him," Esther said. "What's the big idea?"

"My father's," Brock shrugged his shoulders. "It's a sort of punishment for talking out of my turn. Talking big and doing little—according to him."

"How?"

"Well, you see," Brock lingered to explain. "I've been expensively educated. Like some vaccinations, it didn't take. I know a great deal about a lot of things that Dad has very hazy notions about, but I don't seem to know anything that he considers worth a hoot. I don't know what he expected me to be, but he's powerfully disappointed and rather contemptuous with what I am. So he's taking the roughest, toughest way of making a cowpuncher of me. Of course I'll never, in his eyes, be the cowman Matt is, but if I knuckle down I may eventually become useful to the WP."

He grinned cheerfully at this picture of his own painting.

"Polk doesn't like you," Esther said thoughtfully. "And anybody Polk doesn't like gets a rough deal where he has any say-so."

"How do you know he doesn't like me?" Brock inquired.

"I know Polk," she said. "The way he spoke to you just now is enough. Besides he never did like you."

"Right both ways," Brock nodded. "It's mutual, Esther, sad to say. Still, I don't think your worthy elder brother will hand me any raw deal. Not so you could notice. I'm something of a diplomat."

"You'll need to be," Esther frowned. "For goodness' sake, Brock, don't quarrel with Polk. He was always bad, and now he's worse. Something has got under his skin terribly the last couple of years."

"I know," Brock nodded. "It was that Stark business on the Trinity. It has affected Parsons senior something the same way. They know it's a black mark against them. Well, I'm due to eat dust with that herd. Like old times to see you again. You ought to go north and grow up with the country. It's really a peach of a territory. I was up there last summer."

"I might at that," Esther said. "I had the offer of a school in a settlement just out of Fort Benton last summer."

"You wouldn't teach school long up there," Brock eyed her admiringly. "There's ten men to every woman. Those northern boys swing a wide loop when anything as good-looking as you heaves in sight. Blondes are fatal."

Esther laughed. "All the nice Texas boys are going up the trail," she said. "Maybe I'll have to go too, or be an old maid."

"If it gets serious let me know," Brock joked. "I might come to the rescue. So long."

They shook hands.

It must, Brock decided, be pretty obvious when Esther could size up the situation at such short notice. Polk must either have said something or inadvertently let slip some of his rancor. Otherwise Esther would hardly have warned him so bluntly. Only Brock needed no warning. The Nueces was barely two weeks behind and the atmosphere was electric already. Nothing much said. Nothing done. Just atmosphere, a look, a tone. Brock grinned as he joined the other riders on the flank of that grazing herd. Dude! He laughed to himself. As if a few years in an eastern school weakened a man's arm, made his eye less sure, his brain less alert. Brock felt that Polk Munce was always eyeing him slantwise, looking for an opening to flick the whip of authority, to make him look and feel cheap if he could. Just once, the bushwhacking killer! Brock had very definite ideas, very positive feelings about Polk. He knew various things about himself, about his own capacity, which Polk Munce couldn't possibly know. Let him learn!

Meantime he held up his end without any particular effort or coaching, somewhat, he secretly observed, to the surprise of the others in that trail crew. Among themselves they had started out by christening him the "dude cowboy." Polk had started that. Brock smiled and let it pass. So long as he made a hand with the herd, Polk could do nothing except eye him sourly. If he went beyond that he was looking for trouble. Considering which, Brock merely shrugged his shoulders. Polk and everybody else seemed to have forgotten that Brock Parsons had been born on a Texas ranch, that he had done for play or sport ever since he was small the very things the range rider did for a living.

Rivers to cross! In the path of a trail herd from Texas to Montana there was always one more river to cross. The Nueces, the Colorado, the Brazos, the Trinity, the Red River of the South. Swirly water. Swimming water. Bogs. Quicksands. Hissing currents and sluggish streams of brackish water. The WP longhorns breasted them all, passed on triumphant, gaining in flesh and spirit as they crossed each degree of latitude. It was not a drive so much as a sixteen-hundred-mile graze, expertly managed to bring the cattle to a northern range that fall in good shape to face the rigors of winter. Adventure, hardship, good, bad, and indifferent going, were incidental to that purpose. Industry, like an army, drives at its objective undeterred by minor casualties.

And so in the fullness of time Polk Munce's chuck wagon encamped on the Canadian river, which is a long way from Canada. Various things occurred to Polk that particular day. A twenty-eight-mile drive over a waterless plateau under a sun that fairly scorched. A fall that jarred the bones of his ancestors when his horse put a forefoot in a badger hole. An irritating touch of indigestion.

Polk had a weakness for fried steak, hot biscuits, and strong coffee. He was like an angry bee by night, ready to sting anything that moved within his ken.

It happened that Brock Parsons chose that evening to be gay and facetious, to talk continuously while the crew ate supper.

"For God's sake," Polk snarled at last. "Close your trap an' give our ears a rest."

It was not so much what he said as his tone. Tired men make allowances for other tired men. And Polk was boss. Within reason he had a right to demand quietness—if he could enforce it without making it a personal issue. But he flung that at Brock like a calculated insult and a hush fell on the men scooping food off their tin plates. They had no way of gauging Brock. But they all knew Polk Munce.

Brock knew that the expected crisis had arisen. He had seen it coming for days. If he let that slide, Polk would make it stronger next time. Not only as a matter of policy but as a matter of instinct Brock took the bull by the horns like a flash.

"Are you ambitious to cut another notch on your gun, Polk," he asked, "that you speak to me in that tone of voice? Don't do it. It's my privilege—any man's privilege —to talk when and where and as much as he likes."

"Not around me." Polk hunched himself forward. "I don't give a damn if you was the apple of Bill Parsons's eye. When I tell a man to shut up he shuts up."

"Try shutting me up," Brock said calmly, "and see how it works."

Considering the time, the place, and the men, Brock's open challenge left Polk only one thing to do. He had overreached himself and he had to go through—according to his own light upon such matters. As a backing to his statement he reached for his gun—and halted his hooking fingers halfway.

Because in some mysterious fashion Brock had a white-handled Colt in his right hand trained steadily on Polk's midriff. At a distance of ten feet even a dude could hardly

miss. Polk Munce hadn't survived a variety of personal
encounters without using his brains as well as his gun.
There was something deadly about the unexpected speed
of that draw. A green college dude shouldn't be able to
get the drop on him like that—nor be cool enough to hold
a six-shooter in one hand and balance a dinner plate in the
other without a tremor. Nor did Polk misinterpret the
glint in Brock's blue eyes.

"Hell," he said with a forced grin. "Why the lightnin'
gun play? You don't reckon I'm goin' to stage a fight with
any of the Parsons family, do you? I was just tryin' you out,
kid."

"Oh, were you," Brock said mockingly. "How sweet of
you, Polk. Well, since you've tried me out, kindly remember that I've been tried and not found wanting. Likewise
try to remember—when you speak to me, hereafter—that a
little common politeness is expected even from a tarantula
like you."

Polk stepped over to a pot simmering on the fire by the
Dutch oven. He poured himself a cup of coffee.

"Go ahead," he said with simulated indifference. "Talk
all you want to. I won't stop you."

"You couldn't, if you did want to," Brock snapped at
him. "And I'll show you why."

He had been squatting on his haunches. He hadn't even
altered his position except for that one swift movement of
his right hand. Now he arose, thrusting the gun back into
the holster belted around his lean hips. He emptied the
scraps off his plate, took the ten-inch disc of tin and tossed
it high in the air. As it spun, flashing, thirty feet above his
head, he whipped the forty-five out and let go three shots.
The last made the plate leap like a rabbit as it touched the
earth. Horses picketed surged on their ropes. Polk, cattleman in spite of his anger, his mortification, glanced uneasily to see if the snuffy herd had been startled by those
shots. Then he looked at Brock and at the plate which
Tommy Slater ran to pick up.

There were two holes in the middle of it and a long
gouge where the third bullet had struck it edgewise as it

hit the ground.

"That's shootin'," Slater held it up for them to see.

Brock helped himself to another cup of coffee. The others drifted away to uncoil *reatas*, for the horse wrangler was bunching the *remuda* to catch fresh mounts. Polk Munce squatted on his heels, brooding. Brock, walking by him, halted to say in a tone that didn't carry beyond Polk's ears, "I staged that for *your* benefit, Polk. As a trail boss you have a right to fire me for any reason that strikes your fancy. But you can't make breaks at me and get away with it, Mister Munce. Next time you make a play at me and I have to pull a gun on you it'll be smoking when it comes in sight."

Brock went on middle guard that night with Tommy Slater. There was a round bright moon. The cattle lay on a broad flat, a dark blot washed by silver. They would have slept through those midnight hours with no rider near. An all-day march meant an all-night sleep for longhorns on trail, unless something frightened them. All Brock and Slater had to do was put in the time. They ambled around the sleeping herd side by side through their watch.

"Where'd you learn to be lightnin' with a gun thata-way?" Slater asked finally.

"College course in small arms," Brock chuckled.

"You don't say," Slater commented. "Hell, I thought all them colleges did was learn you things outa books."

Brock laughed. "Shucks," he said, "you fellows ought to get rid of the idea that going to college makes a man plumb useless. Even my father sort of nurses that idea. It's a mistake. The fact is, Tom, I was always crazy about horses and guns. Even in civilization there's plenty of chance to learn the use of firearms if you crave to. A man doesn't have to be born and raised in the shade of a chuck wagon to learn a quick draw. If I'd paid more attention to books and not so much to fooling around I'd be better off. I was practically kicked out of Yale in my junior year. That's why the old man is so sore on me. I'm not either one thing nor the other, according to him. But it hasn't ruined me altogether. I think I can hold my own most places."

"You're sure a humdinger with a Colt. You ride good enough. You *sabe* cows almost like you'd been raised with 'em," Slater mused. "I don't see nothin' wrong with you, nohow. Seems like old Polk does, though. You keep your eye peeled for Polk. He turned that off pretty smooth. He's foxy. But he won't forget you took the play away from him. He knows you made him look like a sucker. He holds a grudge worse'n any man I ever saw. He'll be figurin' ways to jump you whenever he thinks the sign's right."

"I expect he will," Brock said lightly. "In which case I might have to promote myself to be trail boss and take this herd through to its destination."

Tom Slater sat sidewise in his saddle and blew a puff of smoke at the fat, silver moon overhead.

"Well," he said. "Far as I'm concerned he wouldn't be missed."

Chapter Eight

FIRST BLOOD TO POLK

THE LONGHORN TEXAS STEER has the spirit of his Spanish ancestry, the fighting bulls of Andalusia. He has in his long legs the speed of a horse. In certain respects he has less brains than a sheep. Generations on the plains shifting for himself, running from wolves and whooping riders made the longhorn brother to the antelope when it came to taking quick alarm and departing hastily from the scene of said alarm.

The WP herd under Polk Munce was made up of twenty-eight hundred two-year-old steers. In ordinary flesh when they left Nueces that spring successive degrees of northern latitude saw them wax fat, sleek, high-spirited. They grew "snuffy," as the cowpunchers say. Their bellies were eternally crammed with rich grass. Their blood pressure began to run uncommonly high. They became as skittish as colts. So that they had to be handled as a trained nurse handles a nervous patient, with tact and finesse. Every trail hand knew that if those longhorns ran once off the bedground, they would run again at their own shadow in the moonlight, at a cough or a sneeze, for no reason at all, except the mysterious contagion of fear. Life would become a burden as soon as night fell. Twenty-eight hundred brutes at a gallop in the dark is a sight and a sound never to be forgotten. It is the bovine equivalent of a theater crowd trampling each other underfoot in a mad rush for exits at the cry of fire.

Polk Munce was a cattleman from his thin hair to the ornate boots on his feet. He could think like a cow—only faster. He moved that herd day by day, bedded them at night in a spot of his own choosing, with an eye single to delivering them in Montana for the WP profit and his own prestige. His men patterned their behavior after him, being practically as competent as Polk himself. No rider ever went on guard without having in mind the contingency of that herd leaping to its feet with a clatter of dewclaws, a clashing of horns, and the thunder of a blind rush that would shake the earth for a radius of two miles.

On an unnamed fork of the Republican River, Brock and Tom Slater took the middle guard one muggy, sultry night. It wasn't particularly dark. Scattered clouds partly obscured the stars. Once properly bedded, a trail herd normally lay in a compact mass till dawn, the sound of its collective breathing like a vast intermittent sigh. Except to turn back an odd straggler suffering from some form of bovine insomnia, men on night guard had only to amble around the fringes of the herd, to keep awake and moving, to be there if something happened.

Middle guard began at eleven. At one-thirty they would call the relief. Brock and Slater circled the herd in opposite directions, meeting and passing twice in the round. Occasionally they pulled up to exchange a word. Mostly they rode that unending circle at a slow walk, crooning interminable chants, not because they desired to sing, but merely to keep the cattle aware of their presence so that a vague bulk looming suddenly with a jingle of spurs and a clink of bit chains would not startle them.

At twelve or thereabouts, Brock and Slater drew side by side. Before either had opened his mouth to speak an ominous rumble like a growl of thunder began at the far end of the herd.

"They're off," Slater cried. "Keep to one side, Brock. Oh, this is goin' to be plumb wicked."

It was. An avalanche of flesh and blood, hoofs, horns and glistening eyeballs swept across that plateau as if all hell clamored at their tails.

No need to warn the outfit sleeping around the chuck wagon. Slater knew and so did Brock. The earth tremors, the pound of ten thousand hooves on the dry turf would rouse them like a pistol shot over their beds. They would be running for their picketed horses now. Presently Polk and ten riders would be on the flank of that herd forging up to the leaders.

Swing the lead, once the stampede strung out, back on its own tail, let it run itself down in a circle, mill until weariness or the strange working of the longhorn brain settled them down again, to lie still and chew their cuds. And the rest of the night lost to sleep for saddle-weary men who seldom got sleep enough.

In theory the method of coping with a stampede was simple, in practice difficult. First turn your leaders. A Texas two-year-old sound in wind and limb can run like an antelope and run a long time, and when flying in panic from some obscure night terror has a tendency to forge straight on regardless of obstacles.

Brock and Slater lay up against the lead of the run. If a horse put foot in a hole or stumbled to his knees! A cowpuncher who began to think of things like that in the face of a stampede soon quit punching cows. Neither Brock nor Slater reckoned that chance. Slater had seen plenty of runs. Brock had experienced one or two the season before. They knew what to do and they were feverishly intent on the doing.

Away back they could see the drag of the herd, the less fleet-footed. They heard the other riders yell to show they were coming. Slater called to Brock. Both drew their guns and began to fire across the face of the leaders to frighten them into swerving aside.

They didn't turn easily. Brock couldn't tell how long they ran, how far they ran, but they kept running. He had used half the .45s in his belt. For a change he unlimbered his slicker and pressed close in, yelling lusty-lunged, waving the oilskin like a banner. It seemed to him the tongue-like point of the herd began to bend back upon itself. A glow of satisfaction shot through him. He had turned the stampede by himself. Not so bad for a dude. He wondered where Tom Slater was. Probably his horse had slowed down.

Then he became aware of a shape like pale gold thundering behind him, a rider on a buckskin horse. Polk Munce himself, cursing like a mule skinner, like a drill sergeant, roaring blasphemous obscenities. Brock knew

Polk's night horse even if he hadn't heard those shouted oaths.

"That you, Slater?"

"No. Parsons." Brock yelled above the hoof thunder. Polk ranged alongside. His profanity ceased. The buckskin lay about at Brock's stirrup leather. And the herd was certainly swinging. Polk hung right at his flank. Brock found time to wonder why, to wonder at that sudden silence on Polk's part.

A six-shooter cracked so close to him that he could smell the powder. Farther back other guns were popping to frighten the cattle into the turn that would end the run. But that was a secondary matter to Brock, a sort of subconscious perception. Because he had felt the wind of that bullet across his neck.

"Watch where you're shooting, you crazy fool!" he shouted at Polk. "I'm not a steer."

"No. But you're my meat!" Polk snarled, and his gun cracked again. This time Brock felt the lead sear him under one arm. Polk's buckskin was almost alongside. Brock's hand came up and turned to shoot back. Polk struck the gun out of his grasp with a venomous blow of his own heavy weapon. Brock could hear the sharp intake of his breath. He whirled his horse. Death was galloping beside him and he knew it—a fraction of a second too late. He hadn't imagined such a possibility, such form of attack. Weaponless now, Polk could finish him unless he got back to the other riders. Polk headed him off. He was making quick motions with his right hand. Brock heard the whistling swish of a rope. The yellow shape of Polk's buckskin shot off sidewise. Brock felt his own horse go out from under him, almost as if some unseen hand had snatched the saddle from between his legs. He sailed through the air like a diver from a springboard.

In that parabolic curve before he struck the earth Brock's brain apprehended that Polk had roped his horse by the feet and jerked him down. He got a quick, clear terrifying picture of that herd pounding over him, trampling his helpless body into a shapeless mess with their hoofs. Then he smashed on the baked earth so hard that he ceased to think, to see or feel.

The sun on his face stirred him to consciousness. He sat up, puzzled at first, bewildered, shot through with pain. He couldn't understand for a few seconds why he was there alone in that grassy emptiness. Then he remembered.

He took stock of himself. Left arm broken midway between wrist and elbow, badly swollen. A raking bullet wound under one armpit. A lesser rip across one thigh. A variety of scratches and contusions. A splitting headache, Agonies of pain from his broken arm shooting through all that side of his body. A thirst that made his throat and mouth feel like sandpaper.

He stood up on unsteady legs, to look about, to peer off, turning slowly on his heels, at the unending horizon, a vacuity of flatness that ran out to the edges of a blue bowl decorated with a ball of fire. Sun, sky, grassy plain. Nothing else.

"Man overboard," he muttered. "And no lifeboat."

Between pain and shock, a probable touch of fever, it was difficult for him to think straight. Plains-bred for all practical purposes, Brock's instincts and his intelligence still served him. Afoot, unarmed, injured, his first thought was for his gun. He didn't know how far he had galloped trying to dodge Polk after that fuming murderer had knocked the six-shooter out of his hand. He looked for tracks, and found a confusion of them, sod torn by shod hoofs. Close by, the track of the running cattle was like a harrowed swath across a field. Everywhere else the grass stood six inches high. Hopeless to find anything that didn't bulk large.

He gave it up. He had to get to water soon or go mad. He felt nauseated, dizzy from the few rods he had traversed looking for his lost weapon. Sitting down for a minute to rest, he tried to reconstruct the lay of the land.

The herd had been bedded on the south side of a nameless creek that flowed easterly, known to debouch into the

Republican farther on. So far as Brock could recall, the trend of the stampede had been southeast. Therefore if he held straight north he must eventually reach that creek again. That was a certainty. Anything else was a chance. It wasn't the sort of country to nourish springs. The western Nebraska plains were too hotly ironed by an unremitting sun for surface water to lie in pools or sloughs so late in the summer.

He turned north. His head ached over the problem. Polk must have nursed a deeper grudge than Brock realized, or he would never have grasped that opportunity to kill him. And no one in the outfit would know that. Probably they wouldn't credit such a thing, even to Polk, a known killer. Brock would simply be missing when the outfit counted noses at daybreak. And Polk wouldn't just shrug his shoulders and move on. He wouldn't dare. The WP cowpunchers wouldn't let him. They knew how such things happened. They would take it for granted his horse had gone down in front of the stampede. They would find his mount with an empty saddle and reins trailing. Polk was too foxy to fail sending a search party to find and at least bury the remains.

Brock was a mile and a half on his way, spurred by that terrible craving for water, when he got it all straight in his mind. He reflected that he was acting stupidly. Naturally the WP riders would backtrack that stampede to find him dead or crippled. They wouldn't look for him to be anywhere except where the herd had plowed with its sharp hoofs. All he had to do was sit by those cattle tracks and wait. They should be in sight now. The sun was swinging high.

Nevertheless Brock was suffering more for water than for anything under high heaven. Presently it would be unbearable. He knew. He hesitated between turning back and moving on toward where that creek must certainly be. He reflected that a man walking could be seen at a mile or two.

He had halted on a barely perceptible rise. And as he pondered, finding his wits slow, and a decision difficult, he saw, unless the mirage was in his brain as well as on the plains, a line of trees to the north that must mark a watercourse. And to the south he saw a cluster of dots taking form. Dots that must be riders.

Brock watched these closely. Riders spread out. The WP looking for what was left of him. They came up fast, following the plain trail of the running cattle until they were parallel with him a mile and a half or thereabouts to the south. Brock got to his feet. He started for them eagerly.

In the reaction he hurried too much for a man wounded and weakened as he was. In the center of a low swale, where the grass stood knee-high, as rank a growth as clothes a farmer's hay meadow, he stumbled and fell. Fell heavily on that broken arm. Pain shot through him like molten fire, sickened him, sapped his waning strength. He lay still, shuddering, setting his teeth against that agony.

When it eased at last he lifted his head. His body was almost buried in the tall grass. He looked through a fringe of coarse blades before his face.

And what he saw was Polk Munce sitting on a sorrel horse, sitting there alone, half turned in his saddle, looking down into that swale.

The shallow saucer shape of that dip in the plains cut off everything else. Brock lay flat. If the other WP riders were far enough away—and Polk spotted him—he would ride down and finish the job. And ride on. Brock felt sure of that. He was helpless. He didn't dare show himself to that killer sitting on his horse so near that Brock could see the expression on his ugly face. If another rider joined Polk, he would rise and yell. If not, he didn't dare expose himself to Polk Munce alone.

For a minute or so Polk surveyed that grassy hollow. Then he swung his mount. Brock crawled to where the long grass thinned, went on all fours from there to the crest of the low slope beyond.

Polk was loping swiftly to join his riders. Brock could see them off in the distance, one or two pairs coming back to join the main group, now bunched, sitting still. Brock stood up. He had no coat. He had no hat. Painfully he eased off his shirt with the one good arm and waved it like a flag.

But the riders had turned as soon as Polk joined them. They were riding slowly back along the path of that stampede. They had covered the outermost limit of the run and were working back. Either he couldn't be seen or no one happened to look that way. He watched them ride until they faded to specks, into nothing, as if the plains had swallowed them.

Out of nine riders looking for him, this would-be murderer to whom Brock didn't dare show himself had to be the only one to come within hail. If he had only been armed!

He turned north again. He had to rest frequently. Also he had to reach water while strength and sanity lasted, or perish. Brock recalled afterward that he talked to himself a lot on the way, as he trudged and rested, licking his lips with a tongue that felt salty, like a rasp, wooden. It was a long way and he was very weak. The sun reached mid-heaven, beating on his bare head as if to further addle his brain. His broken arm swelled and swelled in the neck-scarf he tied around it for a sling. The two bullet scores felt as if red-hot pokers were being drawn across his flesh.

Still he kept going. Sometimes things were hazy, sometimes he knew precisely what he was doing and why—and the only question in his mind was whether he could make that dark line which spelled water. After eons of time he staggered down a little bank to willows fringing a lukewarm stream. Gnarly limbed cottonwoods stood like sentinels on guard in that immense silence. Brock lay on his belly and drank, bathed his throbbing head. A meadow lark lit on a willow over his head and burst into throaty song. Bees hummed over a clump of lupins in late bloom. He tugged off his boots and soaked his blistered feet in the water.

Then he felt himself getting faint and ill. The sky and the willows and the valley of that stream began to spin with slow gyrations. He drew back from the creek, crawled twenty feet into the shade of an enormous cottonwood, and stretched himself there.

Afternoon waned, dusk fell, dark closed in. Brock roused once or twice to mark stars twinkling in the velvet night. But it was all very inconsequential to him. Even when day broke and the sunbeams slanted in under his cottonwood tree, he still lay in that stupor of pain and weakness. Once he crawled to the creek, drank, and crept back to the shade, to lie with his head pillowed on his good arm while the sun wheeled to its zenith.

Chapter Nine

MARCH OF THE HORNED LOCUSTS

OUT OF THE SHADOWY DESOLATION of the *Agua Malo* the point of the Long S herd crawled to the level of the plains, a slow, shifting, elongated thing like some monster reptile twining from its lair to meet the sun. Dawn had broken across the high land but the blasted course of the *Agua Malo* was a blur of shade as if night were loath to quit the place and bare its barrenness to the searching eye of day. For nothing flourished in that drab hollow, no blade of grass, no tree, only stunted sage and greasewood. A long meandering depression threaded by a slinking stream whose waters were bitter in the mouth. Because of that water, precious in an arid waste, the herd had lain there overnight. Now, rising from the bedground in the half-night, the cattle climbed through a coulee in orderly procession to the grass-covered plains—a regiment of hoofed and horned beasts two thousand strong.

A hundred yards back from the long-horned vanguard two riders moved sedately, one on each side, guiding and controlling the line of march as a helmsman holds a ship on her course. Farther back so that they were as yet hidden in the hollow from which the herd debouched rode two more. And back at the drag where bulked large the mass of those who lacked the pace of their more ambitious leaders, three other horsemen moved in the thin haze of dust ground up from the dry earth by eight thousand hoofs.

Presently these were all clear of the low ground, spreading as they began to graze, a huge dark blur on the gray-green of the plain. In the east a blazon of rose and red and orange faded to tints on a scattered cloud bank. Westward a lone butte flashed a cap of gold. And now from this same coulee whence the herd had crawled a wagon came creaking, rattling, swaying, as the four-horse team stepped at a brisk trot. Behind crowded the *remuda,* scores of clean-legged southern horses, sleek-bodied, ears up, alert. A tinkle of bells rose from the leaders. At their heels a boyish figure on a slashing chestnut horse encouraged the *remuda's* progress with a trailing rope end.

As these all won clear of the *Agua Malo* the sun cocked a segment of his yellow eye above the sky line. Long shafts of light stabbed like golden spears across those miles of grassland, flashing and glittering on every rise, setting forth by contrast the black shadow in every dip below the general level. It played upon the silver-inlaid bits and spurs of the riders. The herd seemed no longer a neutral-colored mass but stood forth in its scores and hundreds of units, red cattle, black cattle, white cattle, spotted, buckskin, roan and dun, with sunlight glinting on a myriad of long curved horns.

"Hoo-yah, ponies!" the wrangler cried. "There's trees for shade and some real water at the next camp. Drift, you *caballos.* Split the breeze!"

As chuck wagon and *remuda* pulled abreast of the herd, the driver waved a hand to the last driver. He held straight north. The horse wrangler crowded his saddle bunch close on the rolling wheels. In half an hour the trail herd was a dark blot far behind. Chuck wagon and *remuda* topped a low rise. Miles ahead a thin, dark line wound across the prairie.

As they rolled down to this at a headlong gait the dark line resolved itself into a fringe of willows interspersed here and there by thick-trunked, branchy cottonwoods, green with foliage. A small stream laved the roots of these, coming from a rolling height of land far on the west, winding away into the blank, unending levels on the east.

The wagon halted. The horse wrangler turned the leaders on the creek below and loped to the wagon. The driver was already unharnessing, freeing his work-horses to join their fellows. The two, working swiftly without words, dumped a miscellaneous lot of stuff off the wagon, stretched a square of canvas awning-fashion from a mess kit built on the trail end of the wagon box.

The driver, a stripling of less than twenty, turned to cast an appraising eye over the camp ground.

"Clay gave us the right steer," he said. "This water looks pretty good. Let's fill the barrels before the sun gets too all-fired hot, Lou. Gosh, when I get to wherever we're goin' I aim to find me a ice-cold spring and camp by it for a month. Seems like ten years since I had a drink of clear, cold water—water that don't stink or taste like a dose of salts."

Lou chuckled. "If I'd known you'd be so thirsty, I might have arranged for one of those Kansas City icemen to make regular deliveries along the trail this summer," she said.

"If you'd arranged for a barrel of cold beer to be delivered here an' there, been more like it," Gene Stark grumbled. "You wouldn't think of nothin' like that. You got all the best of it, bein' a female. Dad wouldn't let *me* ever get to Kansas City. A man's got to stay with the outfit, ridin' after these blamed cattle, while you go hellin' around havin' a good time."

"Town's no place for a cowpuncher," Lou observed.

"That's how you got to go, wasn't it?" her brother snorted. "You settin' yourself up for a stockhand, just because you're goin' up the trail with us? You got to do more'n shingle your hair, Sis, and wear leather leggin's to be a cowpuncher."

"I'm a better stockhand than you are, Mister Gene," the girl teased. "If I weren't, you'd be wrangling horses and *I'd* be juggling the Dutch ovens."

"A cook's the most important man on either roundup or trail," Gene grinned, satisfied at having got under his sister's skin in this exchange of pleasantries. "Every cowman admits that. Cowpunchers don't punch cows worth a cent if they ain't well fed at regular periods. Go on bein' proud of yourself as horse wrangler, but help me fill these water barrels and rustle me some wood."

"Fill your own barrels, Mister Important Cook," Lou replied impertinently.

With that she swung up on her horse and loped out for

a turn around the fringe of her grazing *remuda.*

Gene went whistling about his work. He dug a shallow trench, started a fire therein, drove a forked stick on each side of the fire in the crotches of which he placed a heavy iron rod. From this he suspended two or three pots. Having made sundry simple preparations for dinner, he took pails and carried from the creek water to fill the barrels slung on each side of the wagon box. The top of each he covered with a wet sack to keep it cool. With the chill of night air on the water it was not so bad, though at best the stream ran sluggish and tasted of vegetation. But the hot sun swinging across the sky would turn that stream lukewarm in another hour or two. And presently those who toiled in the dusty wake of that herd would descend on camp with baked throats.

Lou dragged up a bundle of dry wood on the end of her *reata,* flung more pert remarks at her brother, and trotted off again bent upon exploration of this wooded bottom, a pleasant place after weeks of slow journeying across bald, sun-stricken plains.

Away at the top of the low rise behind them, the lead of the herd crawled into view, drew nearer. The cattle had ceased to graze. They were walking, sniffing water from afar. When the slow-moving mass ranged within a couple of miles, three riders detached themselves and came tearing campward. Then by an effortless crook of the elbow they brought the cowhorses up all standing in two jumps, swung down, and stripped off saddle and bridle with deft movements. Then concertedly they stormed the water barrels.

And just as they settled themselves in the shade of the wagon, each with cigarette material in hand, Lou came thundering across the flat, the hoofs of the big chestnut beating a patter on the baked turf. There was an astonishing resemblance in the faces of the four men as they stared at her with that squinting keenness of vision that comes from looking out across great distances in the eye of the sun and the teeth of uncurbed winds. Alike they owned rather high cheek bones, straight, thin noses, eyes of a peculiar steely gray, thin, curved lips, a certain lean wiriness of build. All were above average height.

"What's your hurry, Sis?" one asked as Lou pulled up with a jerk almost on top of them. "You trainin' Redskin for a quarterhawss? Or did you see Injuns in the timber?"

Lou's gray eyes were wide and startled.

"Indians my foot," she said scornfully. "I found a man layin' under a cottonwood down there. He looks like he might be dead."

Chapter Ten

THE MAN WITH A BROKEN ARM

"G'WAN," DRAWLED THE IRREPRESSIBLE GENE. "You took a nap under a tree an' dreamed that scary tale."

"Quit your foolin', Gene," the oldest of the riders cut in. "Where is this dead man of yours, Lou?"

"About four hundred yards down the creek," she replied. "Come on. I'll show you."

"Well, I reckon we better take a look at this here corpse," her brother said. He seemed a little dubious.

"Go ahead. Take a chance. We'll bend her over the wagon tongue an' *chap* her if she's takin' a fall out of us," one of the others said.

Lou swung about. The three followed her, grumbling a trifle that she hadn't come before they turned their mounts loose. Gene remained at the wagon because his dinner preparations were under way and not from any lack of curiosity, for all his open belief that Lou was merely stringing them. Already the lead of the herd was pouring down the slope, and dead men or no dead men the riders must be fed.

The girl led them straight to a cottonwood standing in a space clear of the bordering willows close on the trench-like channel of the creek. While they were still at a little distance they could see that she had given no false alarm—of which the three had been none too sure, since all the year was April first to Louise Stark where her brothers were concerned. It would not have been the first juvenile prank she had played on them since they crossed the Texas border heading north. But for once she had not cried "Wolf!" where there was no wolf.

The man lay face down, his head pillowed on one arm, the other arm extended full length. That side of his face which showed, however, was not the face of a dead man, for it was flushed and stained with dried blood. So was the light cotton shirt he wore. He was dressed much as the three men looking at him, in overalls and riding boots, with a pair of very beautiful silver-inlaid spurs glittering above his boot heels. About his hips a cartridge belt was buckled, but the holster was empty. He was minus a hat. The silk handkerchief, or bandanna, according to taste, that ordinarily flutters about a cowpuncher's neck was tightly bound about the extended arm midway between elbow and wrist.

Dave shook him gently.

"Hey," said he. "Come alive, old-timer."

He did not elicit so much as a grunt. Dave slipped a hand under him, feeling for his heart.

"He ain't dead, that's a cinch," Dave remarked. "But he's out. Certainly hurt. He's been in some sort of mix-up. Funny, they ain't no other outfit in sight."

"Of course he's hurt," Lou said. "Why don't you-all pick him up and pack him into camp? Can't do anything for him here."

"I reckon we better," Dave agreed. "Lay holt of him by the shoulder, Wally. Git your arm under his middle, Ed. I'll take him by the feet. Easy, now."

Halfway to the wagon Lou, riding close, saw a pair of dark blue eyes open momentarily. He grunted and his teeth shut on his underlip. Then his head lopped sidewise against Wally Stark's shoulder. They spread out a roll of bedding in the shade of the chuck wagon and laid him down to catch their breath. The stranger was deceptively heavy for his build and it is no easy task to carry a limp burden carefully.

From the herd now pouring in to shade and water came two more riders bobbing into camp. Another unmistakable scion of the house of Stark, a boy scarcely more than sixteen and a man of fifty-odd whose long white mustache and growth of beard could not hide the facial pattern wherein his numerous sons were cast. The two swung off their mounts just as Dave and Wally succeeded in forcing a spoonful of whisky between the stranger's teeth.

Between movement and stimulant, the man presently

opened his eyes. A blank uncertainty, as he struggled for recollection, was shortly succeeded by a puzzled stare at the circle of faces bent over him. A humorous twist wrinkled the corners of his mouth.

"Great Jerusalem!" he whispered huskily. "Are you-all a flock of twins?"

The Starks chuckled.

"You looked for a spell as if you were ready to be planted. But I reckon you ain't, quite," Dave observed. "Where you hurt? Shot up any?"

"I'm nicked just under the shoulder blade, and on one leg, but that don't amount to a hill of beans," the man responded. "My arm's broke, though. That's what raised Cain with me. Ouch!"

"Lemme see that there arm," old man Stark put in. "We're a blame long way from medical men, m'son, but I've set a bone or two in my time."

Stark unbound the handkerchief, slit away the shirt sleeve, and revealed a fearfully swollen arm.

"Get me a pail of hot water, Gene," he commanded. "Have to soak this till some of the swellin' goes down. Whilst she's steepin', might help if you'd eat a bite, eh?"

"It sure would," the wounded man replied. "So would a drink of water. *And* a smoke. To tell the truth, when I bedded down under that tree I wouldn't have given two bits for my chances of either eating or smoking again. I didn't suppose there was a living soul in fifty miles."

Gene brought the water, in which the man immersed his broken arm. Dave rolled a cigarette for him. Mike, the youngest, a man doing a man's riding for all his youthful slenderness, watched the stranger with questions on his face that the older men concealed.

Lou stared at him surreptitiously from a seat on the wagon tongue, shyly aloof. For the first time in a month she was uneasy in Mike's clothing, with Gene's chaps encasing her legs. When a turn of the man's head brought his gaze speculatively upon her she looked quickly away to the longhorns enfilading upon the water.

Gene announced dinner with a laconic "come an' get

it." Lou mounted her horse and broke away to gather in
the *remuda* so that the riders could catch fresh mounts as
soon as they had eaten. If she had an eye to effect in the
highly professional manner in which she marshaled her
charge of a hundred and fifty-odd head inside the rope
corral, staked knee-high from the wagon for their deten-
tion, it was altogether lost. The good-looking young man
she had discovered unconscious beneath the cottonwood
tree was devoting himself wholly with his one good hand
to a plate of fried beef and cornbread.

When men are engaged upon momentous business they
eat to satisfy hunger and they seldom linger at the job. By
the time Lou had her horses bunched, old man Stark and
his sons were ready with *reatas* looped out ready to throw.

Four of them rode out to relieve those on herd. These,
upon reaching the wagon, caught and tied up fresh horses.
Lou was free to turn her saddle bunch loose.

The Stark herd had made fourteen miles since dawn.
Twenty miles or more lay between them and the next
water. For a mixed herd traveling under a midsummer
sun that was a long day's march, with a dry noon camp,
even though they started with the first crack of light in the
east. And since it was a forced all-day journey the herd
would lie the rest of that afternoon and that night on this
creek.

Lou sauntered up to the chuck wagon to eat her dinner.
The stranger sat with his broken arm immersed in the
pail of hot water. Her father smoked placidly, content to
sit in the shade of the wagon. For another hour he rested,
while Gene occasionally poured more hot water in the
pail.

Then Lou held her breath while old man Stark, splints
and bandage made ready, stretched that broken arm till
the fractured bone went into place under his sinewy fingers. The man's face broke out in a film of sweat with the
pain, but his features stayed set in the semblance of a grin
till the job was done. Then he sighed and asked for another cigarette.

Old Eugene Stark stood admiring his handiwork. He

grew reminiscent. "One time I was up at the head of the Pecos in midwinter with Saul Parker," said he. "Just the two of us. Horse fell on Saul. Busted his leg. There we was —three hundred miles from nowhere, me just a kid like Mike here. Saul knowed what to do, but I had to do it for him. Saul rode outa there in two months with his leg as good as ever. That arm won't ever trouble you none, stranger."

"My name's Brock," the young fellow said.

But he didn't say Brock what, or what Brock. Lou marked that. She thought it queer. It was rather more than queer that a man should lie unconscious, with a broken arm and two wounds that though slight were palpably bullet scores, in the heart of an uninhabited waste. Lie there—how long?—wounded and unconscious without a horse by him, or a gun, or a hat to his head. How did he get there? There was not, he had himself said, another outfit within fifty miles. From her brothers' talk Lou reckoned that there was no town, no settlement, no ranch anywhere within a radius of three hundred miles. No white man had ever planted his rooftree in that region. It was a waste, thinly grassed, sparsely watered, untenanted save by antelope, prairie dogs, wolves, and rattlers. Trail herds from Texas to the Northwest crossed it of necessity. How did the man come here alone in that state, and why? Louise Stark wondered. If her father and brothers also wondered, like her they said nothing.

"My name's Stark," old Gene replied.

"I'd say you're all Starks, by the looks," Brock smiled.

"Yes," Stark senior admitted. "These here are all my boys. Seven of 'em. Here's the only girl in the Stark family, an' she's passin' for a boy herself till this trail herd hits Montana—or wherever we locate."

"Ha," Brock grinned broadly at them all, Lou included, before his gaze came back to the old man. "You raised a trail crew of your own to start north with. Darn few cowmen could do that."

"All riders," the old man said with pardonable pride. "Every last one of 'em. We left the Trinity in April—

South Fork."

Lou Stark wondered why Brock looked at her father searchingly and why his eyes dwelt on the shoulder of her chestnut horse standing near on trailing reins. He was nice-looking, Lou decided, even though his face was dirty, streaked with a mixture of dust and dried blood, covered with the stubble of three weeks beard. He had glossy brown hair with a decided wave in it. His blue eyes seemed to smile even when his face was set in sober lines. Any girl who has grown up surrounded by seven competent brothers is apt to use them as a measuring stick for other men. Brock lost nothing by comparison. Miss Louise Stark found herself intolerably curious about him. But personal questions, as yet, were not in order. `

At daybreak next morning the Long S moved off that pleasant creek bottom. When the herd was an hour gone, spread wide and grazing north by slow stages, the chuck wagon passed by. Brock rode on the high spring seat with Gene. Lou trailed with the *remuda* as she had done for weeks that were becoming timeless, so much did one day seem like another. From western Kansas until the northbound trail herds struck Wyoming they were like sailing ships running their easting down the trades. Bald, flat, grass-grown plains as far as the eye could reach. Now and then a butte or a ridge broke the endless level, but beyond these the flat country spread away again.

Far ahead of the Long S herd, the Stark wagon made a noon halt. When the cattle drew close, half the riders would come in, gulp water out of barrels slung alongside, eat fried beef and drink coffee, change to fresh horses, and push on. It was hard on horses and cattle to go sixteen hours between water holes, but God who made creeks and rivers to cross the great plains did not arrange them for the convenience of cattlemen making the great trek from the Texas Panhandle to the Big Muddy.

Gene, young Brock, and Lou Stark sat in the shade of the wagon. All about them saddle horses grazed. The herd was a blot on the southern sky line, marching now, not grazing. They could tell that by the banner of dust lifting like thin smoke. Far westward Brock pointed out another dust cloud faint on the horizon.

"Herd over there," he said. And after a minute. "If we could see two hundred miles instead of twenty, we'd see a lot."

"You reckon?" Gene commented. "Prairie dogs an' antelopes an' a few coyotes. Maybe a few Injuns off the reservation lookin' for scalps."

"Probably," Brock murmured. "But you'd see herds, too. Trail herds going north like the Israelites moving out of Egypt. I'll bet within two hundred miles of where we sit there are a hundred thousand longhorn cattle trailing north. Moving up to a new country. Horned locusts. It's immense."

He stared at the horizon, off across that hushed, empty grassland, as if he saw more than was bared to the eye. It was ten o'clock. The sun had come to full strength. Heat waves shimmered here and there. The daily mirage put lakes and timbered them where no lake or tree had ever been. While they watched, the twin dust clouds, half a day's ride apart, one drawing near, the other soon to fade, began to assume fantastic shapes, to take form and color that shifted and changed. Over that grassy sea the mirage-distorted bovine argosies sailed to new, green pastures, a two-thousand-mile voyage.

"Immense," Brock repeated after a pause. "I saw thirty herds leave the Rio Grande one day last March. Where are they now?" He waved his good hand. "Specks somewhere in this wilderness."

"You talk like a poet," Gene said.

The three of them laughed, a little self-consciously. Gene rolled a cigarette for the broken-armed rider and set a match to his laid fire under the Dutch oven. Dots that were Long S riders came bobbing in toward the camp.

"Dave an' Ed will go scoutin' water ahead tomorrow," Gene remarked.

"You should be a hundred miles west to hit the best going," Brock said abruptly.

"Oh, you know this country, do you?" Lou asked.

"Up the trail last summer," Brock told her.

"We're follerin' accordin' to directions given Dad by men that's driven herds north," Gene declared.

"Better to the west, just the same," Brock persisted. "But in two or three weeks it won't matter. You'll be in a good country. This is a barren stretch. Bad water country. Still," he ended thoughtfully, "hard-looking as it is, in ten years it will probably be cluttered with people."

"They'll starve to death unless they can live like the jack rabbits," Gene snorted. "Shucks, it won't even be cluttered with jack rabbits. A jack rabbit would have to pack a canteen to cross most of this here region. It ain't worth a damn—not even for sheep. Not the last ten days we've traveled. I reckon the wind would blow a man plumb off the earth here in winter. They say the snow gets powerful deep, too."

"You'll see," Brock said quietly.

"We'll not be here, that's a cinch," Gene said. "We're headed for a better country, where there's mountains with pine timber on them, grass like hay on the ridges an' prairies an' oodles of good spring water, they say. Gosh, I wish we was there now."

The bobbing riders drew up, unsaddled, drank thirstily. The herd crawled abreast, steers strung a mile in the lead now, cows and young stuff bunched in a bawling drag, grinding up the dust. Four riders punched the drag. Ed, Dave, and Mike rested in the shade. Gene senior, Wally, Clay, Pete swallowed the dust. In an hour all seven had eaten, were mounted afresh, riding on the flanks of that moving herd.

Although it was past noon and the sun beat on them without rest or mercy the cattle walked, no longer with heads lowered to nip a blade of grass here and there, but with noses out sniffing for water. They would neither rest nor feed till they found it. Like columns of spearmen, horns glinting, they marched, were marching steadily under their dust banner when the Long S chuck wagon and *remuda* passed.

Dave Stark rode ahead to pilot the wagon to water, a

string of sloughs in a shallow drag. There they halted and Dave rode back to join his fellows at the herd. Gene and Lou unloaded by these brackish pools. Gene filled his barrels. Sundown found the cattle stringing in. In an hour the sloughs were muddy wallows and the Long S herd lay in a mass about the banks, too weary and footsore to graze. Twenty-seven miles from water to water. Ninety in the shade. Over soil hot enough to blister a man's feet.

"Trail drivin'," Dave Stark tugged at one boot that night in the dusk and grunted to Brock, with whom he shared his bed, "ain't no snap in these parts."

"Pioneering never is," Brock murmured.

"Pioneerin' my foot," Dave remarked casually. "This ain't pioneerin'. We're just movin' north to better range. Little tough in spots, that's all. Why, when the old man was on the Pecos, about the time I was born, they had to fight Injuns every little while. The buffalo was a darned nuisance. They had nothin' but muzzle-loadin' guns. Why, man alive—*this* ain't pioneerin'. It's just work. Where was you raised, anyhow?"

Brock didn't answer that.

Chapter Eleven

GUNS OUT IN LOST RIVER

DAY AFTER DAY IN ENDLESS PROCESSION. Hot sun. Parched earth. Vegetation bleached yellow-gray. The only green thing in all that waste a few blades of grass by the edge of a water-hole, stunted willows by some sluggish creek. Heat waves shimmering away to beautiful pictures painted on the horizon out of nothing by the mirage. An atmosphere at noon like the hot breath from the stokehold of a liner.

And through this burning emptiness, without chart or compass, feeling their way by throwing scout riders a day's move ahead to locate water, the Long S outfit shoved its herd north. They bore west by Brock's advice and so traversed a less desolate region. He was useful, this crippled man of mystery. He had the lay and nature of the land in his head.

His arm bone knitted. It was almost well when they trailed down a long watershed in the eastern Wyoming to a river and civilization of a sort. For here they crossed the Union Pacific railway and the smoke of town chimneys greeted their eyes from afar. Also, upon this river bottom half a dozen other herds were converging to make the same crossing of a treacherous stream.

The Long S set up camp a mile below another outfit whose white tent looked on the river. Before their supper fire was fairly crackling two riders loped over.

They did a curious thing. When they came to the outer fringe of the Long S *remuda*, they pulled up short, sat like statues for ten seconds, swung their horses about, and rode straight for their own camp. And when Lou Stark—only she and Brock and Gene were by the wagon—turned to Brock with a comment on this curious behavior, she saw him staring after them, frowning, his lips curled. Anger seemed to glow in his eyes. He didn't even mark Lou's glance at him. He put his good hand deep in his pocket and stared, scowling, after those riders.

The lead of the Long S cattle came down to water. When the entire herd had taken its fill, the Stark riders moved the herd well back on the flat, to good grazing.

The relief sat down to supper. Eugene Stark said to his sons, "Nobody's goin' to town tonight. Keep your eye peeled. That next outfit above us is a Parsons herd."

"Don't worry me none," Ed Stark shrugged his wide flat shoulders. "If they want to stir up more trouble—"

Lou saw Brock flush a little. But he didn't lift his eyes from his plate. And when he had finished his supper he said to old man Stark, "You've been darned good to me, all you folks. I'm about ready to use my arm again. I can quit you here and shift for myself. Or would you consider me making a hand with the herd to wherever you-all are headed for?"

"Why, we could use you, I reckon," Stark said. "We been workin' short-handed all the way. But you ain't got no ridin' rig."

"Stake me to a couple of horses for an hour or two," Brock replied, "and I can remedy that."

"Why, Gene'll lend you his hull for this evenin', I expect," the old man replied. "Reckon you can get a saddle an' such in Lost River."

Brock reckoned he could.

Ten minutes later he was mounted and riding. Lou watched him go. He gave the Parsons herd and camp a wide berth. The Stark men noticed that.

"He don't advertise himself none, that *hombre*," Dave remarked. "An' he ain't no fool either. Wonder if he knows anything about the fuss between us an' them."

"Probably more concerned with whatever fuss he was in himself," Dave's father observed dryly. "But I'll bet he ain't no slouch at nothin' he undertakes, that young feller. His private business is none of ours, no more'n ours is his. If he wants to stay with us he'll be useful, an' welcome."

"I think he's got his eye on Lou," Gene suggested impishly. " 'Nother scalp. Time we cross the Yellowstone he'll be askin' you to name the day, Sis. Terrible to have that fatal beauty. Gosh, these cowpunchers is soft. If he only knew you like I do."

"What if he did?" Lou retorted. "Maybe he could do worse."

"Here, here," Stark senior remonstrated mildly. "You two carry a josh too far. You ain't either of you done school yet. Talkin' about fellers. Shucks. Wait till you're growed up."

"If I'm grown up enough to wrangle horses for the Long S from the Texas Panhandle to Montana, I should be grown enough to pick a man for myself, shouldn't I?" Lou asked pertly.

"Oh? Did you aim to pick *him*?" her father asked quietly.

"Why, of course not," Lou retorted. "I ain't picking nobody. But I like Brock, just the same, in spite of Mister Smarty here. He's nice."

"Sure, nobody denies it," the old man grinned. "Decent speakin' an' actin' every way. Nobody's runnin' him down. But if you're goin' to get partial to him, I'd kinda like to know who he is, where he's from, an' how he come to be stranded an' shot up on the bank of a creek in Nebraska a hundred miles from nowhere."

Lou rode out around her horse herd. She had found Brock on the bank of that lonely stream much as the daughters of Pharaoh found the infant Moses in the bulrushes. That in itself gave her a sort of proprietary interest in him—which she frankly admitted to herself. Lou was no shy, rustic beauty, with a heart that palpitated in the presence of personable young men. Texas had population, history, culture peculiar to the Southwest. Neither cattlemen nor their families were hermits. The very nature of their calling, the scope of their pastoral affairs, made them alert, responsive to both mental and physical stimuli. They covered a lot of territory. They were not strangers to nicety of living. Many a man who drank thankfully of brackish water stagnant in a cow track on trail and roundup knew also the taste of good wine and better food. And their women were sometimes as modish, as aware of the world beyond the cattle country, as their sisters of the Atlantic seaboard. Wealth is wealth anywhere, in any form, bonds, gold, land, wheat, or cattle. It gives those who command it assurance and dignity. So Louise Stark, having seen range, ranch, and cities throughout the Southwest, from Santa Fe to New Orleans, a region old and populous when Illinois was still a savage frontier, did not fret herself over the family's chaffing, nor try to evade the fact that she liked young Brock better than any man she had ever seen.

The mystery that attended his presence merely piqued her curiosity. She knew her father and brothers were equally curious, but it was not range form to admit a burning curiosity about any man's private concerns. No one in the Long S would ever ask Brock why and how he came to be in that plight, unless it simply had to be inquired into.

But Lou was quite fanciful enough to wonder if he would come back. He might be just an unfortunate stockhand. He might be a man with a price on his head along the Rio Grande. No one could tell a frog's jumping capacity by the way he sat on the bank. No one knew better than the cattlemen that riders could never be judged wholly by appearances. They didn't. They gauged men by their actions. A man's reputation carried little weight unless he lived up to it, nor was complete lack of known reputation a demerit.

So it occasioned no comment and little surprise when Brock failed to return at sundown, nor crawled into the bed he shared with Clay during the night. No one mentioned him. He had Gene's saddle, two Long S cowhorses. He might be on a "bust" in Lost River. He might have jumped the country. Time would tell.

Above them the Parsons herd took the river at daylight. Their cattle rose dripping on the north bank, trailed up to the bench, vanished.

Old man Stark issued orders after breakfast.

"We'll lay here today. Take in this town and load supplies," said he. "Water that herd at noon an' then hold 'em well back. We'll make the crossin' at sunup."

The Stark wagon rolled into Lost River. Lou herded her horses by the camp. She rode with her brothers around the grazing cattle. The character of the country had begun to change. A richer growth of grass lay underfoot. The river ran clear as crystal, a swift stream with a gravelly bottom, swimming deep. Away off on the edge of things mountain peaks stood purple against the blue. Lou stared at them longingly. She knew little of mountains and pine trees and singing creeks. They were more to her liking than the hot plains where she had spent most of her years. North, the country seemed to lift in great undulations. Grassy ridge after grassy ridge yellow in the sun. Her brothers told her that the trail from now on lay across rolling country with patches of prairie. Sagebrush and cactus still held its own. But there would be timbered creeks. The monotonous level and the bad water lay behind them now. They tried to alarm her, too, by grave discussion of a bad Indian country, the haunt of Cheyennes, Ogallalas, Crows, Sioux, even the fierce, raiding Blackfeet. But she only smiled.

The chuck wagon, replenished in Lost River, rattled back to the camp ground. There was fresh fruit, newspapers, vegetables, by grace of the Union Pacific freight trains. Stark senior, Clay, and Dave had been in town. They sat by the wagon now, resting until it was time to relieve the day herders. Old Gene didn't go on day herd himself. He continued to read.

When the relieved riders had filled their plates and squatted in the shade, Wally said to his father, "Clay tells me Lost River's a right smart little town. Reckon we'd get dehorned if we-all ride in this afternoon, for a spell?"

"Why, I dunno's there's any great risk," old Eugene grinned. "They's two good stores an' a hotel. The saloons have beer on ice. Go to it, son. Only don't liquor up too strong."

"I could do with a few knickknacks myself, Dad," Lou suggested. "Suppose I ride in with the boys?"

He nodded assent.

Gene made mysterious signs to his sister. She joined him

where he sat smoking a little apart from the others.

"Boys tell you about Brock?"

She shook her head.

"Well, this protégé of yours, Sis, sure gave 'em a touch of high life last night. They told us about it. A feller with one arm in a sling, they said. Brown, wavy-haired *hombre*. He killed a Parsons trail boss an' rode outa town cool as a cucumber."

"I wouldn't care if he shot up the whole Parsons tribe," Lou replied. "Good for him. That's why he didn't come back to the wagon. Are they after him?"

"Why, there ain't no officers after him, if that's what you mean," Gene answered. "When trail hands tangle, the county authorities don't mix, if they go on about their business afterward—so they say in Lost River. Sheriffs has troubles enough in their own line without chasin' men outside their own territory. He left a note for the old man, with a storekeeper."

"What did he say?"

Gene shook his tawny head.

"Dad just grinned when he read it an' put it in his pocket. That's all I know."

Lou rode off to Lost River half an hour later. Wally, Pete, Mike, and Ed commented on the story of this killing as told them by their brothers when they took over the herd. It left plenty of room for speculation. Details were scanty. Brock apparently had ridden into town, bought himself a gun and other things he required. He was lashing a new bed on his pack horse when three Parsons riders jogged in. The man with his arm in a sling flung one short sentence at the Parsons trail boss. Both reached for their guns—and the trail boss would drive no more herds. His two men stood aside. They shrugged their shoulders and went back to their wagon. Brock concluded his business, then he, too, rode out of Lost River, unmolested by anyone.

"Cool hand, that," Ed remarked. "Maybe we'll never see him again. But I'd admire to make him a gift of two of the best cowponies in the Long S *remuda* every time he drops one of that Parsons crowd, whether he ever shows up again or not."

"I'll bet you a new hat Brock'll finish the drive with us," Lou declared impulsively.

"What makes you think that?" Wally asked.

"Because he said he would," Lou flung back, a touch of color rising in her cheeks.

And for once her brothers looked at her with faint smiles and forebore to tease.

Chapter Twelve

WAR PAINT

WHETHER BY FAITH OR INTUITION, Lou was right. Two days north of Lost River, as part of the Stark crew sat eating their noon meal, Brock rode into camp.

He had a good stock saddle, not new, but of a famous Wyoming make, a bulky bed lashed across Gene's old saddle on the extra horse. He had new clothes from his neck to his heels. An expensive Stetson replaced the battered old felt Dave Stark had loaned him. And as Lou surveyed this equipment, she saw that the once empty holster on his belt now carried a brand-new Colt with a white bone grip. Nor did Brock carry his arm in the sling. He still wore the bandage and splints but he was using his hand.

"Go easy with that," her father warned. "You strain that knittin' bone an' you'll have trouble."

"I won't," Brock smiled. "I'm favoring it all I can. But I've got to use my fingers now and then. Feels good, too, after being one-handed so long."

When the wagon broke away to follow and pass the herd to the next water, Brock rode ahead as pilot. They had a fairly short move. When the creek came in sight of Gene driving the wagon, Brock dropped back to ride with Lou at the heels of the *remuda*. The leaders' bells tinkled in that empty void with a sweet silvery sound. The cattle were a trailing mass far behind. Ahead opened a beautiful prospect. They were dipping into a miniature edition of the valley that housed the town of Lost River—only no railway bisected this timbered depression, nor did any smoke from a chimney flutter like a pennant against the sky.

Brock pointed away northwest. A faint series of pale blue peaks broke the sky line, a jagged line a shade bluer than the sky itself.

"Big Horn Mountains," Brock told the girl. "If you

could see far enough to the northeast you could glimpse the Black Hills in South Dakota."

"It's an awful big country, isn't it." Lou flung out one gloved hand. "There's no end to it. We travel a week and come to a river. Cross it, trail on another week, and come to another river. And we've been doing it all summer."

"And still seven hundred miles to go," Brock remarked. "Well, the worst is behind us. From here, we have good country ahead. Kansas and Nebraska is tough going for trail herds. This is more like a white man's country."

"Lots of Indians, too, aren't there?" Lou asked. "They outnumber the whites yet, I've heard."

."Oh, sure. But they're all penned on reservations," Brock replied.

"Except when they jump off to go on a raid, eh?"

"Uncle Sam's cavalry is never far behind them when they do," Brock assured her. "Ten years ago we might have had to fight every other day crossing this country with a herd and over a hundred good horses. It's safe enough now—far as Indians are concerned. Some young bucks might try to sneak a few ponies on a dark night. So far as pitching into the outfit and cleaning us up goes—"

He shrugged his shoulders. Yet that expressed optimism didn't prevent him from scanning the creek bed thoroughly. They were in the country once fought over by both Cheyennes and Crows, not wholly beyond the outermost range of the fierce Sioux. The last of the buffalo still roamed in decreasing herds. Doomed like the carrier pigeon, the buffalo still drifted over miles of the Northwest in their aimless migrations. Brock had seen fresh wallows and rutted trails that morning. Where there were buffalo there might easily be Indians, either hunting parties or raiders. He did not want to alarm Lou Stark, but he had mentioned that fact to all her brothers as soon as he rejoined them. Only the season before a trail outfit had fought forty Cheyennes for two days on this same creek a few miles to the west. Horses were wealth. A white man's scalp still brought honor to a warrior. Cavalry couldn't keep track of every small raiding party that stole out on the plains.

So Brock kept an eye on the reaches of this pleasant valley as they made camp. Four miles behind, the Long S herd was on the crest of a low divide, coming in long files, eager for water. Brock left the wagon and rode a little way up the creek. As he turned a bend, a mass of lumbering beasts filled the hollow by the stream, hundreds of them, brown, shaggy, hump-shouldered brutes lying on water, grazing like longhorns after a day's march. They looked at Brock unmoved, small eyes peering through matted fringes below their black, shiny horns. Brock crossed the creek. On the bench he found the marks of killing—fresh killing.

Two buffalo carcasses, with part of the loin meat cut away off one, and the tongues. Only hunters traveling light did that. The hide hunters skinned their kill. A meat-hunting party of Indians left little but head and hoofs. And any legitimate hunting-party would have been harrying that band of buffalo yet.

Brock stared at this sign for a minute, looking backward at the bison scattered along half a mile of creek. He eyed the earth about the mutilated carcass. Four unshod ponies. Moccasin prints. In his mind's eye Brock could see four braves, glaring splashes of color across each one's aquiline face. Out for scalps and plunder. Prowling like wolves across the plains. Hanging in the path of the trail herds on the chance of a trophy.

It made him slightly uncomfortable.

He loped back to the wagon. The lead of the herd was still far up the slope. He left his horse standing on the reins. Gene was making his supper preparations. Lou sat beside the wagon. The *remuda* was scattered, grazing all about them.

Brock's eyes marked every object near, small clumps of aspen shivering in the summer airs, willows hugging the stream. It was beautiful, that particular spot, grass like a cultivated sward, rich loamy soil, the stream clear on a gravel bed. Two men and a girl—and a hundred and fifty head of well-broken saddle stock. A dozen of those range-bred horses would be a rich *coup*—to say nothing of three possible scalps. It was, he considered fancifully, like leaving a bag of candy in the same room with a small, spoiled child.

Only of course, that was absurd. He wasn't afraid. He was scarcely uneasy. Nevertheless he had a very clear apprehension of his time and surroundings and he was very watchful. Buffalo and Indians went together. He knew that the Starks poohpoohed the chance of Indians striking. The hostilities in the Southwest were tamed these many years. But the north was not so tame, Brock knew.

So, remembering the moccasin and pony tracks, his eyes roved.

As if his faculties had been sharpened for that purpose he saw quite distinctly less than a hundred yards away a sagebrush move as no sage should ever move of its own accord.

"Gene," he said in an undertone. "Come here, will you?"

The range man is accustomed both to giving and obeying commands, inured to instant action in emergency. Gene didn't question. Perhaps Brock's tone warned him of something amiss. Louise looked up and Brock motioned her to be still. Gene moved over to the wagon wheel.

"Don't seem to pay any attention or look about you," Brock said to the boy. "Stand still for a second, just as you are. Indians. *Sabe?*"

Gene nodded imperceptibly. His eyes brightened as at some new game to play.

"Stretch as if you were sleepy, Lou," Brock ordered, in the same casual tone. "Then lie down flat, and edge in under the wagon, behind the wheel. Got a rifle handy, Gene?"

"On the tail gate," Gene answered.

"Get hold of it and be ready to take to cover," Brock told him. "I have a new Winchester under my stirrup leather. When you have your gun in your hand, I will move. I don't know exactly what I will do. But neither of you leave the wagon shelter whatever I do. I saw signs. I'm pretty sure they're sneaking up on us through the sage. I have one spotted. Cough when you're ready. Don't make any false or hasty motions to show 'em we're alarmed."

Out of one corner of his eye Brock watched the girl while Gene sauntered around the wagon and stealthily got hold of a single-action .45-90 Sharp's. Louise caught Brock's eye, smiled. She lay on her face, half-hidden behind the spokes and a roll of bedding. She carried, like her brothers, a Colt in a holster. She held it now in a two-handed grip. She looked pleased and eager. Brock smiled.

Then Gene coughed. Meanwhile that sagebrush had moved again, inching nearer. There were probably other clumps of sagebrush creeping nearer, Brock surmised. But he had that one located and he did not lose sight of it while he ambled three steps to his horse. He was a shining mark for the red brother as he laid hand on the rifle in its scabbard. But he wasn't nervous. If there were four Indians only he knew about what their probable strategy would be—creep close unobserved, so close that their first surprise shots would drop him and Gene. Then a short rush to grab the white woman, seize and mount the two saddled horses, cut off what horses they could handle from the *remuda*—and be far away with scalps, booty, and prisoner before riders from that herd could reach the wagon, much less pursue.

Brock's fingers closed on the grip of the rifle. He swung the sights low on that sagebrush which had acquired a mode of motion foreign to sagebrush in general and pulled trigger.

Something glistening like dull copper straightened up and vanished again with a weird screech of anguish. Ten yards apart two similar forms sprang from cover and raced for the Long S wagon, yelling like fiends, carbines spitting as they leaped.

Gene's .45-90 roared like a young cannon. Brock's carbine popped like a whip. Both braves flattened forward. And Brock knew neither was playing 'possum. He cast himself on the ground.

"There's another yet," he warned Gene. "Keep your eye peeled."

There might be more. Brock didn't think so. With reinforcements at hand, that pair would never have staked their lives on a frontal attack. But there was certainly a fourth. And Brock looked sharply. They had killed three. If one escaped to tell his people, the Long S would be harried for the next two hundred miles.

He might have been mistaken in the number. The maker of the fourth track might have separated from his fellows. Or he might be lying within a hundred yards waiting a favorable shot.

While Brock speculated, waiting eagle-eyed for sound or movement, water splashed, hoofs drummed the turf across the creek. He caught the flash of a spotted pony, a rider lying low along his neck. A shrill yell of defiance carried back as both he and Gene shot at the flying enemy.

Brock didn't waste ammunition. He rose to his feet, reached for his stirrup. "That's all of 'em," he shouted. "You two stay tight under cover."

Ten seconds later his horse hit the creek with a splash. He gained the top bank in time to see the Cheyenne or Crow, whichever he chanced to be, with a quarter-mile lead. He was running for the buffalo herd. If he swept down on those beasts yelling at a gallop they would stampede. In the dust and confusion he could lose a pursuer and cover his tracks till darkness hid him. Also, farther up the creek heavier timber gave good shelter.

But he was in plain view still, his piebald pony like a painted beast in the eye of the setting sun. And Brock, on a more powerful, far faster horse, set sail after him.

Half an hour later, in the gathering dusk, Brock rode back to the Stark wagon. The herd was on the creek. Dave Stark stood guard on one bank, Clay on the other. The others were bunched by the wagon, and the *remuda* was packed in the strung rope of the corral. Old man Stark came over to Brock as he dismounted.

"Didja get the last varmint?" he inquired.

Brock nodded.

The old man stroked one point of his long white mustache and grinned at Brock.

"Seems like you saved a hunk of the family bacon, young feller," said he. "I didn't reckon on Injuns. They'd 'a' got these kids of mine, only for you. Gene told me. They ain't had experience with hostiles, Lou an' Gene. Glad you rounded up that last one. We'd had to do some tol'able fightin' the next day or two if he'd got back to his own lodges."

"I figured it that way, or I wouldn't have tore after him," Brock said. "I hadn't lost any Indians—and I'm not a killer."

"Go eat your supper," old Gene said. "We won't take no chances. We'll move outa this creek bottom after dark an' make a dry camp by the herd on the open bench."

Lou dished Brock up a plate of fried beef and cornbread. As she stooped to fill his cup from the coffee pot, she murmured, "You don't know what Dad said about you. You've made a hit with him."

"That's fine," Brock answered under his breath. "But I'd be a lot happier if I knew I'd made a hit with you, too."

"That," Lou breathed, "is something you'll have to find out for yourself."

Brock smiled. He opened his mouth to reply—and bit the sentence off at the first word. Thereafter he finished his supper in absolute silence, staring thoughtfully at his plate, while from her seat on a bed roll Louise Stark regarded him with an expression of intense curiosity until he rose and, in so far as he was able, began to help getting the outfit ready to move up on high ground—against the contingency of a night attack by other predatory aborigines. Brock scowled as he worked. And when he was not scowling it seemed to Lou Stark that he looked very unhappy about something.

Chapter Thirteen

LOCATED

SEPTEMBER, WITH THE DAYS SHORTENING, nights touched with a frosty chill, overtook them at last. But the end of the long trail was in sight. The Long S cattle were fat as seals. For the last six hundred miles they had grazed on rich buffalo grass from water to water. The Yellowstone lay behind them. The Yellowstone and Miles City, where they crossed the Northern Pacific fresh from the hands of its builders. Jim Hill had not yet laid his two streaks of rust on a right of way from St. Paul to Puget Sound. The Canadian Pacific was still a thing of plans and blue prints. Between the Stark outfit and the North Pole, men and goods went and must still go by wagon and pack, by river steamer or canoe. Not so long since this was the red brother's domain, and his cattle, the bison, still roved in small bands. The Long S riders ate buffalo meat more than once between the Yellowstone and their destination. But after that brush with the Cheyennes they saw no more Indians abroad in paint and feathers.

They pitched camp one evening in a winding valley full of willows, poplar, service berry, cut by a small river knee-deep and crystal-clear, looping in and out between meadows of natural hay, ripe for the mower.

"Shucks, we're walking right over one good location after another, Dad," Dave said to his father "What's the matter with driving stakes right here? Farther we go north the farther we have to trail our beef to a shippin' point. What's the use of gettin' three hundred miles from the only railroad in the country?"

"I figured to get north of the Missouri," old Gene said. "Bill Sayre told me he'd heard from reliable men that that North Montana country was hard to beat. Still, I got to admit that this stretch is mighty attractive."

"You better let Brock rave in your ear about the Bear

Paw mountains," Clay suggested. "Seems like he passed through there last fall. Accordin' to him, it's God's country. Only two outfits in a range of hills thirty miles wide and seventy-five miles long, an' both outfits small."

"I get plumb curious about that *hombre* sometimes," Dave remarked. "He's a cowpuncher from the ground up. But he's sure an educated man too. He can certainly sling language when he has a mind to. I wonder what his name is besides Brock?"

"He never said an' I never asked him, an' I don't care," Clay said carelessly. "He's all right any way you take him, an' his personal history is his own concern."

"I've heard him mention the Bear Paws," old Gene ruminated. "I'll find out what he knows."

Old man Stark remembered that when Brock came off day herd for supper. Brock, it transpired, knew a good deal, which he imparted with enthusiasm that grew as he talked. He pointed to a purple smudge straight north of them, and a farther break in the skyline, a jagged line just a little bluer than the sky itself.

"Those first hills are the Little Rockies," said he. "And the blue that you can just see miles beyond them is the Bear Paw range. It's a paradise for cows, waiting for people to walk in and take possession. The cream of the country waiting to be skimmed. There's pine timber for buildings and corrals and pasture fences, spring creeks everywhere. And grass—bunch grass and buffalo grass and bluejoint meadows. I know a spot—"

He paused to stare off at those distant hills.

"Then you lead us to it," old Gene made his decision. "Dave an' Ed's kinda partial to locatin' here on the Musselshell. But I've had the other side of the Missouri in mind somehow from the beginnin'."

"You can't go wrong there," Brock declared. "The Musselshell's all right, good range and all that. But it's got one thing against it for your purposes."

"Oh? What might that be?" old Gene inquired.

"The WP from the Nueces has established a headquarters on the Judith river a day's ride west of here,"

Brock said slowly. "You'd be rubbing elbows with them all the time."

"Oh," said Eugene Stark, and both Dave and Ed lifted on elbow to stare at Brock. It was the first time he had ever mentioned the Parsons outfit. "An' what do you know about *that?*"

"Enough," Brock answered briefly. "I take it that where there's a world of room you'd as soon not have the Parsons outfit for near neighbors."

"That's true enough. I reckon we-all would rather confine our energies to gettin' on in the cattle business," old man Stark said thoughtfully, "than waste 'em in a senseless private war. I didn't know Parsons was startin' business up here. I thought he was just trailin' beef north to fill army-post contracts."

"The WP is here and here to stay, I imagine," Brock said positively. "I started north this spring with a WP herd from the home ranch on the Nueces. I was up the trail for them last summer. They are building a ranch on the Judith. Bill Parsons has other herds on trail. He will have thirty thousand cattle on the Judith river before snow flies."

"No matter," old Stark said abruptly. "We'll have the old Missouri an' a hundred an' fifty miles of territory between us. I reckon we can keep him off our grass. An' he can hardly say we moved in on his range lookin' for trouble—not if we are located in the Bear Paws."

Old Gene wrinkled his brows and looked at his sons. Dave and Ed nodded agreement. Clay said nothing. He was looking off into the dusk. And the others knew what he was thinking. They seldom mentioned the Trinity now, nor the bloody sequence of events that had driven them forth. It seemed a trifle remote, almost unreal, here in a new country fifteen hundred miles as the crow flies from the Trinity river in Texas.

Northwest from the Musselshell, the Long S crossed a rolling country that pitched at last down into the vast confusion of the Bad Lands, a ripped and torn area that spreads irregularly in a broad band on both sides of the

Missouri River. The outer fringes of it began as small creeks and shallow coulees, ended on the river flats as yawning canyons. In between was a maze for roughness, a topsy-turvy world. They came down to the big river eventually. In a dozen places throughout that weird region they had passed the impassable with their chuck wagon, where no wheeled vehicle had ever gone, where no wheeled vehicle could go except as it was lowered and hauled and yanked bodily by a dozen mounted men handy with ropes. In that strange desolation it seemed as if God must have grown weary in his world-making and left the place unfinished and all askew.

They made a night camp on the south brink of the Big Muddy. The Missouri was half a mile wide there and everywhere swimming deep. But the Long S cattle had come to many rivers and left them all behind. They would face this one boldly at dawn.

"That's a steamer landing over there," Brock pointed to a huddle of buildings on the north shore. "We should be able to get a scow or boat from them to get the wagon across without having to make a raft ourselves. There's a freight trail runs up to the level country."

Dark came on. Across the river, lights blinked under five-hundred-foot valley walls, cut sheer by the titanic plowing of time. The river bottoms spread ghostly gray, the Missouri itself looped through this grayness like a silver snake, hissing softly where the four-mile current swept gravelly shores. The Starks watched and talked, grouped by a fire of pine sticks.

"You could straddle a log and float down to New Orleans," Brock said apropos of nothing. "This river is like a highway through the heart of the United States. This old stream could tell tall tales. Fur deals since the time of the Northwest Fur Company. Placer gold in wooden boxes, buffalo hides by the million. And now the cattlemen are moving in. After us the railroads, then sheep, then farmers. The longhorn will go like the buffalo."

"Not in our time," old Gene said casually.

"I'm not so sure of that," Brock murmured.

He sat with his back against a roll of bedding. Within arm's length Louise poked absently at the fire with a stick, sending up little flames that cast a golden glow on copper-brown hair in two braids twisted about her head. Brock's gaze kept turning to her. Clay sat between them with a faintly amused smile. Brock and Clay Stark had grown to be very friendly in a silent wordless way of their own. They slept in the same bed and stood guard together. They seemed somehow to speak the same language although they used different terms. Clay apprehended much that he didn't mention, that neither his brothers nor his sister seemed to see. He never teased Lou about Brock the way young Gene frequently did, and sometimes the others. Clay never said much about anything. He was almost pure act. Nevertheless he had as keen a brain as any in that group. He had been the most difficult of all Eugene Stark's sons. Something that ran in his mind now kept a faint smile flickering on his dark, lean features.

A loud hoarse blast startled them, made picketed night horses snort.

"What in Sam Hill is that?" Dave exclaimed.

"River steamer—must be," Brock said. "This is the head of navigation, except in the high water. There's shallows and rapids above here. But they can always unload at Cow Island."

Around the first bend below came a shape glittering with lights, puffing audibly. In the velvet night the thresh of paddle blades beat like a flail. She came forging up, abreast, without halting at the mouth of Cow Creek. Lights from the freight camp hurried to the river brink but the steamer neither slowed nor turned from midstream. Her port light glowed ruby-red among yellow gleams. The smoke banner from her tall stack trailed darkly over the pale river. The thresh of the huge paddles on her stern was like some amphibian monster slashing the water foam-white with his tail. Then she was gone around a jutting point a mile above.

"Gosh, that's the way to travel. Say, did you hear that

music?" Gene commented. "I'd like to ride on one of them. I never did yet."

"She must be light and the river must be high," Brock said. "Generally those stern-wheelers only make it to Fort Benton on the spring freshet."

The river *was* high. But high water or low the Long S cattle took it like veterans. Brock and Clay swam with the lead of the herd. They sat dripping horses on the opposite bank and watched the herd string up out of the shallows. Then they rode over to the freight camp. As Brock had prophesied, they found a small scow available to ferry their wagon.

"No more rivers to cross," the Starks said thankfully when they hitched their four-horse team on the north side.

They made camp a few miles up Cow Creek that night in the gut of a great hollow floored with sagebrush. The high earth walls that lined this Bad Land gorge loomed above them, banded with varied-colored strata of clay, yellow and red and brown. Scrubby pines clung precariously here and there. The water in Cow Creek was bitter with alkali. The Bad Lands spread all about them, mysterious, desolate, forbidding to the eye. But the Bear Paw Mountains lifted purple, saw-toothed peaks, with darkly green lower slopes when they looked northwest at dawn.

Two days later the Long S herd grazed without watching riders, along a creek made by the Almighty to gladden a longhorn's heart. Grass a foot high, a yellow carpet unsoiled and untrampled. A broad stream whispered knee-deep over pebbles that shone in the crystal-clear mountain water. A background of hills, garmented in bunch grass and pine forest, lifted between them and the Canadian line, peak after peak, canyon after canyon, a seventy-mile east and west barrier against the northern blizzards.

Brock squatted on his heels by the wagon looking over a small pencil-marked map. Eugene Stark, Dave, Clay, and Lou peered over his shoulder.

"This here creek should have a name," old Gene said.

"Big Birch," Brock answered. "West Fork called Little Birch. Cow Creek heads away to the east. Twenty miles west is Eagle Creek with the Block S owned by a man named Adam Sutherland. Home ranch just in the edge of the timber on Eagle Creek. Fifteen miles farther around the hills on Sandy Creek is the Cross Seven. Nothing else in all the length and breadth of the Bear Paws till you get out on the plains northwest of the mountains toward Milk River. There's a military post there—Fort Assiniboine. Indian reservation lays off to the east from the foot of the Little Rockies—Gros Ventres."

"We'll look around some," old Gene said. "But right here is good enough for me."

That look around took them a little way up Birch Creek in the afternoon, under the shoulder of a butte that thrust a black, rocky spire above timber line. But its lower slopes were thick with massed battalions of straight lodge-pole pines. Birch creek widened a little here. They turned a bend and came on a beaver dam with a hundred acres of valley land flooded, and hay ripe for the mower growing in a wide band all about the water's edge.

"For irrigation purposes, an' for pickin' dam sites the beaver has some civil engineers backed off the map," Dave Stark smiled. "Gosh, that's a pretty sight."

"Man," Clay murmured to Brock, "you sure did lead us into the Promised Land."

Brock smiled. Old Eugene Stark sat with his gloved hands resting on the horn of his saddle staring at earth and grass, timber and water, which was his to take if he chose. Then he rode silently over to a patch of chokecherry bush and broke off a dry stick ten feet long. He came back to where his sons were grouped and thrust the stick like a lance into the rich black soil.

"We're located," he said. "Here on this flat we'll build us a home. Boys, we can take this creek from its head to where it drops into the Bad Lands, land, water rights, an' timber—an' hold it ag'in all comers. We'll make us a ranch an' we'll be a cow outfit again in spite of Bill Parsons an' all hell combined!"

Chapter Fourteen

"BE KIND, MY SON."

SEPTEMBER PASSED, days strung like golden beads on a chain of crisp starlit nights that left hoarfrost white on leaf and blade and windows at dawn. Tiger Butte, looming over the Long S, swathed its black rocky head in a white cap the first week of October. That white shroud crept lower with every fleet of clouds that sailed the high divides of the Bear Paws. But the snow held off the lower ground for a long time. And before it came, the Stark boys climbing up among the pines on Tiger after venison could look down on a sprawling house of peeled pine logs, a roomy stable, a great haystack within a tight pole fence. Nine pairs of sinewy hands, skilfully directed, using sharp tools and machinery, can accomplish miracles of industry in five weeks.

Lou cooked, and young Gene did a man's work outside. There were no more horses to wrangle. The *remuda*, all but necessary work teams and a saddle horse for each man, was loose on the range. Until spring round-up came, the ponies would paw their living in the snow, root like the longhorns for buried grass, live like the deer that haunted the slopes of Tiger Butte in the pine thickets.

While Lou fed them and kept the house in order and labored with sewing machine and fabrics in her spare time to give the place an atmosphere like home—in which she was presently aided by Ed Stark's wife and Dave's— her father, brothers, and Brock were by turns carpenters, haymakers, freighters. Fort Benton lay eighty miles west. All that they used and needed came in wagonloads from that trading center. Food, machinery, luxuries even. Over rutted trails made by the bull teams plying between Cow Creek and the Fort.

They were a microcosm complete, self-contained, when the wives and children of Stark's two oldest sons came by train to Miles City, and thence by wagon to that Bear Paw ranch. The world outside their immediate environment might have ceased to be in those months, and they would have known nothing of it, nor have been inconvenienced thereby. Ed had two boys and a girl. Dave had three girls and an infant son. Wally's wife came with them but they were a childless pair. Brock, lounging in the separate bunkhouse he occupied with the bachelors of that family, Peter, Clay, Mike, and young Gene, sometimes smiled to himself at the riot of those six juveniles either indoors or out. The Long S was like a clan housed in a village of its own, set apart in the wilderness. And Dave Stark had laughed when Brock called it pioneering.

"If we had a couple more kids the government would send us a school-teacher," old Gene remarked one morning at breakfast.

"There is a school on Eagle Creek. A gunshot above the Block S," Brock volunteered. "I stopped in there yesterday. Sutherland has a girl. Likewise he has three or four married men working for him. And there's two or three youngsters from the Cross Seven that ride across the hills to that school."

"Have to send some of these young devils over there with a camp outfit in the spring, I reckon," Dave said. "Yeah. That's what we'll do."

"How's them cattle rangin'?" the old man asked Clay. Clay and Brock rode abroad more or less. They were restless. They were both deadly with a rifle and there were buffalo wolves in the low country, and deer in the mountains. They hunted both, incidentally keeping an eye on loose stock to see how they fared.

"They ain't rangin'," Clay answered. "The outside fringes of 'em ain't five miles from the ranch yet. All they do is to eat an' lay around. They don't have to travel now. I reckon them longhorns think they been turned loose in some farmer's hayfield the way they hang close to Birch Creek."

Brock could look up and down Birch any time and see a thousand head of cattle grazing on the benches or stringing slowly in on water. They had traveled enough that summer. They neither needed to be herded within bounds nor even watched. Fat as pigs from rich grazing, a northern winter meant little hardship for them, not the ordinary run of northern winter. There were rumors abroad, based on the experience of trappers, miners, Indian legends, that once in a decade or so a hard winter hit that country. Deep crusted snow, blizzards, forty-below-zero weather weeks on end. That was a chance the cattleman took. If it came, he was wiped out.

Brock sauntered about this particular morning with nothing much to do, wondering why he stayed on, why old Gene kept him drawing wages. The Long S was housed for the winter, snug against all rigors of climate, six months' food supply in its larder. Nine men with nothing to do but cut firewood and feed a dozen stabled horses three times a day.

There was no occasion to stay. Yet Brock hated to go. The Long S had picked him up a wounded stranger on that fork of the Republican. He had become one of them. They were like a clan under a hereditary chief. Right or wrong, they stood by each other. Even Clay, who had the temper of a fiend and the brooding quality of some dark, aboriginal ancestor, accepted the family discipline, believed in and lived by the fact that each was in a sense his brother's keeper.

Curiously, Clay seemed closer to Brock than any of the others. They had grown that way on trail. Each had the same quality of getting the other's thought, meaning, with scarcely a word said. Whether they worked or played or hunted, their minds seemed to run naturally along the same groove. Which is probably why Clay alone knew what Brock and Lou Stark kept unuttered with their lips and said continually to each other with their eyes. It amused Clay to see this and to know that all the rest of the Stark family were totally blind to what these two masked by seeming indifference. It made him wonder perhaps why Brock did his courting with his eyes only. He had that perfect self-possession that makes a man competent to face any issue, whether in love or war. And it wasn't Clay's business. It was theirs. He would watch them unobtrusively, with tolerant amusement, wondering sometimes, humorously, if they knew what ailed them. Clay considered the matter and decided that Brock would be a good man to have in the family. Clay knew his charming, tempestuous sister very well indeed. Brock wasn't any fool. Why then didn't they get together?

Clay was to get the key to that by and by.

When Christmas was three weeks distant old Gene said to him, "You'n' Brock pull for Benton an' bring in a load of stuff. I made out a list. There's some things I forgot. 'N' we have to celebrate. She's been a good winter so far."

There was a scant two inches of snow on the ground. In many long stretches the winds had blown it all bare. The land was flint hard with moderate frost. Their wagon wheels rattled behind a trotting four-horse team and the two men perched on a high spring seat wrapped in fur coats. Eighty miles. One night camp. They made Fort Benton the afternoon of the second day, loaded their supplies before sundown—supplies that included by a miracle half a dozen turkeys imported by an enterprising dealer for the Christmas trade.

After dinner they loafed in the bar of the Grand Union hotel. They met other cattlemen, cowpunchers, swapped yarns, played poker. And drank a good many sociable drinks. Clay grew morose and thoughtful as the bourbon whisky accumulated under his belt. Late in the evening he drew Brock aside.

"They tell me there's three WP men in town. Let's go after 'em."

Brock talked him out of that. It took all his persuasion. The old sore was festering in Clay. In the corner by the bar, in the lobby, on the stairs when Brock was easing this liquored-up son of the house of Stark up to their room, it was touch and go whether the combined alcohol and that deep-rooted hatred of everything connected with the Parsons outfit would not lead Clay out to make a round of the saloons looking for his enemies.

And as they lay in bed together, Brock listened to Clay's heavy breathing, sleepless himself, knowing what he knew. It would die hard, that blood feud.

Sober at daylight, Clay—recalling quite clearly what he did and said the night before—sat up in bed and rolled a cigarette. With his knees hunched up under the blankets and his lean brown hands clasped over them he looked at Brock with a friendly grin.

"You're like Con was," he said abruptly. "He could always talk me out of anythin' foolish when I was lit. I miss that kid. You wouldn't think with six brothers I'd miss one—but I do. We all do."

Brock lay silent. There was nothing he could say.

"So you go right ahead an' take me by the ear any time I show signs of hittin' the war post thataway," Clay continued. "I'd take it off you where I wouldn't off anybody else, I reckon. It's plumb foolish for me—for any of us to hunt trouble. I promised the old man I would never stir up this Parsons war again, if it could be dodged. Let them start it, says he. And he's right, too."

"Of course, he's right," Brock commented.

"We whipped Parsons an' his hired men fightin'," Clay went on thoughtfully. "He skinned us alive in the courts. His money talked louder 'n' longer'n ours. But he can't fight us with damage suits an' injunctions here. This is unorganized territory—likely to be for quite a spell. No courts, no sheriffs, no windy law-sharps. I wouldn't ask nothin' better than one good round with the Parsons outfit on the open range—just us Starks. But it's up to them if it ever comes off. They got to start it—an' this time we'll finish it right."

"There's Federal law," Brock pointed out. "And cavalry at various military posts to enforce it."

"Cavalry don't move in civilian affairs without orders from Washington," Clay retorted. "An' there's no civil machinery much. A United States Marshal with two or three deputies, for a territory four hundred miles wide an' six hundred miles long. Shucks, two outfits could fight a pitched battle anywhere in Northern Montana an' it would be weeks before the authorities even heard of it. No, if Mister Bill Parsons comes north of the Missouri to pick on the Long S he'll get his bellyful this time."

"I don't reckon he will," Brock said—but he lacked in his heart the conviction of his words. "No WP cow is likely ever to show her brand on this range. The Judith Basin is a long way south and cattle don't cross the Missouri unless they're forced."

"Just as well if they don't," Clay nodded. "Maybe it ain't Christian, but some of us boys ache now an' then to play even. It wasn't a square deal nohow. If the WP hadn't been so high-handed nobody woulda got killed. I miss Con when I get to thinkin' about them things. Well, I guess it's wiser, as the old man says, to forget. We lost a lot down on the Trinity. Still, we've made a fresh start here. I don't hone for trouble, really. Only the WP *is* in the country. And sometimes when you're not lookin' for trouble it comes an' hunts you up."

Brock discovered the truth of that before so very long. Christmas loomed on the calendar. For the first time the Starks broke the shell of their isolation. True, they ate their Christmas turkey and mince pie under their own roof, nine men, four women, six children, a patriarchal tribe, embracing three generations. Of the eighteen souls Brock Parsons was the only one not blood kin to someone else there. They were merry under that snow-laden roof. A bowl of Tom and Jerry stood golden-frothed in the lamplight. A young pine picked for symmetry lifted a green cone in one corner, brave with cotton tufts and tinsel, with scarlet cranberries and colored candles to delight the children. There were two guitars, a mandolin, and a banjo, and most of the Stark boys could pick melodies. So could Brock. But he didn't.

Something got under his skin in this hour of feasting. Somehow he felt on the outside looking in. The blue devils got him early in the evening. When he could, unobtrusively, he slipped away to the bunkhouse, to sit on his bed staring at the floor of hewn pine slabs. Why did he drift on that tide? For he had been drifting since that day in

Lost River when he shot Polk Munce off his horse. He had stood there in the dusty street, not so much considering that act of retributive justice, as deciding whether he should go his way or rejoin the Long S. And the Long S had pulled hardest. It would have been better all around for him to ride alone. He had told Tom Slater and Bill Thye why he killed Polk. He had told them to elect a trail boss and go on to their destination. He had said that he had ridden his last for the WP. He should have taken that herd himself. But he had come back to the Starks. Why? Oh, he knew well enough why. Only—Brock sighed. He shouldn't be there—drifting.

A foot touched lightly on the threshold. Brock looked up. Louise stood there. She had flung a coat over her shoulders. Her feet were white where she had run through the snow that twenty steps that separated bunkhouse and kitchen door.

"What hit you all of a sudden, Brock?" she asked. The tenderness in her voice sent a pang through him.

"Nothing much," he denied.

Louise came over to him.

"I know better," she breathed. "You can't fool me. I was watching you. Homesick?"

"A man can't be homesick when he hasn't got a home—not in the sense that you-all have," Brock told her. "I have people. But they're far away. Only one of them means anything much to me. And I'll probably never see them again anyway. No, I'm not homesick. Not that way."

Lou put her hand on his shoulder. She smiled down at his serious face, shook him gently.

"What way then?" she asked. "You're one of us. You know that. Or you could be, if you wanted."

"I'm afraid not."

"Why?" Her voice held a note of anxiety.

"I can't tell you," Brock said. "Not now. Sometime, maybe."

He took that small, soft hand off his shoulder and held it between his own for a second, staring searchingly into her face. What he saw there, what he had had glimpses of now and then for weeks, troubled him in the same breath that his heart quickened. He could feel the slight tremor in those imprisoned fingers. He knew she was waiting as a woman waits for a man to speak, to act. And he couldn't, not without telling her who he was, what he was. Better to say nothing at all than that.

Brock bent his head and pressed a kiss in her palm. He shut her fingers close over that and freed her hand. They were silent for a second.

"You had better run back," he said. "They'll miss you."

"Yes, I must get back," Lou whispered. "Come on over and be one of the bunch. Don't mope here. Please. It makes me unhappy. I'm sorry, Brock, whatever it is."

"So am I," he said simply. "Run. I'll come presently."

Which he did, and no one knew that for a little while they had been all but in each other's arms. Brock knew that. A Parsons man and a Stark woman. With all that spilled blood on the Trinity between them. No, he had to save Lou from that. Maybe time would iron it out. But it was still all too fresh, like a gaping wound. Time—if he could have patience—and wait. And patient waiting had never been an attribute of Brock's, whose blood could run like fire in his veins with love, or anger or excitement, no matter how outwardly cool he might seem. That was the sort of thing that ran in his mind until he came back to the bunkhouse with the other Starks to turn into his blankets.

That resolution got a testing he hadn't foreseen. Adam Sutherland came over the day after Christmas to ask his new neighbors if the entire Long S would come to a party at his ranch on Eagle creek on New Year's day. The Cross Seven would be there, every soul in the Bear Paw mountains. There was plenty of room. The three outfits could muster a dozen women. They could dance. Winter was time for play.

The Starks left their ranch deserted on New Year's. Men, women, and children, they trekked by saddle and homemade sleigh across the hills to the Block S on Eagle Creek, to make merry in that sprawling, big-roomed log house. Sutherland had been first in the Bear Paws. He had been there four years. He meant to stay. He had ranged cattle in Texas, Colorado, Wyoming. He was middle-aged and he was making his last stand. When the Northwest settled up there was nowhere else, he said, for cattlemen to go. So he had built accordingly. He had room for everybody, and everybody was welcome. There in this sprawling log castle of a rising cattle king they danced the old year out and the new year in to the music of a squeaky fiddle and Wally Stark's banjo. Outside the fiddler, and they forgave him gladly, there was no discordant note anywhere. There were hard men jovial as children, their hardness sloughed for the time being.

Brock lay in his bunk when they got home with Starks all about him snoring in healthy tiredness. And he himself was wakeful, daydreaming and tearing his dreams to tatters with bitter logic as they formed.

He couldn't avoid dancing with Lou Stark, not without comment. Brock was a marked man among all those gathered there. He was no Greek god, but he was a good-looking youth. His education, his language, his manner, unconscious in its simple good breeding, made him stand out among his less literate fellows. He didn't realize that most of the time. To be one of the Stark crowd and avoid dancing with the daughter of the house, where every other young man competed for that favor—well, he couldn't do that. And to hold her in his arms, to feel that involuntary yielding of her body to his own, was at once a delight and a torment. If they kept their lips closed, the language of the eye is as old as passion and as easily understood.

She wants me and I want her, Brock told himself truly, turning uneasily in his blankets. *Why should all this stuff that neither of us had a hand in come between us like a wall?*

It shouldn't. But it did—it would. Not with Brock. The Parsons household had been a divided one from his childhood. There had never been bred in the Parsons menage that unquestioning solidarity that was part of the Stark bone and flesh. They were primitive folk—the very salt of

the earth—and Lou was one of them. She could not be anything else. Proud, passionate, loyal. And she loved him.
She knew he loved her. She wondered, in her innocence,
why he kept his distance, why he held back.

Well, then he would hold back no longer. He would
tell her who he was, what he was, what he felt about it—
and take his chances. Presently—presently he would tell
her. In the spring. It would be less a grief to ride on when
new grass was lifting like green velvet and the blue wind-
flowers opened their petals to the sun. It was something to
be here, where he could hear her laugh and see her smile.
That storm cloud which his father had brought to the
Trinity with its deadly play of gunpowder lightning had
sent no echoes here yet.

But Brock's hand was forced from an unexpected quarter and Clay's dictum that a man didn't have to hunt
trouble because it would find him soon enough proved all
too true.

With time beginning to lie heavy on their hands, with
plans for that ranch in the making, the Starks began to
slash and haul poles from the pine forest that clothed the
lower slopes of Tiger Butte.

Brock came in at noon one day in early February with
Wally and Clay and Pete. He noticed a saddled horse
standing by the bunkhouse door. Old Gene left woods
work to the younger men. He came now bareheaded from
the house to tell Brock as they put their horses up, "Feller
waitin' in the bunkhouse to see you."

"Look like he's got a warrant?" Brock laughed.

"No. I reckon not," old man Stark said slowly. A queer
expression flitted across his lined face. "Were you expectin'
a officer with a warrant?"

"Lord, no," Brock smiled. "I'm not on the dodge. Did
he say who he was, that wants to see me?"

"He's ridin' a Sutherland horse," Eugene Stark said
gravely. "But he ain't no Sutherland man. He don't say
his name—but I know him. Go an' see what he wants with
you."

Clay turned toward the bunkhouse with Brock.

"You heeled?" he muttered.

"No. I never pack a gun at work," Brock said. "Why?"

Eugene Stark called sharply, "Clay." Brock saw him shake his head at his father's imperative gesture to come back. For a second or two Brock scarcely comprehended why Clay kept step with him. Then his wits functioned.

"Shucks, Clay," he smiled. "I don't imagine it's anybody after my scalp. If he is, it's my funeral, not yours, old-timer."

"You killed a Parsons trail boss in Lost River last summer," Clay said quietly. "Sometimes a dead man has friends or kin to take it up. I'll just saunter in with you. If it's a love feast I'll amble on. If it's trouble, why, I'll be a—a witness that you only acted in self-defense."

He grinned broadly.

"No friend of Polk Munce's would dare come here to tackle me," Brock declared. "You don't do anything half-way, do you, Clay?"

"Not where my friends or my kin is concerned," Clay replied.

The bunkhouse door opened as they drew near and a man stepped out. Brock's heart rose in his throat, for the man was Matt Parsons.

"Hello, Brock," he greeted casually.

"What in the name of God are you doing here?" Brock demanded. "Are you crazy?"

"No. I got a message for you, that's all," Matt said. He looked at Clay indifferently, nodded a polite "Howdy." And Clay looked searchingly at him, looked once at Brock, and went into the bunkhouse. Over his shoulder a glance showed Eugene Stark, Wally, Ed, Pete, in a group by the stable door. Every eye was turned on himself and his brother.

"You *are* crazy," Brock lowered his voice in an undertone, "to come here."

"No crazier than you are," Matt replied. "Anyway, it was somethin' I promised to do personal."

"What is it?"

"How long since you heard from Mom?" Matt asked

abruptly.

"A while before Christmas."

"She's dead." Matt didn't soften the blow. "She left you what she had. A matter of ninety thousand dollars all in cash. She wouldn't trust the old man. She put it up to me. There's fifty thousand on deposit in San Antonio. The rest I have put to your credit in the First National in Helena. I'm the sole executor of her will. Here's the papers. It's all settled. She made me promise to hunt you up an' deliver this an' a package with my own hands. Otherwise I wouldn't be here. Your business is your own. But it seems to me you've got mixed up queer. What happened to you an' Polk Munce?"

"Plenty to justify me," Brock said. "No time to tell you now." He took the package wrapped in brown paper from his brother's hands. Old Gene Stark's words ran in his mind like a sinister refrain: "He don't say his name—but I know him."

"Get on your horse an' ride," he said. "There's seven men within speaking distance would as soon kill you as not. They know who you are, Matt. Mount and ride."

Matt looked startled.

"None of these Starks ever saw me before," he protested. "I knew you was usin' your first name. I asked for you by that. They don't know me for a Parsons."

"Old Gene does know you," Brock snapped. "Hit the trail while the hitting's good."

"What about you?" Matt asked as he turned to his horse.

"I can take care of myself," Brock told him. "Move. They don't love their enemies, these Starks."

Matt moved. From his saddle as he tightened his reins he said, "One thing more. The old man foams at the mouth when you are mentioned. Tuck Munce has made his talk. Tuck's boss of that Judith Basin layout. Keep your eye peeled for him if you stay in this country."

"I can take care of myself," Brock repeated.

"Looks like you can," Matt said. "I'll be in Fort Benton for ten days or so, if you want to know more about things. So long."

Eugene Stark and six of his sons stood by the stable door, immobile, except that their heads turned to watch Matt Parsons out of sight over the rim of Birch creek. Brock went into the bunkhouse. Clay sat on a bunk, staring at his toes. He looked up at once and then he looked down again. He didn't speak.

Brock sat down. He turned that package over in his hands. His eyes smarted. He felt very much as he had sometimes felt when as a small child he had been punished and left alone to brood in a dark room, forlorn and deserted. He had loved his mother. He had pitied her, too. And she was beyond either affection or pity now.

He opened the package at last. There were the documents covering the money she had bequeathed him, the remnant of her father's fortune which Bill Parsons hadn't succeeding in absorbing. And there was a flat blue, velvet-covered box, quite old and worn about the corners, which when Brock opened it revealed a sheet of paper covered with his mother's shaky handwriting—and a string of pearls such as Brock had seldom seen.

He read the letter, with a deadly heaviness in his breast, because he had been very close to that bed-ridden woman on the Nueces, and he knew what it must have meant to her to know she was dying with him half a continent away. She wrote:

My son, when you get this I'll be gone. I wish I could have seen you once more. I am leaving you some money. Matt will attend to that. I can't trust your father any more, not where you are concerned. He sent you away from me and I can't forgive him that. You didn't know, but he knew, that I had not very long to live.

You have been a good boy, my son. Be a kind man. There is so little kindness in this world.

. Your father has raved and cursed you but I think you have done well to do as you did. I am sure the Starks are good people. I knew Lavina Tree when she was a girl, before she married Eugene Stark. In the end your father will somehow suffer for what he has done to them, as well as

*other people who have stood in his way. Brutality brings
its own reward.*

*These pearls my mother wore when she married. So did
I. When you marry, Brock, put them around your bride's
neck with my blessing.*

Good-by, my son. God keep you from all harm.

Brock stared at the words till they blurred before his
eyes. Then he became aware that Clay was standing beside
him, that he was rather white about the mouth, that his
dark eyes had a hurt, angry look.

"That," Clay stated, "was Matt Parsons. I know. He
was pointed out to me an' the old man in Houston just
before the last of them trials. You favor him a heap. Are
you, for God's sake, a Parsons, too?"

"Yes," Brock said lifelessly. "I'm a Parsons, too. Bill
Parsons's youngest son."

Chapter Fifteen

DOUBLE-DAMNED

"I SEE." CLAY LOOKED AT HIM FIXEDLY for a few moments. "I see."

But what it was he saw he didn't say. And there was nothing Brock could say, nothing indeed that he wanted to say. A man can be shocked into numbness by his own emotions as effectually as by a bullet. Brock sat staring at those pearls in the faded velvet case, at his mother's letter, thinking. Wheels within wheels. Crossed threads. Tangles.

"I don't *sabe*," Clay said fretfully at last. "If you're Bill Parsons's son, what are you doing here? What's the object?"

"No definite object," Brock roused himself to explain. "My father and myself are about as friendly as a porcupine and a hound. He dislikes and resents what I happen to be. I dislike and resent what he is and some of the things he does. I tried to play the game with him but it just didn't work. If he doesn't like anybody his instinct is to make them crawl. He sent me up the trail this spring under a man I despised, just to give me hell, to tame me. That was Munce. Polk tried to kill me one night in a run on that fork of the Republican. That was how I came to be stranded there with a broken arm and a couple of bullet scratches. That was why I went after him on sight in Lost River. No, there isn't any object, Clay. You people were good to me. I liked you all. That run-in with Polk Munce finished me with the WP. Since the day Lou found me under that cottonwood I've just been drifting. It was pleasant."

"It is not goin' to be so pleasant, I don't think, not for Lou, no more," Clay murmured.

"Nor for me," Brock said. "How could I foresee that? And I have kept my distance, knowing what I know. I would have ridden on in the spring, and you all might never have known you'd had an enemy's son for a friend.

I didn't really fly false colors. You never asked me to account for myself. I used my own name, only not all of it. You knew me as Brock Jefferson. I'm Brock Jefferson Parsons."

"Oh, hell," Clay exclaimed. "I thought you were one of us—or goin' to be. Now—"

He threw out his hand with a gesture of finality.

Brock closed the jewel case, stood up, thrust his mother's letter at Clay.

"You and I have been like brothers," he said. "Read that. It may explain me better than I can myself. You can hardly *sabe* a divided family, looking at everything with different eyes. You Starks stand shoulder to shoulder by instinct."

Clay read, handed it back. "Why, yes, I reckon I can see your position," he said slowly. "Still—"

"It doesn't make it different," Brock admitted. "Blood's blood. I know that."

He turned to his bed, drew the canvas tarp off and stretched it on the floor. He laid blankets and clothing, all that he possessed, on that canvas and folded it ready to pack across a horse. Clay watched a few seconds then left him alone in the bunkhouse.

When Brock finished that task, he walked over to the stable. The Starks were standing in a group about their father. He knew they were discussing him. He passed them in silence, his head up. Pride stirred in him. After all he was an innocent party. And he would suffer for the sins of the WP probably a great deal more than they.

He saddled a mount and rode out into the foothills. He had acquired two good horses against just such a contingency. In the back of his mind had always lurked the disturbing certainty that some day he might have to ride away from the Long S leaving his welcome behind him.

He found his ponies ranging under the shoulder of Tiger Butte by mid-afternoon. At four o'clock he was packed and saddled by the bunkhouse door. No one had spoken to him since he came in. Brock hoped no one would. He knew, or thought he knew, how they felt. He twitched his shoulders with impatience over that. But to them it was grim fact. He belonged by birth and blood in the camp of their enemies. And the Starks did not love their enemies. They accepted quite literally the principle of an eye for an eye.

Yet as he stood by his horses ready to mount, with a heaviness in his heart that he had never experienced before, old Eugene Stark and Clay came out of the house. The others, Brock knew, were about the place. They hadn't even gone out to their woods work that afternoon. He looked at the two approaching. Then he saw that old Gene had a green slip in his hand.

"I see you're leavin' us," the old man said evenly. "Here's yo' time up to date. We're under considerable obligation to you personal, one way an' another, or I'd have more to say."

"There's not much use saying things, is there?" Brock replied. "I can't help being who I am. I'm not responsible for what my father did, or does. I'm only accountable for my own actions. And I've never done you any harm. If you know me at all, you know I wouldn't. You have no occasion to hate me."

"We've got no reason to love your tribe," old Gene said. "Your kin has done a lot to us that's hard to overlook."

"I know." Brock looked him in the eye. "I can see your side of it better than you could possibly see mine."

Pete, Dave, Ed, Mike, Wally, young Gene, seemed to converge from different parts of the ranch. They walked past Brock, to stand in a knot on the stoop before the bunkhouse. They didn't speak. They looked at him not so much in hostility as with a curious sort of surprise, as if he had suddenly taken on an entirely different aspect from the man who had laughed and worked with them in the dust and heat of that long trail, through months of hard going. It cut Brock deep.

For a second, glancing over Clay's shoulder, he caught a glimpse of Lou Stark, her face pressed against a kitchen window.

"Did you tell *her?*" he asked, with a gesture toward the

house.

"I did," Eugene Stark said coldly.

"I should have told her myself," Brock muttered. "But I couldn't. So long."

He swung into his saddle, turned his horse. The pack pony capered on the lead rope. He passed the house, not daring to look at those curtained windows. And as he faced toward the west bank of Birch Creek he heard someone call his name. He looked back. Clay was running after him, through the crisp, powdery snow. Brock pulled up.

"Hell, I couldn't let you go like that," Clay thrust up his hand. "We been friends. There ain't no war between you and me, Brock."

A lump lifted in Brock's throat. His fingers shut down on Clay's lean, brown hand.

"There never will be," he said. "Nor between me and any Stark. You tell Lou that for me, will you, Clay?"

"Uh-huh," Clay nodded. "I *sabe*. I wish you didn't have to go like this."

"Maybe I'll be back," Brock hazarded.

"Not too soon," Clay told him. "Give the old man and the rest a chance to settle down. It's all right with me. It jolted me at first. I'd fight Bill Parsons and the WP single or in a bunch, anytime, anywhere. But you ain't the WP."

"No," Brock said. "If I had been it would be different, now. *Adios, amigo.*"

"So long. Good luck to you." Clay gave his hand a last shake.

Brock made the Block S on Eagle Creek in winter starlight, snow crunching under his horse's feet. He rode early and late the following day and walked into the Grand Union Hotel in Fort Benton that evening, saddle-weary, chilled through heavy clothing by a lance-toothed north wind and twenty-below-zero atmosphere. And when he walked into the Grand Union bar to get a hot whisky, there, leaning against the polished wood, glass in hand, stood his father, Matt, and Tuck Munce.

If hunger tames a lion, weariness dulls any man's fighting spirit. Brock had ridden two days with grief close at his elbow. The trio at the bar hadn't seen him. He could turn back, go to his room, and postpone a clash, even avoid it altogether if he so desired.

But he didn't. If Tuck Munce had made his talk he might go through with it and again he might not. Men like Tuck and W. J. Parsons could only be impressed, held in check, by something they could grasp as a manifest danger. He had to face Tuck sometime, if he stayed in Montana. And Brock meant to stay.

He was within two steps before they saw him. Tuck saw him first, turned slowly to face him, wary as a crouching cat. Brock's white-handled gun slanted in the holster on his hip. His dark blue eyes bored into Tuck's small, mean ones, with a mixture of contempt and hostility, partly real, partly assumed.

"I understand," he said evenly, "that you consider you have a grievance against me. That you have made a sort of war talk. If you have any idea of opening up a package of trouble I'm here to help you cut the string, Tuck."

No man can ever say precisely what goes on in another's mind. Brock could only make a shrewd guess at Tuck's reaction. At his father's, too. Tuck would take a chance, but not a desperate chance. Brock had made a deliberate attempt to buffalo a thoroughly dangerous man, and he knew he had succeeded. Temporarily, at least.

"Why, seems to me you're the one huntin' for trouble," Tuck said finally. "An' I don't want to have no trouble with any of the Parsons family. I got too much regard for 'em."

"How considerate you are," Brock sneered. "After making a crack that you'd get me for getting Polk."

"I never said that," Tuck grunted.

"You lie!" Brock challenged. "You did say so, before two trail crews."

Tuck looked appealingly at his employer. Bill Parsons glared at his younger son. The blood mounted to his florid, beefy face.

"You young hound," he said thickly. "I wish you was the size when I could take you across my knee an' larrup you. I'd learn you. You ain't never been nothin' but a bunch of trouble. Is this what I get for raisin' you, educatin' you? I send you out to be made a man of, to be some use to me, an' you lay down on your job an' throw in with people you oughto be ashamed to have any truck with. I—"

"Hold your horses a minute," Brock interrupted. "You," he addressed Tuck Munce, "move on. The Parsons family is going to have a private conference."

Tuck moved on. His look was venomous and Brock kept one eye on him when he edged away to the lobby. But he had no fear of Tuck taking a crack at him in Fort Benton that night. Tuck would wait his chance. The surprise on the faces of both his father and Matt at Tuck's sullen withdrawal amused Brock a trifle.

"Now," he said to his father, "that that tarantula is out of hearing you can say whatever you like to me. I didn't lie down on the job. You sent me out with Polk to break my heart, to make me knuckle down. Be reasonable, Dad. Nobody can make me eat out of his hand. For the last five years no matter what I did or said it was wrong, or piffling, according to you. Why don't you give me the same chance you give Matt?"

"You ain't worth it," Parsons stormed. "You was raised wrong. I disown you. Go back to your damn Starks. I'll boil you all in my kettle one of these days. You can tell 'em I said so."

He thrust his jaw forward aggressively.

"In the spring I'm moving north of the Missouri," he declared. "I'll take the Bear Paws like I took the Trinity. I'll run the Long S outa Montana like I run 'em outa Texas. An' I'll wipe you off the map if you horn in."

"What do you want me to do?" Brock asked patiently. "I'm your son. I've never really defied you yet. I've tried to play the game, and I'm still willing to do that, if *you* will. Be reasonable, Dad. You're declaring war."

"I am." Parsons drained the glass in his hand and set it on the bar. "An' I don't give a damn who knows it. You ain't nothin' to me. *Sabe?* You cut yourself off from the

WP complete an' final when you killed my oldest trail boss an' threw in with the Starks. Get outa my sight, you over-educated, no-account pup!"

"You're the only living soul who would think or say such things about me," Brock said bitterly. "I've always done what you told me to do, even when I didn't like it. You have no license to talk to me like that. You put me in a position where I had to kill a snake that tried to bite me. As far as the Starks are concerned, they picked me up in Western Nebraska wounded and helpless fifty miles from nowhere. They took care of me, treated me as if I'd been one of their own. When I got on my feet I merely tried to repay their kindness. If that makes me a disgrace to the Parsons family then I don't know anything about logic or psychology or even common sense."

"I'd sooner they left you to rot where you was," Parsons bellowed. "By God, I hate 'em! An' I despise you!"

Before that strange, unreasoning passion Brock could only stand in dumb wonder. And as he stood gazing at his father's distorted face Bill Parsons ripped out an oath and struck at him. Matt caught the swinging arm. Brock seized him by the other. Young, powerful men as they were, for half a minute their father threw them this way and that as a bull might shake two terriers hanging on his flanks. Then weight and strength told and they pinned him helpless, panting, against the bar.

His red face worked. His eyes were glassy with rage. His mouth opened, filled with obscene curses. Brock could feel his body shake and quiver. Then his cursing died away to a mutter. He seemed almost to slump and become uncertain on his feet.

Matt motioned his brother aside. Brock let go. Matt led Parsons away. Brock stood there watching them go through the lobby, disappear upstairs, his father leaning on Matt, taking each step uncertainly, with dragging feet.

Brock turned to the bar for a drink. He was shaking himself, burning with shame and anger. A dozen men had looked and listened with lifted eyebrows.

While he stood with that whisky sending a warming

glow through him, Matt came back.

"Better keep out of his sight, Brock," he said. "He's leavin' town in the mornin', anyway. Were you goin' to put up at the Grand Union?"

"I'll stay at the other hotel," Brock decided. "Walk over with me."

When they were alone in a hotel room three blocks distant, Brock observed, "That was rather ghastly. Has he gone *loco,* or what? That was like a man being insane."

"He's pretty well tanked, for one thing," Matt replied thoughtfully. "Been drinking all day. Still, even cold sober he has spells. If he's crossed he wants to stamp everybody into the earth. You know his temper. I warned you at the Long S."

"I didn't suppose he'd be up north, or in Fort Benton. Yet I didn't feel as if I had to sneak to avoid him. When I spotted the three of you there, I figured it would be a weakness to side-step. It would be fatal for me ever to let Tuck Munce get the idea I would walk around him."

"You know, in your own way you're more like the old man than I am." Matt looked curiously at his brother. "I'm considerable older than you are. I've lived a lot rougher. I'm supposed to be high-handed. But I've never killed nobody yet. You as good as declared yourself about Polk before you left the Nueces. And it was over this Long S business. How did the play come up between you and Polk, anyway?"

Brock told him.

"The old man would never believe that," Matt mused. "Polk made a good many men jump through his hoop in his time."

"No matter. Those are the facts. Polk rode me from the start. I gave him an even break in Lost River, which he didn't give me that night on the Republican. And I have no regrets about it. He was as much responsible as Dad for all that Trinity trouble."

"You got awful set ideas about that Trinity business," Matt commented.

"It was a rotten deal from start to finish," Brock

declared. "Pure aggression, and you know it as well as I. Those Starks are the whitest crowd on earth. Everybody in Texas knows the WP hamstrung them. Do you think he really meant what he said tonight?"

"I'm afraid so." Matt frowned. "He's plumb *loco* on that subject. You know what he's like when anything gets under his skin. Stubborn as a bull. Yes, I know he's planning to put an outfit somewhere in that Bear Paw country in the spring. Just to take a fall out of the Starks. Tuck Munce is eggin' it on."

"Why?"

"Well, for one thing, Tuck toadies to all the old man's weaknesses. Always did. For another he was in that Oxbow fight, an' got pinked in the ribs, an' he's a grudge holder from hell. As bad or worse than Polk was. Since you killed Polk an' threw in with the Long S you're reckoned same as a Stark by both of 'em. But I have another suspicion about Tuck, too. I wouldn't dast say it to anybody but you."

"What?"

"You recollect the Palos Verde war?"

Brock nodded, remembering a bloody clash between two outfits over water rights on the upper Nueces when he was barely thirteen.

"While that ruction was in full swing," Matt said reflectively, "there was a lot of stealin' went on in that section. The *vaqueros* on both sides saw a chance for good pickin's. Tuck and Polk was both in that scrap from start to finish, with the Lazy K. Tuck come out of it with six or eight thousand dollars. He gambled it all away. He's never had a stake since. I think he has ambitions to repeat. There's no organized law north of the Missouri yet. I reckon Tuck has ambitions to make another stake thataway. When riders get to fightin', things get sort of disorganized on a range. All a man needs is a running-iron an' a long rope."

"Why don't you tell the old man?" Brock said. "He has all the confidence in the world in you."

Matt shook his head. "He'd just hoot at me. Nobody

can tell him nothin' when he gets his neck bowed. You know that. Besides, all I have said about Tuck is a hunch."

"My hunches are generally sound," Brock replied. "Oh, it's damnable. I hate to think of my own people and the Starks tangled in a bloody mess again."

"You can't stop it. I can't." Matt shrugged his shoulders. "Not if he reckons to go through with it. He's got money, an' he can get men. It's like when we sent herds up through Kansas. If there was a farmer's fence in his way he shoved right through it. He'll crowd in on the Starks an' put them outa business."

"Where do you stand?" Brock asked.

"I'll stand by my own outfit naturally," Matt said without enthusiasm. "I got to. He's always favored me. I got ten thousand cattle under my own brand on the Trinity right now. But I won't be in on this. He don't want me in. I'm runnin' the Nueces end. I wouldn't even be up north now if I hadn't promised Mom I'd tend to that for you. That there whim of hers to leave you the last few dollars she had in her own name made him pretty savage too. Gosh, darn it, it's a pity."

"What is?"

"That you're at loggerheads with the old man. You'd be a right smart addition to the WP." Matt looked at him with a friendly, almost admiring grin. "You sure turned out to be a surprisin' sort of a dude. Only you shouldn't 'a' throwed in with the Starks. He'll never forgive you that. Take a fool's advice, Brock. Get outa Montana before the fireworks begin. You can't stick with the Long S against your own kin, very well."

"They wouldn't let me if I wanted to," Brock said grimly. "I had to tell 'em who I was the day you were there. They were good to me. One of those boys, the nerviest, deadliest one of the bunch, ran after me to shake hands and tell me he was my friend even if I was a Parsons. What the hell can I do? And I've got to do something. I can't let the WP make the Bear Paws a shambles to satisfy a grudge."

"You can't stop it," Matt declared. "All hell wouldn't

stop him. It's a mania. He broods over it. And he has a bunch of men around him that would welcome trouble for reasons of their own."

They pondered that in silence for a time.

"Well, I got to get back to the Grand Union. Leavin' on the stage to the Judith tomorrow. Keep your eye peeled for Tuck, old kid. Say, what's the matter with you coming back south with me? I think you an' me could get along. This ain't your war, nohow."

But Brock could only shake his head sadly. It wasn't his war. But he knew that willy-nilly he would be tangled in its red snarl if it began anew.

Chapter Sixteen

IN TIME OF PEACE

BROCK SAT IN THE SHADOW cast by his horse looking up toward Big Birch, where Tiger Butte made a green cone thrusting loftily against the spring sky. New grass shot a myriad tiny blades up through the old winter-bleached growth. Wherever he looked, cattle grazed. His cattle, with a new brand peeling from their ribs: Diamond B. A mile south of him on a bald flat between two deep coulees slanting east to' the Bad Lands the yellow of peeled pine logs made a golden flash in the sun. Figures of men moved about there. The *chuck, chuck* of ax blades on wood carried in the thin air, air as clean and uplifting as old wine. From his ranch location the plains rolled west to Chip and Eagle creeks, far off against the horizon, to the immensity of Lonesome Prairie. East, the Bad Lands spread their desolate, forbidding area, like a dark sea frozen in grotesque contours. Twelve miles south, the Missouri cut like a great gash out of the westward plains into the maze of the Bad Lands.

But Brock's gaze remained fixed on the north where his thoughts were. And so looking, he presently saw a moving speck become a rider and watched the rider grow into Clay Stark astride a black horse coming straight to him.

"Well, I'll be darned," Clay said when he swung down and put out his hand. "Never expected to come across you down here. Where you been an' how goes everythin'?"

"So-so," Brock answered. "Been south and back. Bought a herd of two thousand mixed cattle on the Yellowstone early this spring. Locating here on Chase Hill. I'm sort of glad you happened along. I wanted to see you, or somebody from the Long S. How does the family feel about me, Clay?"

"We-ell." Clay seemed to hesitate. "Nobody says nothin'. You know how it is. These things is unfortunate, but there they are. You're a Parsons an' that don't sit well after all that happened on the Trinity. Still—shucks, no use harpin' on that."

"Come over to the camp," Brock invited. "It's getting on for noon. I want to talk to you. You're not in a rush?"

"No," Clay told him. "We're just loafin' before we start calf round-up, which ain't no great task with what stuff we got. Although the old man has bought a couple of thousand more head, that are to be delivered at Miles about July. I heard a new outfit had pulled in an' located here. So I ambled over to size 'em up. No idea it might be you."

"My mother left me some money when she died last winter," Brock explained. "So I decided to go into the cow business myself."

"With your education," Clay remarked as they jogged along, "I'd think you'd try somethin' in town."

"I like this," Brock said simply. "I always did. I went to school all those years to please my mother. Now there's nobody to please but myself. I like the life and I think I can make money at it. And there are other reasons besides."

They dismounted by the chuck wagon, turned their horses loose to graze with the *remuda* scattered around the camp. Clay stared about. Nothing escaped his gaze. His keen dark eyes lingered on the ranch house, walls ready for roofing, the foundation logs of a stable, a set of corrals already complete. From a distance that site looked like a bleak, waterless plateau. But a spring boiled out of the earth ten steps from the corner of the house, flowing like a tiny river through a grassy channel to the southward coulee. The house kept drawing Clay's eye. The wall logs were huge, timbers sixteen inches diameter.

"You buildin' a fort?" he asked lightly. "An' why in Sam Hill didja pick a location where the wind'll blow your eyeteeth out when there's all kinds of sheltered creeks?"

Brock only smiled.

"Meet the boys," he said.

Besides Brock and the cook, seven men gathered to the noon meal. Four were capable-looking youngsters about Brock's age. The other three were past thirty, silent, thin-faced men. Clay shook hands with them all. He looked sharp at one fair curly-haired boy, and the rider chuckled.

"You didn't sort of expect to run across me up here, eh?" he said. "Looks like all Texas is moving north these days. These here's cousins of mine, Clay—Joe, an' Del Pickett."

"They as useless an' ornery as you, Lin?" Clay grinned.

"Heap more so," Lin Pickett assured him. "Plumb worthless, all three of us. That's why we're here. Brock's charitable."

They ate and went back to work at the house. Clay and Brock loafed over cigarettes. Two riders with a pack horse came in sight on the far ridge of the plateau, rode to the corrals, unpacked, unsaddled. Brock walked over, talked to them a few minutes. When the three came back to the chuck tent, Brock said, "This is Bill Spear and Reg Hardy, Clay. This is Clay Stark of the Long S."

They nodded and loaded plates with food. One was a gorilla-built person with a square face and tremendously long arms. The other was a very mild-looking middle-aged man. They finished their food and sauntered away to the shade of a few willows by the spring and stretched themselves in the grass. Clay looked at Brock curiously.

"You have sure picked a crew of right smart gun-toters," he said. "I know Spear and Hardy by reputation. Bert Hargrave I have heard about too. Three years back Lin Pickett rode for us on the Trinity. He wasn't but eighteen or nineteen then, but he had a reputation. The whole Pickett tribe is like that, I understand. They look like lambs an' are dynamite when the occasion arises. You have certainly got a picked crew."

"Yes, hand-picked," Brock said. "It took me all winter to gather them up. If you know something of most of them, you know that if they are gunmen with reputations, you know also that not one of them ever did a mean or crooked thing in his life."

Clay nodded agreement.

"And probably," Brock continued with a smile, "you wonder a little why I pick a ranch site with water at the corner of my house out on a bald flat where a jack rabbit couldn't approach within half a mile without showing himself. And why I have built a house that struck you as being like a fort."

"Well, there's no law agin' wonderin'," Clay drawled. "Long as a man keeps his wonderin' to himself. Maybe you aim to promote a war, or stand a siege or somethin'."

"I'll tell you why," Brock said. "Tomorrow I would probably have ridden up to the Long S. I might not have been welcomed by the rest of the family but I figured I could talk to you."

"You can always talk to me," Clay said softly. "I don't reckon the rest of the family would be hostile—only kinda sorry. We ain't unreasonable folk."

"I know that," Brock replied soberly. "I wouldn't be here if I were not sure of that. Well—it's like this."

He paused to wrinkle his brows and poke absently at the soil with the sharp heel of his boot.

"Hell is going to pop in this part of the country, soon or late," he began finally, "and I'm partly the cause of it. When I pulled out of here last winter I went to Benton. I wanted to talk over certain things with Matt. We were never exactly like brothers, but we can get along without flying at each other's throat. Matt has some sense about me. But I ran into my father and Tuck Munce first thing. Tuck has set himself to get me over my run-in with Polk. The old man has disowned me completely because he regards me as having gone over to the enemy just to spite him. He seems in his old age to feel that he is ordained by God to wipe out everybody who gets in his way or crosses him, whether he is right or wrong. That Trinity business sticks in his crop like poison. Tuck, who is running the northern end of the WP since Polk faded out, has got his ear and is ribbing him up to things. It's rather a horrible thing to say, but it seems to me that my father wouldn't give a damn if one of his hired men did kill me off."

Clay looked at him soberly. "That's a hell of a situation in a family," he remarked.

"It doesn't sound natural, but it's true, I'm afraid," Brock replied. "Some of that's hunch, with me, and some of it's based on what the old man himself has flung at me. But there's no hunch about one thing. The WP is deliberately moving in on this range to take a fall out of the Long S."

"You sure of that?" Clay asked sharply.

"Would I be likely to make a statement like that if I were not reasonably sure?" Brock countered. "Tuck Munce was over here with three men looking around as soon as the snow went off this spring. You saw Bill Spear and Reg Hardy ride in just now. I've had them out for a week keeping tabs on the WP. They've staked a ranch on Chip Creek about ten miles due west of here. They have crossed three herds at the mouth of the Judith. They are going to shove about twenty thousand cattle in here."

"Well," Clay grunted, "I don't think the WP'll buy no bargains off the Long S in a country where Colonel Colt is judge an' jury. If they come askin' for it they'll get it. Still—"

"Oh, it's so senseless," Brock exclaimed.

"Some people are like range bulls," Clay ruminated. "They lock horns once, rest awhile, an' go at it again. It's their nature. We moved outa Texas to keep peace an' avoid trouble an' killin'. We won't move no more. We don't have to. But where do you come in?"

"I don't know yet," Brock answered. "I have wanted to make my home in this Bear Paw country ever since I first saw it. The stake my mother left me enabled me to make a start for myself. I can't help the way my father feels about me. I can't help what Tuck Munce has in his mind because I killed his brother. I'm a little bit like you. I don't feel like side-stepping just because certain people undertake to crowd me."

"Yeah," Clay said, "but you had all the Northwest to pick from. Why camp right in old man Trouble's yard? If the Parsons outfit starts anything with us it won't be pleasant for you. You don't aim to fight us—an' you don't want to fight your own people over somebody else's quarrel."

"Tuck Munce and a bunch of hired gunmen are not my

people," Brock said. "Tuck publicly announced that he'd get me for getting Polk. It's sort of tangled. There is one outstanding reason why I want to stay in or around the Bear Paws. You know why as well as I do. I don't propose to side-step anybody who dislikes me any more than you do. I'm here attending to my legitimate business, like the Long S. We were here first. If the WP moves in here aiming to walk over everything in sight—well—"

He made an impatient gesture with his hands. He had said his say, all he meant to say. He didn't tell Clay what Matt had suggested, that Tuck had an ulterior motive in stirring up the Parsons-Stark feud again. Time enough to add that to the score when Tuck began to show his hand.

"I reckon I *sabe*," Clay nodded. "These here boys you got on your pay roll ain't just a happenchance. Nor your location on this open bench. Nor these buildings that look like they'd stop a bullet from anything but a cannon."

"I am merely using what brains God gave me," Brock said. "It is my ambition to live and prosper, to grow beef and ship it to market. If it happens that Tuck Munce elects to take a crack at me, I'm pretty sure he'll try to make it safe for himself. If the WP tangles with the Long S I'm liable to be in the position of the innocent bystander. It is also a sort of ambition with me to shoot square with my friends and confound my enemies."

"Likely you will," Clay nodded. "If other people I could name was like you—oh, well, a man's got to take things as he finds them."

"Things, yes. And men," Brock muttered.

"And men," Clay agreed. "Well, life ain't likely to be monotonous around the Bear Paws. Not with three cow outfits located within thirty miles of each other with their backs arched an' tails wavin', all primed to claw each other like tomcats."

They smiled at that picture. It seemed to fit the case and yet to verge on the ludicrous. They rolled fresh cigarettes and sat listening to Brock's men laugh and talk as they worked. The cook whistled over his dishpan. Off north the Bear Paws lifted green lower slopes and purple heights. Over the heavy grass and scattered sagebrush on that plateau, a lone plover swooped in circles crying harshly for his mate. A meadow lark warbled in the willows by the spring. And they sat in that placid atmosphere thinking of battle, murder, and sudden death.

"Lou's up at Sutherland's." Clay broke a long silence with an apparently irrelevant remark. "That school opened the other day. They got 'em a real good-lookin' school-ma'am from Benton. Gene told me. Dave an' Ed sent their kids over. Lou's staying there awhile to look after 'em. You been up around the Block S lately?"

Brock shook his head.

"Good head, old Adam," Clay went on. "You'd oughto look in on him. Well, I reckon I'll ride."

One of the men bunched the saddle horses. Clay saddled and mounted. Brock roped a fresh horse. He stood staring after Clay until he bobbed out of sight. Then Brock rode straight for the notch in the hills where Adam Sutherland's home lay hidden in a pleasant valley.

Five miles below the Block S Brock rode up to the rim of Eagle Creek. He pulled up to admire. Down on Chase Hill, and all the way up he had ridden over a rolling terrain, void of tree or any green thing but grass. Up here where the foothills came down to meet the plain every watercourse was wooded. Green leaf and waving bough, thickets of wild rose that would bud in June, pale-trunked groves of quaking aspen where dryads might be at play. The plainsman loves trees the better for his days spent in the hot, dry, shadeless wastes. Brock rested his gloved hands on the horn of his saddle, and half wished he had built in a place like this.

Something spatted on the fork of his saddle with a force that jarred him. A bit of flying lead cut his wrist. The embossed leather of his saddle ripped in an ugly tear. Simultaneously a gun cracked below.

He wheeled his horse back from the edge of the bank. Two jumps took him out of sight of whoever had fired that shot from cover. Brock's teeth clicked as he flung himself off the horse. He had a carbine thrust in a scabbard under his left stirrup leather. He yanked that out, dropped flat, and wormed his way back to the rim of the bank, lay peering through a fringe of grass, mad as a hornet, with no idea who had shot at him or why, but primed for reprisal. He was not hurt, but that was no fault of the hidden rifleman.

Yet, though he watched the north and south reaches of that creek bottom and all that spread below, he saw nothing move except a few Block S cattle stringing in to water. A man cannot fight vacuity. Brock had the patience of an Indian on stalk. He stared until his eyes ached. And then far down the creek he saw a horseman galloping south, weaving in and out among scattered patches of brush.

He tried the old device of raising his hat crown into view. Then slowly he lifted his head. After that, his body. Finally he stood up. That rider slipping away beyond his reach was almost surely the would-be assassin. But if he gave chase and overhauled him he had nothing to go on, no proof. The fellow had kept in brush and timber until the timber ran out. Brock shrugged his shoulders. That particular incident was closed.

So he mounted and rode on to Sutherland's. It wasn't reassuring to be shot at from ambush. Even more disturbing not to know why, or by whom. Still, it was there. He gave the creek a wide berth until he came in sight of the Block S, with that episode still troubling both his mind and his temper, with a shallow scratch across his wrist to remind him that it had been a close shave.

When he rode into the dooryard of the Sutherland ranch at four o'clock a woman was walking toward the house. Brock had an eye like an eagle. She was bareheaded. Brock stared at that mop of yellow hair, at the cast of her face. Unmistakable. Esther Munce—whom he had last seen on the Trinity River in Texas. Incredible; nevertheless it was Esther. And seeing her, Brock had one of these strange certainties which he termed a "hunch," which in his experience so frequently proved correct. He spurred up his horse and intercepted Esther at the house steps. She was a Munce and he had killed her brother. She might regard him with distaste, perhaps even with bitter resentment. But Brock had a question he wanted answered.

If Esther had ever cherished any feeling on that score it didn't exist now, Brock knew as soon as her eyes turned on him. Her face brightened with a smile. She held out both hands to him as he dismounted.

"Why, Brock Parsons," she cried. "Where did you spring from? My, I'm glad to see you again."

"I'd hate to tell you how tickled I am that you feel that way," he told her. "I didn't know—I thought—"

"You mean about Polk?" she said. "Why, I was sorry you had to be the one to do it, that's all. I don't think I'm cold-blooded. But I didn't grieve for Polk. He was so mean he hated himself. It was only a matter of time till somebody had to kill him. If it doesn't worry *you*, it certainly doesn't me."

"Tell me," Brock asked bluntly, "Was Tuck here and did he ride down Eagle Creek an hour or two ago?"

"Why, yes," Esther admitted. "He did leave here not so long ago and he did ride down the creek. Why?"

"Oh, nothing much," Brock answered casually. He had tied a handkerchief around his wrist and he could account for that slight cut simply enough if he were asked. And he didn't want to worry Esther Munce. "I saw a rider that looked familiar enough to give me the idea that it was Tuck."

"Probably was," Esther nodded. "The WP's putting an outfit in south of here and Tuck's range boss."

"I know," Brock said. "Their headquarters is only about ten or twelve miles from my ranch."

Adam Sutherland came out to greet Brock genially. He stabled his horse. He sat with Esther and Adam on the porch for a time. Then they went into a log-walled room where a fire glowed in a cavernous fireplace of rough stone. They talked. Brock told Sutherland of his start in the cattle business.

"It's bound to grow," old Adam said placidly. "Pretty soon—in less'n five years—the Bear Paws'll be full of cattle. Grab all the creek bottom and hay land you can, Parsons.

An' water rights, while you can have 'em for the askin'. Land an' water. Cattle an' land an' water'll make us all rich if we use our heads."

Presently old Adam sauntered off.

"I wonder why the WP crowds in here where the Starks are, where you are?" Esther pondered. "Have you all buried the hatchet?"

"How would I know?" Brock countered. "I'm at outs with my father. That's why I'm on my own. I don't know what his present intentions are as regards me. But I know that he still has his knife out for the Long S. Say, how did you happen to take this school?"

"I told you I was coming north, didn't I, because all the nice Texas boys were emigrating." Esther smiled. "I got an offer of a school in Fort Benton. Then after I got there I met Mr. Sutherland. He persuaded me to take this one instead."

"Like it here?"

"I love it," Esther said. "I never lived in the mountains before. It's beautiful."

"Some of the Stark children are in your school, aren't they?" Brock asked.

"Yes. They're staying here with an aunt, Louise Stark, taking care of them. I like her awfully. Have you met her at all, Brock?"

"Why, yes," Brock said dryly, "seeing that she found me half dead under a cottonwood tree in western Nebraska, and that I came up the trail from there to the Bear Paws with them and lived at their ranch on Big Birch until February. Yes, I suppose I could be said to know Lou Stark. She never happened to mention me?"

Esther shook her yellow head. She regarded Brock rather questioningly. Perhaps his tone gave her some clue.

"Lou and I just don't talk much about anything connected with that trouble on the Trinity," she said. "Polk and Tuck were both in that. She knows I'm a Munce. But we're friendly in spite of that. If the Starks are all like her they must be a fine family. And according to all accounts, they are a fighting family. How did they come to take you to themselves? It's a wonder they didn't kill you on sight."

"They didn't know I was a Parsons," Brock explained, "until they'd sort of accepted me for myself."

"I can understand that." Esther looked at him appraisingly. "But I've spoken about you, and she never even batted an eye."

"She wouldn't," Brock said. "Where is she now?"

"Somewhere around the place," Esther told him. "She'll be here at supper, anyway. Are you deeply interested, Brock?"

"Yes," Brock replied simply. "I am."

"You poor kid," Esther murmured. "You shouldn't be. You know what these family feuds are. You'll be torn to pieces by both sides. What does *she* think about it?"

"I don't know," Brock said. "That's what I rode in here to find out."

"Then you'd better go and find out right now," Esther told him, glancing over his shoulder, "because she's coming up the steps."

Brock went to the door. Lou didn't see him. Her eyes were on the steps until they came level with his spurred boots. Then she looked up. Her hands went to her breast. The blood seemed to recede from her face for a matter of seconds. Then it flooded back in a rush of color. And her gray eyes took on a curious glow. But she didn't speak.

"I didn't have a chance to say good-by." Brock sank his voice. "But you knew I'd come back, didn't you?"

"It would have been better if you hadn't come back," Lou said.

She moved as if to pass him. Brock's fingers closed on her arm.

"Sit down here," he commanded. "I've got to talk to you."

"I don't want to talk to you," she flared. "You lived a lie!"

Nevertheless she sat down. His grip on her arm compelled her. Brock had a temper as quick and fiery as her own. That last stung him.

"I did not live a lie," he said tensely. "I know what you

mean. I am not the WP. I'm not W. J. Parsons. I'm myself. And I love you. I loved you from the beginning. I never told you. But you knew it, just the same."

"You shouldn't. And I shouldn't," she protested.

Brock's heart leaped at that tacit admission. Yet he had known well enough..

"Some day," he told her, "all these grudges will be forgotten."

"My father will never forget nor forgive." Lou shook her head. "Nor my brothers. I don't know that I could myself. It was too terrible, Brock. You weren't in it. You don't know what it was to see your men come in bleeding. To see one of your brothers brought in dead like a sack of flour across a horse. To live for months in constant fear of what might be happening to them. To have to face ruin and run away as we did out of Texas. It's no use us caring about each other. My people would destroy you. They'd sneer and look at me with contempt. I'll never go back on my own family."

"Clay doesn't take it like that," Brock said.

"Clay isn't the whole Stark family," she answered. "Clay's always been a law to himself. If he hadn't taken a liking to you he would be the deadliest of the lot. I'm glad he feels that way about you because otherwise he'd kill you on sight. But the rest aren't like that. They aren't extremists like Clay. You're a Parsons. That's enough for them."

"There's no sense in that," he declared. "They took me for what I was, and liked and respected me for months. There's no sense to turning against me for something I had no hand in."

"There's not much sense in anything, it seems to me," Lou said sadly. "You mustn't try to see me. It'll only make trouble."

For half an hour Brock strove to persuade her that they were not bound by the feud between the Long S and the WP. He only wasted his words. The sun slipped behind Shadow Butte and shade settled over the valley and still they talked.

"It's no use, Brock," Lou said wearily. "I love you too. I admit it. I'm not ashamed of that. I wish I didn't. It's made me suffer. I know it's made you suffer too. I used to wonder why you looked at me the way you did and never said a word. When they told me who you were I understood. You know too. We can't get anywhere."

And Brock, suddenly recalling why the WP was shoving into the Bear Paw country with arrogant malice, to walk on this girl's people again, felt a chill come over him, and a wave of passionate anger.

"By the Lord we *will* get somewhere, sometime," he gritted. "If you do love me, if you give me a chance to play my hand I'll get us somewhere in spite of all this."

"I do love you," she answered steadily. "Sometimes I've almost hated you because I did. If you hadn't stayed with us long enough for me to know you, I wouldn't have a heartache. And I know you well enough to know you'd play your hand anyway. You're made that way. But you can't turn the clock back, nor undo what's been done."

"You can always have a new deal," he muttered.

Lou's hand rested in his. She squeezed his fingers gently, looked quickly over his shoulder and kissed him. There was a bright wetness in her eyes. She rose.

"They have called supper," she said. "And—good heavens, there's Clay!"

Her brother had just turned the corner of the house on the same coal-black horse he had ridden to Brock's ranch that forenoon. Lou glanced at Brock apprehensively.

"He saw me kiss you," she murmured.

"Why, there's nothing to worry about," Brock told her. "Clay was at my camp for lunch today. In fact he told me you were here."

"I wonder if there's anything wrong," she said. "Clay never rides up here. I have a funny feeling there is."

But there wasn't, judging by Clay's tone and manner. He came up to them from stabling his mount, with Adam Sutherland, a faintly amused flicker in his dark eyes. He stood tall and straight, slender and imperious as a lance, on the top step and nodded to Brock and kissed his sister.

Sutherland led them into the living-room.

Esther Munce, rising out of a deep chair like some exotic flower, golden-haired, blue-eyed, skin like cream tinged with roses, stared at this dark-eyed rider, almost, it seemed to Brock, as if she had been expecting Clay Stark and was glad to see him. Yet they were just being introduced. They had never laid eyes on each other before.

Adam Sutherland showed the two men to rooms at the end of a pleasant evening. Brock was tugging off his second boot when Clay came in and sat on the edge of his bed.

"Well," said he. "You take a hint as quick as anybody. Maybe I'm speakin' out of my turn but I didn't tell you Lou was staying at Sutherland's just to be talkin'. What kind of reception did you get?"

"About the kind a Parsons man would naturally get," Brock admitted.

"I was afraid of that," Clay murmured. "She's a Stark an' she's a woman besides. I reckon I'm the freak of the family."

"It's that old Trinity fight," Brock said. "If it wasn't for that— Damn it all, why do such things have to happen? She likes me. But—oh, hell!"

"I know," Clay said. "It *is* hell. It was hell for us too, if you stop to think. I'm with you, Brock. I can't be a halfway man. But if that's the way Lou feels you can't do nothin'."

"No," Brock agreed. "Only wait."

"An' a fresh batch of trouble brewin' outa the same old kettle," Clay continued with a frown. "Gosh darn it, you don't have no luck, do you, Brock?"

"Would you consider it luck to have me in the family?"

Clay merely grinned. He rolled a cigarette, contemplating the bright pattern of a black and scarlet Navajo rug on the floor.

"Did I get that girl's name right?" he finally asked. "Esther Munce. Is she kin to them Nueces Munces?"

"Sister to Polk and Tuck," Brock told him. "But she ain't to blame for that any more than I'm to blame for being the son of my father."

"Hell's bells!" Clay muttered. He put his head in his hands for a minute, a trick he had when he struck a mental snag. When he looked at Brock again there was resentment and something like a hurt in his dark eyes.

"I may seem foolish to you, but I was always kinda sudden," he said. "We're gettin' into quicksands, you an' me, Brock. You killed this girl's brother last summer. He fought us on the Trinity. In fact he was the dirty dog who started the trouble. If you have sized the latest WP move up right, one or the other or both of us will sometime maybe have to tangle up with brother Tuck. Where do you stand with her? She seems friendly about you."

"I've known Esther since she wore little yellow pigtails down her back," Brock explained. "She knows me and she knows her brothers. Esther has brains. And she's fair. She *sabes* probably better than anyone else could just why and how Polk and myself locked horns. She doesn't hold it against me. She isn't that kind."

"Oh, damn!" Clay swore softly and stared at the floor.

"Go to bed and sleep on it," Brock advised. "If it happens that you like her and she likes you, just forget Polk and Tuck."

Clay went out silently. Brock sat boot in hand, concentrated on that tangle. Things didn't work out right. Instead of growing simpler they grew more and more complicated.

And when all those WP riders and herds were loosed in the Bear Paws and Tuck Munce began to lead his roundup across the range they would become more complicated than ever.

Nature doesn't care a whoop how she gets the business done, Brock thought wistfully. *I don't know about Clay. But I do know about myself. It'll be tough going for this young man, all around, I'm thinking.*

Then he blew out the lamp and turned in. A man couldn't solve a problem by staring through the dark in dumb protest. Not the sort of problem that involved heartaches, being shot at from ambush, because a mean man held a grudge, and a selfish man craved despotic power to use at his will, against anyone who crossed his purposes or stood in his way.

Chapter Seventeen

First Blood

CLAY AND BROCK LEFT THE SUTHERLAND RANCH at sunrise. Lou didn't appear until breakfast, and after she rose from the table Brock didn't see her again. But Esther Munce laughed and chatted with them while they smoked. She walked with Clay to the stable, watched him saddle up, and waved farewell when he rode away. And Clay took off his hat and swung it at that figure in the yard when they climbed out of Eagle Creek bottom.

"I don't give a damn nohow," he said defiantly, as if he had reached a conclusion and voiced it to the world at large. Nor did he need to tell Brock what he meant. Still, Brock looked at him curiously.

"You *are* sudden, all right, Clay," he said at last.

"I always was," Clay replied frankly. "But never about a woman before. What the hell is it hits a man, Brock? Was it like that with you and Lou?"

"No," Brock told him. "It just sort of grew."

"I wouldn't 'a' believed it of myself if anybody had told me," Clay said wonderingly. "But there it is. Like touchin' a match to powder. An' she likes me—she likes me."

He uttered that phrase with a note that could only be described as sheer exultation. After that he said nothing for a long time. Not in fact until they topped a rise well west of Eagle Creek. Then he pointed with one gloved hand and pulled up short.

"What in Sam Hill has broke loose down there?"

Down on Chase Hill a billow of smoke lifted against the morning sky. One glance told Brock it rose in the vicinity of his camp. Prairie fire was an old story to the plainsman, a sinister flower that bloomed and left destruction behind. But a spring fire was not so bad. The new growth would still mature to pasturage.

Brock stared, frowning. That smoky banner wavered,

pearl-gray on top where it was touched by the slanting sunbeams. Otherwise it was black, angry-looking. The mixture of green grass with the bleached last year's growth made a thick sooty smoke, bitter in the nostrils.

"That's around my place or near," he said and shook up his horse. Clay loped beside him. They covered the intervening miles in less than an hour. The smoke shrank in volume as they neared. From a distance of a mile they could see the figures of men beating out the last flickering tongues of flames with wet sacks.

But the plateau surrounding the ranch buildings lay a charred waste between the north and south coulees, black as ebony, giving off faintly acrid odors.

Lin Pickett and Bill Spear were nearest them. They had finished the job. In that quiet dawn there had been no wind to fan the flames, to send fire shooting across miles of grass.

"Somebody get careless with a match or cigarette butt?" Brock asked Lin.

"Yes. I reckon somebody was right careless with a match, all right," Lin Pickett growled. His white teeth showed something like a snarl in a face blackened with sooty ash. Bill Spear didn't open his mouth. He turned toward the buildings, he and Lin. Brock and Clay rode on ahead. Reg Hardy, his squat, gorilla-like body stripped to an undershirt, was building a fire in the trough where the cook ranged his Dutch ovens. Del Pickett sat on the chuckwagon tongue, wrapping a bandage around one hand, with smears of blood staining the white cloth. The others were coming in. Del pointed to a sheet of canvas outspread by the wagon wheel.

"Look-a-here, Brock," he said.

He turned back one corner. The face and shoulders of a dead man bared to the sunlight.

"The only peaceable, harmless, defenseless man in the Diamond B," Del said. "Shot him down like a darned coyote."

The rest gathered about. Three Picketts, Bert Hargrave, Spear, Hardy, Mack Stone, Dave Hull. They stared at that still figure with impassive countenances.

"Who did this? What happened?" Brock asked.

Lin Pickett shrugged his shoulders.

"Search me for who. We was all asleep, a little before daylight. We heard a shot. When we raised up, Baldy was down on his belly hollerin'. He'd just lit his fire. The grass on the bench was burnin' in two three places. First move we made there was more shootin'. Maybe Baldy just got up and set about his fire, or maybe he was takin' notice of this fire they'd started. I dunno. They shot him, and they took quite a few pot shots at us as soon as we made a move. Nicked Del on the hand. That's all."

"It's plenty," Brock growled. "There's only one outfit in the country got an ax sharpened for us. Tuck Munce took a shot at me yesterday from ambush on Eagle Creek. Of course it might have been Indians."

"Indians," Reg Hardy said, "don't bushwack for fun. They don't ride shod horses. I looked for tracks. There was just two of 'em."

Del Pickett covered that immobile face.

"Well, we got to eat," said he. "Can't do nothin' on an empty stomach."

"I'll bunch the horses while you fellows get breakfast," Brock said. "Then we'll make medicine over this."

Clay rode out with him. The Diamond B saddle bunch, a hundred head or so, normally grazed on the bench that was burned to a crisp. They watered at the spring. Now they were scattered north where they had trotted away before the flames. Brock had marked some of them as he rode in. He and Clay gathered a couple of dozen and penned them in the corral.

"You gave that black a pretty hard ride this morning," said he. "I'll let you have a fresh mount to go home."

"I don't know that I was aimin' to go home," Clay grinned.

"You'd better," Brock said bluntly. "I've no way of proving it yet, but I think Tuck and the WP is setting out to put the fear of God in us, mostly for my benefit. He *might* extend his operations to the Long S while he's at it. Even if he doesn't, this isn't your fight."

"These boys *sabe* the situation?" Clay asked. "They'll stand by you?"

"Till hell freezes over," Brock declared. "They aren't just hired gunmen, Clay. I didn't have enough money to swing a cow outfit by myself. I didn't want to borrow from banks. I gathered up these fellows between February and April and made them a proposition. They all had some money. The Diamond B is really a pool. Every man in this outfit has a material interest in it. They went in with me with their eyes open. If Tuck Munce is jumping me, he's jumping a bunch of men who are here because the country looks good to them. They're not here for excitement, but to do some good for themselves in a purely legitimate business. If you know anything about these fellows, you know how they'll take to being harried or driven off a range where they have as good a right as anybody—a better right than the WP, because we were here first."

Clay nodded. "I would sort of like to amble around with you fellows an' look into this monkey business," he drawled. "But I reckon I better take a fresh horse an' drag it for home. It may be that we all got to get organized."

"I'd ride the high ridges and look sharp," Brock advised. "Tuck would probably as soon get you as me."

"I hope he tries," Clay said earnestly, "If any man can get me on the open range when I know there's trouble in the air, he's welcome."

And since Brock had ridden enough with Clay Stark to know how competent he was to take care of himself he did not worry when Clay went loping alone away to the eastward. Instead he squatted on his boot heels to smoke a cigarette and mull things over in his mind. Presently he was joined by his riders. They talked.

"This sort of thing," Del Pickett looked irritably at his sore hand, "can't go on. We can't sit around and be potted like sage hens."

"Can't fight shadows," Brock frowned. "We will not be caught like that again, at daylight or any other time. Either Munce deliberately aimed to stir us up and start us on a raid—in which case he would have an excuse for open fighting—or else it was just pure cussedness. I'm certain he shot at me on Eagle Creek last night. Now we know, we can be foxy, day or night. All we can do is wait and watch till he shows his hand plain. We must get this house and stable finished so that we can sleep safely. Or perhaps," he concluded with a dry smile, "you boys may figure it looks like too tough a proposition to buck the WP and would as soon try your luck elsewhere."

Lin Pickett rose to his slim five feet eleven. He ran his fingers through a thatch of fair, curly hair.

"There ain't no place else we can go to start in the cow business," said he reflectively, "unless we cross the line into Canada. An' the United States is good enough for me. We was here first. There's no place I know of, between here and the Texas Panhandle where some mean cuss won't try to run over you, or take what you got if he thinks he can get away with it. We might just as well stand pat. So quit kiddin', Brock. Let's bury old Baldy. That's all we can do for him now. Then let's get to work. If we finally got to fight, why hell, most of us have had to do that before!"

Chapter Eighteen

No Man's Land

THAT SORT OF THING, as Del Pickett put it, couldn't go on. It didn't go on. But the cessation was as much a mystery as the wanton attack itself. The Diamond B, lacking a mark to shoot at in retaliation, awaited the next move from an unknown but easily guessed enemy. Days ran into weeks. That blackened plateau turned to a sward like green plush. The house took on a roof and narrow windows. The stable became a stout building where one well-armed man could keep twenty at bay. Brock and his riders went abroad on the range in pairs and quartets, in a body. They kept the Diamond B cattle bunched within a radius of a few miles and they got their calves branded. Always one or two men were watchful about the ranch. Wherever they rode someone kept to high ground guarding against surprise. Whatever they were about, their weapons were handy.

And nothing happened. No bullets came whistling about their ears. No hostile riders crossed their trail. WP men kept close to their headquarters on Chip Creek. Neither Brock nor any of his riders met a WP man west of the Diamond B, nor anywhere in its vicinity.

Brock knew where they were and what they did most of the time. Bill Spear or Reg Hardy was always scouting, reading signs, keeping the rest informed of every move the WP made.

It was the same at the Long S. The Starks went about their business with one eye ranging the horizon. Warned by Brock, through Clay, they expected anything, at any time. But no overt act disturbed them as summer waxed toward the dog days. Brock knew that from Lou. The Starks were aloof, self-contained. Only Lou at the Sutherland ranch, caring for her brothers' children, was a link between them and Brock through Clay. Clay never came to the Diamond B again. But Esther Munce was a lure for him at the Block S. Now and then when he rode there to see her he left a brief word for Brock with his sister. Those contacts were infrequent. Brock rode in to see Lou because he craved a sight of her at times, not because she encouraged him to come.

Bill Parsons's drunken boast that he would run the Long S out of Montana as he had driven them out of Texas might have been alcoholic vaporing. Tuck's threat to "get" Brock Parsons for Polk's death at his hands might have lost its force as summer wore on. Except for two significant facts.

The first was that the WP flooded the south side of the Bear Paws with cattle until Adam Sutherland and Eph Marks—who owned the Cross Seven off to the west on Sandy Creek—began to murmur that even a virgin range could be overstocked.

Parsons pushed herd after herd across at the mouth of the Judith. He swam trail herds from the south at Cow Island and loosed them almost in the Stark dooryard. He denuded his Judith Basin range of everything but beef cattle. He must have wintered trail herds in Wyoming, because longhorns flowed in from all the southerly points of the compass until the Bear Paw outfits estimated thirty and perhaps forty thousand WP cattle thrown within a radius of twenty miles with the Long S as the focal point of that circle.

For that season, as these herds were turned loose, they would not be disturbed again by round-ups. They were all breeding stock, Brock's men reported, or immature steers. But in the spring—there would be two full WP round-up crews combing that range, perhaps three. Forty to fifty riders. No law in the country save as they carried it in steel tubes. Unorganized territory. One outfit bigger than the other four combined. Sutherland and the Cross Seven could work with the WP. Brock couldn't, wouldn't, nor would the Starks. And if they didn't co-operate they would clash, as inevitably as the sun rose or the wind blew. The WP would begin to show its teeth then, Brock suspected.

Tuck Munce could be depended upon for that, with power at his hand and sanction behind him for any high-handed proceeding.

At any rate the range swarmed with WP stock and that ranch on Chip Creek became a nest of buildings, corrals, with a big pole pasture for saddle horses on the creek below. An increasing number of riders loafed and worked there as each herd was turned loose.

"There's at least forty riders hangin' around on Chip Creek with nothin' much to occupy 'em," Bill Spear reported. "The WP carries some pay roll. A cow outfit don't generally pay good wages outa charity."

A second and equally significant circumstance came to Brock's knowledge through Bill Spear and Lin Pickett. It had to do directly with Tuck Munce. Recalling Matt's guess at what might lie in the back of Tuck Munce's mind, Brock pondered a good deal over that information, took pains eventually to verify it in person.

The upper reaches of the Bear Paw Mountains embraced as rugged a country as lay outdoors in the Northwest. Peaks lifted above timber line, towering stony crags, split by deep canyons. Mountain meadows lay emerald-green in hollows here and there. There were slopes where grass swept a rider's stirrups and slopes where a mountain sheep needed to watch his footing. A far-spread jumble of mountain, pine forest, canyon, creek, and spring. It ran thirty miles north and south, seventy miles east and west. It stood up out of the immensity of the plains like a turreted castle made for giants. The Long S, the Sutherland ranch, and the Cross Seven squatted in the edge of the southern foothills. North, well out on a barren plateau, Fort Assiniboine, manned by cavalry, guarded a region where Indians still went on forays.

Up into these unoccupied, lonely heights, where no cattle ranged, where snow piled deep in winter, where deer and bear and bighorn sheep never saw a hunter now that the Gros Ventres and the Blackfeet were penned on reservations, Tuck Munce and five men vanished one day with a pack outfit. Bill Spear saw them go, watched for their return. They were gone a week. Only three came back then, Tuck, Ev Sprott, the Guadalupe Kid. Bill followed when this trio rode into the mountains again with another packhorse, trailed them warily, out-Indianed them for three days. He lay in cover and watched. They seemed to do nothing except ride occasionally here and there, and disappear between while into a box-like canyon.

Spear didn't dare to go in there alone. The canyon began in timber on a mountain side. It ran north for a half mile and narrowed to a notch masked by a grove of pine. So far as Bill could see, horses or cattle might scramble into that place down its precipitous southern end, but they could never get back that way. And to the north beyond the narrowest place it gradually opened into a valley threaded by a creek.

Bill Spear hung around there as long as his grub lasted. Then he came home.

"No cattle around there at all?" Brock asked.

"Not a hoof above the foothills. Too many flies. They like to eat me up," Bill said. "Nothin' in them hills but game."

"And they're still up there?"

"Were when I left. They did a powerful lot of choppin' in that canyon. I couldn't see what they were at. But it sounded like they might be buildin' somethin'."

"We'll go up and look that layout over tomorrow," Brock decided. "I'll send Lin over to tell Clay Stark. This might interest the Stark outfit. Tuck Munce isn't poking around up there with his particular pets for fun."

Lin Pickett left for the Long S. He had ridden a season for Eugene Stark in Texas and he was still welcome at the Long S even though he was now a Parsons man, he had once jokingly told Brock. He was back early in the morning.

"Clay'll meet you at the west shoulder of Tiger Butte," he told Brock, whereupon Brock and Bill Spear set out. They took neither pack horse nor bedding. Only rifles under their stirrup leathers and food in their saddle pockets.

Clay rode out of timber as they crossed an open glade.

"How goes it in your neck of the woods these days?" Brock inquired.

"All serene, except that we're about swamped with WP cattle," Clay replied. "We been ridin' like hell, shovin' 'em off an' tryin' to keep our own stuff from bein' scattered all over the map. Sort of looked for the WP boys to jump us for that. But nary a soul has showed his face nowhere. What do you suppose his joblots is doin' up here in these mountains when he's supposed to be bossin' a cow outfit on the flats?"

"I'm curious about that myself," Brock grinned. "That's why we're here."

Bill Spear led the way, keeping now always under cover of the pine forest that made a sparse cloak over most of that country, until at last from the crest of a ridge he pointed to a dark hollow, a sunken spot in the timber off on the west.

"Now, I ain't particular nervous," said he, "but if we want to explore that canyon, Brock, I'd say we want to be darn sure nobody's in it, nor catches us in it. If Tuck Munce aims to collect your scalp that would be a right good place for him to get you corralled."

"The only way to find out is to go there and see," Brock said. "Unless you've got something to suggest, Bill."

"Well, I prowled around there a lot," Bill told them, "an' so got a pretty good idea of the lay of the land around that canyon. Let's work pretty well up to the rim. Then I'll go afoot and do some scoutin'. If the bunch ain't there, one of us can go down while the others stand guard."

"Sounds like wisdom," Brock agreed. "Hop to it, Bill."

Spear stopped them within a hundred yards of the lip of that gorge. He left his horse with them and vanished. Brock and Clay sat on a carpet of pine needles and talked in whispers under that screen of trees. Riders could pass through that forest easily. But they were fairly hidden. A man couldn't see far through those ranked trunks. It was shadowy, cool. The green tufted tops of the lodgepole pines filtered that blazing sunlight.

Spear was gone a long time. Brock didn't get uneasy.

They had time to burn. Spear was as crafty as any woodsman, a resourceful, cautious hunter. Nobody was likely to take him at a disadvantage.

And no one did. He came back as silently as a wraith over that layer of pine needles.

"They've done gone out," he said. "I found their tracks. All six of 'em. Lucky we didn't run into 'em on the way. So I sneaked up through the canyon while I was at it an' climbed back out the top end. Wasn't a good deal of a goat I wouldn't 'a' made it."

"What did you find down there?" Brock inquired.

"Nothin' of no great consequence, except it looks like Tuck was prepared to occupy this here place an' make use of it from time to time," Bill chuckled. "You better go look her over an' draw your own conclusions. I think I *sabe* it myself. But a man can always be mistaken."

Spear posted himself on the brink of the canyon.

"Now I'm right over their hangout," he said. "It can't be seen from above on this side. Maybe you could spot it from the west rim, but I dunno. An' when you're in the canyon you won't see nothin' till you're right up to a grove of pine mixed with quakin' asps. Follow this rim till you come to a draw that pitches down pretty sharp. That's most a mile. It'll lead you to the bottom. If anybody does show up I'll fire three shots quick. When I do, you get outa that box canyon quick as the Lord'll let you, because it ain't no place for them to nail you. In fact I'd say only one of you better go in there."

"I never got into no place yet I couldn't get out of," Clay said. "I'm plumb curious about this. But I think Bill's right, Brock. Only one should go at a time. No use taking chances. Those *hombres* might be somewhere around."

Brock left them lying flat on their stomachs looking down over a cliff that stood four hundred feet sheer. He rode at a trot until he found that draw. He passed through the constricted entrance and found himself in a high-walled pocket, flat-floored, covered with grass and sage, a perfect trap of a place. He scanned the cliff top as he rode. Presently he made out two heads. A hand waved for him to come farther up. Then he ceased to pay attention to Spear and Clay, because he had come to what Bill Spear thought he *sabed.*

Pine and quaking aspen clustered about a spring bubbling out of the base of that cliff. He could see the marks where horses had grazed on picket in the grass. That bunch of timber was the only cover and at first approach it seemed innocent enough. But a second look showed the heart of that grove gutted and cleared. The fallen timber had been used to build a corral of stout poles. Back of this corral a small cabin stood between corral and cliff. All new. Well hidden from aught but a prying eye. As yet unused. The brown leaf mold within the circumference of that corral bore scarcely a hoof mark.

Brock tried the cabin door. It opened on a latch, on hinges of rawhide. Two small squares, guiltless of glass, served as windows. Four bunks filled with grass, marked with the outline of recumbent bodies, ranged against the walls. The ash and charred sticks of a campfire lay just outside the door.

The interior gave Brock food for thought. A couple of sacks suspended from wires to the ridgepole, beyond reach of rats and skunks, contained a considerable supply of staple foods—flour, cornmeal, coffee, sugar, dried apples, a slab of salt pork. Brock examined these without disturbing the arrangement. Then he took a last look at the spring, cabin, and corral and went back the way he had come.

The three squatted on the brink and talked it over. Bill Spear had seen what Brock saw.

"If a man wanted a place to hide out," Brock said at last, "this is good. If he figured on a little rustling on the side it's better. Why should the range boss of a big cow outfit want a hiding-place in a box canyon tucked away in the mountains with a corral big enough and high enough to hold a hundred head of cattle at one shot? I'll tell you how it strikes me."

He repeated to Clay what his brother had told him in Fort Benton. He had told Bill Spear long before.

"It kinda seems to me I heard somethin' about Tuck Munce draggin' the long rope during that Palo Verde war," Bill said. "I thought it was just talk at the time."

"If the WP starts a scrap with *us*," Clay said reflectively, "there'd be lots of opportunities. They could keep us so darned busy we wouldn't have no time to look after cattle. They're strong enough to make us step high, wide, an' handsome. There might be good pickin's for half a dozen riders handy with long ropes an' runnin'-irons. Or maybe Tuck just craves a secluded spot to rest up in now an' then, where he can commune with nature undisturbed."

They smiled at that.

"Well, we know where his hangout is," Brock observed. "And he doesn't know we know. That's something. We'll keep an eye on this."

They got down to the foothills early in the evening. Bill Spear headed home. Brock and Clay turned aside to the Sutherland ranch.

"You an' me," Clay said to Brock, "are both in the same fix. We got no business thinkin' about the women we do think about. The best either of us is likely to get will be the worst of it."

"I've never taken the worst of it from anybody yet," Brock said softly.

"Nor me." Clay's face lighted up. "Esther isn't a Munce any more'n you're a typical Parsons. And while we ain't exactly wolves, I have a hunch that when Tuck Munce an' the WP has done their damnedest it will still be our night to howl."

Clay rode a hundred yards in silence. Then he burst into a ribald song:

> *"Oh, the elephant walked around*
> *And the band began to play!*
> *You boys around the monkey's cage*
> *Had better keep away!"*

Chapter Nineteen

THE GATHERING CLOUD

JULY PASSED. August unrolled its thirty-one days off the calendar. Earlier in the season Brock had secured another cook from Fort Benton. Now from a mining country farther west he imported half a dozen laborers and certain machinery. During the passage of those burning midsummer weeks that cooked the grassy plains to pale yellow and baked the turf to springy hardness, these men labored at haymaking while all the south side of the Bear Paws lay quiet as an Illinois cornfield. It might have been a land void of human life, inhabited only by the cattle that grazed on every ridge, in every hollow, as far as the eye could reach. No man made a hostile move. The Block S and Cross Seven combined on a roundup, that was lost somewhere in that waste as a few sticks of driftwood are lost in the immensity of an ocean. The WP riders never strayed far from that Chip Creek ranch. When they did it was merely to make a great sweeping circle around the outer fringes of the range, throwing back a few straggling hundreds.

The Starks brought in their second herd from the south. They put up hay as Brock did. Stacks grew in enormous wedge-shaped piles at both ranches. The Northwest had a reputation for intermittent hard winters. If that means of guarding against loss occurred to the WP, Bill Parsons didn't act on it. Brock's men kept watch on their Chip Creek neighbors. Either Brock and Lin Pickett, or Bill Spear and Reg Hardy, frequently all four, were abroad. The forty riders at the WP put up enough hay to winter a few saddle horses. Otherwise they did nothing but ride, and little of that. Their cattle were bunched around the Long S and the Diamond B. Brock's cattle, the Stark cattle, were only a few drops in that huge bucket of WP stock.

"What they're probably aimin' at," Clay said to Brock

one day when they met, "is to sort of hold 'em all around us till winter comes on. The minute bad fall weather hits this range stock'll drift. Our cattle'll be scattered from hell to breakfast by Christmas, mixed up with WP's like you'd shook 'em all up in a bag. Spring roundup'll bring somethin' to a head."

"Maybe it'll come before," Brock returned. "I hear the WP has a contract to deliver three thousand dry cows to the Belknap Agency this fall. Indian Department. They'll have to gather. There'll be a stir on this range before long."

"H-m-m," Clay ruminated. "Pay us to keep an eye on that gatherin'."

"W. J. Parsons may be a hard man to buck, Clay, but he will not try to steal your cattle, nor mine, nor anybody's," Brock declared.

"No. But Tuck Munce would, and think it smart if he could get away with it," Clay answered tartly.

"It's our business to see he gets away with nothing," Brock said.

Tuck's activities troubled Brock more than anything else. The WP had a very mixed lot of riders. All of them, as a matter of course, would be loyal to their salt, in any sort of situation. But fully half of that two score were the hardest kind of hard citizens. Some of them were known, personally and by reputation, to Brock's Texan crew. The look of the rest was sufficient to classify them. And Tuck's personal bodyguard, the half dozen who rode with him to that box canyon high in the Bear Paws, were the hardest of the lot. By September Brock's men had definitely spotted what they called the "Munce gang." Tuck and this crowd made trips into the hills. The Diamond B riders followed them. At different times Lin Pickett, Bill Spear, Reg Hardy, and Brock himself haunted the timber above that hangout.

All Tuck and his crew ever did, so far as they could discern, was to ride around. Aimlessly, it seemed.

"They're up to something," Brock fumed. "He hasn't built a corral and a cabin in that hidden place for the fun of the thing. I wish I knew what he has up his sleeve."

"Nothin' that shows, that's a cinch," Bill Spear commented. "They just amble around there like men that was merely making themselves familiar with the country."

"Which is very likely just what they're about," Brock said. "But why?"

When Tuck went off on these expeditions, Bill Spear reported, a Texan named Pickles took charge at the Chip Creek ranch. Spear and Hardy and Bert Hargrave knew Pickles's record, and it was fairly lurid. He was a Nueces man who had been involved in several tumultuous affairs, at various points in the Southwest. A first-class cowman. Likewise a cold-blooded killer. Pickles had never been associated with anything crooked, but he had managed to inject a lot of gun-play into matters that might otherwise have been peaceably arranged. The mere fact that fully a dozen riders of Pickles's stripe were with the WP made Brock sure that his father's threat had been no idle one. The WP was merely biding its time. Tuck Munce was likewise awaiting his opportunity.

Yet it began to seem to the Starks as if perhaps Bill Parsons had reconsidered his intention of running them out of Montana. Brock met Ed and Wally once on his way to the Block S. They stopped and spoke courteously enough. Ed looked at Brock finally and said, "From what you told Clay last spring we sort of thought the WP would be on our necks before now. Reckon that might have been a false alarm?"

"I gave it to you for what it was worth," Brock declared.

"Barrin' the fact that WP cattle swarm all around us," Ed continued, "there is no signs of hostility."

"I hope there won't be," Brock replied.

He went up to Sutherland's thinking over this curiously quiet summer, where he had looked for fireworks. Haying was done. Fall brooded over the hills, an atmosphere charged with that strange spell that is cast over the land when summer is dying. Cool nights, touched with frost. Lazy, still days. Peace and silence.

Perhaps W. J. Parsons *had* reconsidered. But Tuck

wouldn't. Brock was very sure of that. Tuck was the type that once suffering humiliation, injury, craving revenge, never overlooked his chance to play even. The Starks and Brock Parsons stuck very tightly in Tuck's crop. He had lately been jawing at his sister because Clay Stark came to see her. Esther told Brock that.

"Why should I be forced to take sides in a row that began over a lot of miserable bulls?" Esther said to Brock indignantly. "I told him that. Even Clay's people look down their noses at me, and at Clay for liking me."

"Do you like him?" Brock asked.

"Of course I like him—heaps," Esther admitted frankly. "Why shouldn't I?"

"You should if you want to," Brock said. "Don't let anybody sidetrack you, if you feel that way about him."

"I don't think there's any danger," Esther said coolly. "*You're* the one that's getting sidetracked."

"That can't be helped," he sighed. "My father precipitated the scrap. There's a lot they can't overlook. I'm his son. And Lou's a Stark."

"She's a darned chump," Esther said impulsively.

"You haven't any idea what it might mean to her," Brock pointed out. "You don't know what it is to be considered a lowdown renegade by your own people."

Brock got a little further light on what it meant that day when he rode into the Block S. True, he saw Louise Stark. She spoke to him with her eyes rather than her lips, for Eugene Stark was sitting by the Sutherland fireplace when Brock walked in. And after supper old Gene contrived to draw Brock aside for a quiet word.

"I want you should leave my girl alone," he said sternly. "You're makin' her unhappy. There can't be no truck between you two."

"You're almost as unreasonable as my father," Brock declared with a good deal of bitterness. "I'm damned on both sides of the fence for something I had no part in. It isn't me that's making Lou unhappy."

"I don't want to be arbitrary with you," old Gene said grimly, "I don't want to be enemies with you nohow. But the way it is I just can't see no daughter of mine marryin' a Parsons. You know what he done to us. He's fixin' to go at us again, by your own account. You got to be either with us or agin us. An' when it comes to a showdown a man don't fight against his own kin. It ain't natural. So walk around my girl. She's a Stark. You're a Parsons. You can't either one of you get over that."

"She doesn't forget it any more than you do," Brock said wistfully. "But it doesn't loom up like a mountain to me."

"I hope she never does," the old man murmured. "She seen too much blood spilled on the Trinity. An' I'm askin' you to be a man an' give her a show. She likes you. I know that. So do I—but it can't go no further. Don't you forget that."

Brock left him to talk to Adam Sutherland. There was something he wanted to know. He described to Sutherland, without betraying the source of his curiosity, that particular box canyon which Tuck Munce frequented, its location. He asked Sutherland if he knew the place.

"Why, yes, I know of it," Sutherland said. "Old prospector that worked for me the first winter I come into the Bear Paws told me about just such a place. It's on a fork of the Claywater that runs out north to Milk River. Yeah, just such a place as you say. He trapped up in the deep snow one winter. Called that place the Bear Den. Why? You been scoutin' up there? That high country's no good for stock. Too much snow. Flies by the million."

Brock turned the questions off casually. He found himself restless and uneasy in that comfortable room. He couldn't stay in that atmosphere. And old Adam seemed to understand.

When Brock walked into his own house late that night, Tom Slater sat chatting with the Diamond B men. Brock stared. He hadn't laid eyes on Slater since the night of that run on the Republican River, which stood out as the turning-point on that long northern trail, as a turning-point in his life. He hadn't even known that Slater belonged to the Chip Creek crowd. But he was presently made aware of that.

"Hello, Brock," he greeted pleasantly. They shook hands.

"How's chances for a job?" he grinned, after they had talked a while.

"I'm full-handed right now," Brock said. "What's the matter with the WP? They laying off men?"

"I laid myself off," Slater told him. "I don't hitch with Tuck Munce nor Dill Pickles somehow."

"Well, I'll see about that in the morning," Brock promised.

Slater approached to remind him of that after breakfast. Brock drew him aside, out of hearing of the others.

"Look here, Tom," he said, "You've been a WP man for two years that I know of. Probably longer. You must have a pretty good idea just how matters stand between the Parsons outfit and myself. You know that Tuck has made the crack that he'll get me for killing his brother. Frankly I'd be dubious about taking any man into this outfit fresh from the WP. We may have to fight, and we are quite prepared to do that any old time. We're dead sure the WP was responsible for the fire we had here in the spring. And a man was shot without any chance to defend himself. This is a poor place for anybody from the WP to come looking for a job."

"I was only stallin'," Slater grinned widely. "Say, I wouldn't ride in the Bear Paws on a bet. Chances are I'd be potted from ambush myself pretty pronto. I just rode over here to put a bug in your ear, because I like you an' I never had much use for either of them Munces. Tuck's meaner'n Polk ever was, an' he hasn't never had Polk's nerve. He's lowdown. He propositioned me about somethin' an' I turned it down. I ain't got either the taste or the nerve for the kind of stuff he wants to put over. Since I know about it, an' he knows I smell a rat, this country ain't healthy for me no more. So I'm on my way. I just wanted to let you know that Tuck is plumb hateful about you. What he said about gettin' you was just a mouthy break. But you called him for it in Benton. He's got the idea your old man don't give a damn if you were put outa the way. Tuck's on the make. He's hinted about what good pickin's there'll be on this range when the WP starts in to disorganize you and the Long S."

"That's the program, eh?" Brock asked. "Tuck's organizing the WP for a range war."

"Why, sure," Slater said. "I have a hunch it'll break loose pretty soon. There's a picked bunch on Chip Creek that'll do anythin' Tuck or Pickles orders. They're drawing double wages. Bill Parsons himself blew in today. I'd say things is about to tighten."

"But you don't know just what Tuck is driving at, when you say he's on the make, do you?" Brock inquired.

"Well, all I know is that in a general way the WP aims to run out or wipe out the Starks," Slater said. "If you take a hand, and for some reason they reckon you will, they'll clean you up too. That'll leave six or seven thousand cattle on this range that'll do somebody a lot of good if they're handled right. That was the way Tuck put it to me."

"Where's Tuck right now?" Brock asked.

"I don't know," Slate replied. "He's been actin' mysterious. Him an' some of the boys pulled out four or five days ago. Pickles is organizin' to do somethin' or go somewhere. That's all I know. It didn't look good to me. So I'm pullin' for Fort Benton. Maybe I'll catch on with some cow outfit that ain't buildin' up a war. I was in that first Trinity scrap, an' I had plenty. Punchin' cows is my trade. If I want a job fightin' I'll join the cavalry."

"What sort of humor does W.J. seem to be in?" Brock couldn't forbear asking.

"I don't know him awful well," Slater admitted, "but the way he talks and growls I'd say he was a mighty bad-tempered man with a considerable grouch which he don't conceal from nobody."

"I can imagine that," Brock murmured. "Well, I'm mighty obliged to you, Tom, for riding in to tell me."

"It don't seem like a square deal to me," Slater declared. "Polk certainly set out to hand it to you. Tuck's playin' the same sort of game. He's up to some sort of devil-try that don't mean no good to you. An' I kinda liked your style when we was comin' up the trail together. I just thought I'd pass it along, in case you didn't suspicion."

"I have. We're ready," Brock grunted. "Let 'em turn their wolf loose."

"That's all right then," Slater drawled. "Me, I'm pullin' my freight for more peaceable climes. I ain't lost no range wars."

"If they knew you rode in here to warn me," Brock suggested, "it might be darned unhealthy for you."

"They'd beef me, I reckon," Slater shrugged his shoulder, "but I ain't never died a winter yet. Pickles was kinda mean when I quit. Tuck don't know I'm gone. He's up in the hills. Maybe hangin' around Sutherland's. He's got his eye on that Stark girl that's livin' where his sister is teachin' school."

"What?" Brock exclaimed.

"Hell, yes, the old fool!" Slater said carelessly. "I don't suppose she'd spit on him, but he's been talkin' about her for the last month. Ambles around that way just now an' then to look her over. You'd think to hear him talk all he had to do was grab her. They say she's a darned nice, good-lookin' girl, too. Well, I got to ramble. I want to make Fort Benton tonight, if I can."

But the cards were stacked against Tom Slater reaching Fort Benton that day, or ever. Brock told his crew what Slater said as soon as that youth was out of sight—all but Slater's mention of Lou Stark. That sent a queer chill through Brock, and a furious blaze of anger. So he kept it to himself, added it to Tuck Munce's score against the day of settlement. He sent Bill Spear and Del Pickett out forthwith to see if they could determine what that bunch of potential trouble-makers on Chip Creek might be up to. For an hour after they had gone he debated taking Lin Pickett with him to go seeking Tuck Munce and his pets up in the mountains—whither they usually went when they disappeared from the home ranch. In the end he decided against that. Better, if something was about to break loose, to be on his own ground.

That evening, an hour after dark, Spear and Pickett rode in. "Blanket that window," Del Pickett said as soon as he crossed the theshold.

For a long time after that fire and shooting in the spring, they had been wary of lights that would outline a man's figure after dark. Latterly they had grown careless in undisturbed security. But they didn't need to be told twice, to act.

"Pickles an' a bunch of men are up behind a ridge hardly a mile south of here," Bill Spear explained. "We been keepin' tabs on the WP all day. An' that boy who stayed here overnight is layin' dead in a coulee halfway between here an' Eagle Creek. Somebody shot him off his horse as he rode through a draw. He was still warm when we come on him."

"The dirty murdering hounds!" Brock cursed. "They followed him here and figured he might have told something. And you say Pickles and a bunch of riders are camped not far south of the ranch here? Any sign of what they might be about?"

"I ain't no mind reader," Bill replied. "We Injuned on 'em after they left the WP. Had to wait till dark to get in here without 'em seein' us. Looks to me we might be in for a touch of high life around here."

"Get something to eat, you two," Brock ordered. "Then put out all the lights. Bert, and Joe Pickett and Dave, take your rifles and plenty of ammunition and camp yourselves behind that barricade at the outside corner of the haystack fence. Lin, you and Mac Stone hold the stable. That way we cover every approach. They may not intend to tackle us. But if they do we'll give 'em a warm welcome."

Chapter Twenty

ONSLAUGHT

THREE MEN, each with a rifle, a frontier Colt, and plenty of ammunition for both guns, posted behind a barricade of logs laid against just such a contingency. Two men, also well-armed, in a stable with walls thick enough to stop an ordinary bullet. Four resourceful, determined men within that house which was built like a fort. The cook didn't count as a defender. He was an unknown quantity. But he fed the two riders who had just come in, stroked his grizzled mustache, and calmly asked for a rifle. He was a kindly soul, well past middle age, who never had much to say.

"You better lie down on the floor and have a sleep," Brock suggested. "Your job is to feed us, not to fight. We might be penned up here quite a while if this bunch means business."

"Before I took to jugglin' a skillet an' Dutch ovens," the cook said, quite unperturbed, "I was a buffalo hunter, Mister Parsons. I've laid in a buffalo wallow an' stood off Injuns whilst you was still wearin' didys. I'll have me a sleep all right. An' I'll rustle grub whenever it's needed. But if there's goin' to be a passel of folks shootin' at us, I'd like to be fixed so I could shoot back. I bet I don't waste as many ca'tridges as you fellers will, either."

"That sounds all right to me." Brock laughed. "You're one man to the good. Here's a .45—90. And two hundred rounds for it."

"Aha," the old man's eyes gleamed. ".45—90. That there's a gun. She ain't no snappin' Jenny. When she lifts up her voice she roars, an' what she hits is hit good."

They weren't afraid. They weren't even disturbed. They took their positions, one man to each narrow window. Even in the dark no one could come up on them unseen. For a hundred yards all about the ground was denuded of grass by trampling hoofs and wagon wheels. Barring a match to haystacks, they could hold the place against a hundred men.

So they waited, with eyes grown used to the gloom. Half an hour. One hour. Two hours. Nothing stirred near or far. Not the distant jingle of a bit chain, nor a footfall on that dry turf.

"Looks like a false alarm," Brock said at last. "Listen to Zack saw wood."

The cook, rolled in a blanket on the floor by his range, snored in deep, untroubled slumber.

"Takes it easy," Reg Hardy grunted. "He's seen enough wild west, I reckon, not to be nervous over any kind of ruckus. I wouldn't take it as a false alarm yet, Brock. Maybe Pickles don't aim to tackle us. Again he might be waitin' for the middle of the night, thinkin' to take us in the soundest part of our sleep. And again he might calculate to open up a little before daybreak. No WP man has ever set foot on this bench unless he prowled it some dark night. I doubt if they know how well we're fixed. They ain't very likely to figure us standin' on our guns the way we are. His object in bein' here with a bunch of men is all guesswork, anyway. But I'd say we'll either be shootin' before daylight or there won't be no shootin'."

That was a logical enough conclusion, Brock agreed. He turned to his window again, a north window that looked past the stable toward the Bear Paws. His eye presently detected something off in the northeast that lightened and spread, grew to a faint reddish-gold tinge on the sky.

"Come here, Reg," he said.

Hardy joined him, to stare at this phenomenon.

"It strikes me as being just about where the Long S is, on Big Birch," Brock said.

"Yes," Hardy declared. "I'd say so. An' it looks like buildin's or hay burning instead of just grass. Too bright in one spot for a prairie fire."

Brock chewed his underlip. There were women and children there. It was more on the cards that the WP would strike at the Starks than at him. Tuck Munce would perhaps rather hit at Brock to satisfy his own poisonous hatred. But Bill Parsons ordered the WP policy and his rancor was against the Starks far more than against his youngest son. Brock watched that brightness grow with a flame of anger and anxiety burning in his breast.

"You fellows can hold this ranch without half-trying," he said to Hardy at last. "I can't stand this. I'm going to take Lin and ride to the Long S."

"We can hold her all right," Hardy muttered. "But I wouldn't go, Brock. They may not bother us. If you horn into the Stark-Parsons feud personally, we lay ourselves wide open."

"I can't help it," Brock declared. "I've got to know what's happening over there. If they wipe out the Starks, we'll be next on the list anyhow."

"Somethin' in that, too," Hardy said thoughtfully. "Well, be careful."

Brock called to Lin Pickett as he neared the stable. Lin opened the door to let him sidle in.

"Looks like a quiet night around the Diamond B," Lin drawled. "What fetched you over here?"

"The Long S looks like it's all on fire," Brock informed him. "I'm going over to see. I'm worried about that. You want to go along, Lin? The rest of the boys can easily hold the fort."

"Sure I'll go," Lin said. "Three men could hold this place, let alone seven."

"There'll be eight with us gone," Brock said. "Old Zack is cuddling a .45—90 in his sleep and dreaming of what he can do with it."

Lin laughed. They felt about on pegs for their riding gear, got horses out of stalls and saddled them. Brock murmured instructions to the other men. He called softly to those by the haystack, "Don't shoot. Lin and myself are going to ride out."

They led their horses outside, swung up, moved off slowly. The night was shrouded in that peculiar luminous darkness that comes with the haze of Indian summer. They used every caution. Yet softly, carefully as they eased their mounts away from the place, eyes and ears as keen, brains as crafty as their own, were looking, listening, in that outer ring of darkness where vision could not penetrate.

Before they had covered thirty yards a dozen guns roared at them. Brock heard bullets go *whe-e-e-e*, a thin-edged unpleasant whine. The reports cracked like giant whiplashes.

From house and stable and log barricade by the haystack, his own men returned that fire as if they had been waiting with fingers crooked on each trigger, taking as their marks each separate sunflower that spread its deadly yellow blossom for a moment in the darkness, spitting its seed of death.

Brock heard Lin Pickett say, "Hell!" and jump his horse to a gallop. He followed suit.

"Don't fire," Lin cautioned as they plunged forward side by side. "They'll spot us by the flash of our guns if we shoot."

Brock had his .45 drawn. He shoved it back into the holster. There was sense in Lin's counsel.

The drum of hoofs alone betrayed them. For a matter of perhaps twenty seconds a continuous fusillade sounded about that ranch. Once they came right on top of two spitting guns. But to hit a fast running horse in the dark was a matter of chance rather than skill. They ran through the circle, left the crackle and the bright flashes far behind. They galloped for a mile and pulled up to let their blowing mounts get their second wind. The odd shot popped yet. An occasional flash showed like the wink of a fiery eye.

"Gosh, I kinda think it's lucky we made that break away from there," Lin said. "Them *hombres* had worked in pretty close without one of us spottin' 'em. They won't have a chance to rush the place now. Well, we're out in the cold, cold world, Brock. How we goin' to get back?"

"We're not going to try to get back until I find out what's going on over there." Brock pointed northeast, where the firelight on a dark horizon looked now like a small sunrise.

"I'm all for that too," Lin answered lightly.

They shook their horses into a lope. For five miles they

held that gait, let them walk a few hundred yards, and loped again, until they dropped into the gut of Little Birch. When they rode out on the broad bench that spread away to Big Birch and north to Tiger Butte, a long bright line of fire came creeping toward them, flickering little flames. They could smell the smoke strongly, borne on the cool night airs. Out of the hollow of Big Birch a column of flame lifted, snaky tongues of yellow licking at the sky.

"The Long S is sure goin' up in smoke," Lin remarked.

Brock pulled his horse to a stop. They cocked their heads on one side, listening.

"Shootin'," Lin grunted. "Yep."

"That prairie fire has a good start," Brock growled. "If it gets away God only knows where it will stop."

"Hardly a breath of wind," Lin pointed out. "She'll travel slow until the sun comes up. Then if the wind comes —whoof! Well, it sure looks like a big night tonight."

"Come on." Brock spurred his horse. "Let's see what it's all about."

"It strikes me," Lin said as they rode, "that we might find ourselves between the devil and the deep sea. If the WP is stagin' a raid on the Long S an' are still hangin' round there they won't greet us like long-lost brothers if we run onto any of 'em. If they've had at the Long S an' departed, them Stark boys is liable to be darned hard to approach."

"We'll manage it somehow," Brock declared.

After that they rode in silence until that creeping line of fire that wiped out every blade in its path was a dancing fringe before them. They picked a thin spot and ran their horses at it, crossing with no more than a few singed hairs and a blast of heat in their faces. Once through, they were on a black waste where little wisps of acrid smoke drifted here and there. Once they stopped to listen, hearing nothing. That fiery pillar lifted brightly out of the bed of Big Birch. But there was no more shooting.

And as they rose out of the next hollow they rode slap into a group of horsemen. Without challenge, without hesitation, these riders fired upon them. Brock and Lin swerved aside, drew six-shooters, and fired back as they fled. Nor did they fly far. Only a matter of a hundred yards. Then Brock jerked his horse to a stand, flung out of his saddle, and unlimbered his carbine. He could hear the beat of hoofs. He fired at the sound, blind and large in the dark. So did Lin Pickett. Somewhere off there a man uttered a sharp exclamation, a pained oath. They threw lead until their guns were empty. The sound of those hoofs · grew faint, died away.

"I reckon we discouraged any notion they might have had to chase us," Lin said as he shoved fresh cartridges into his magazine. "Wonder if by a fluke we hit anybody?"

"Sounded like it," Brock replied. "Well, they're gone. Let's get on to the Long S."

They looked from the rim of Big Birch down on ruined heaps of glowing red where stables and haystacks had stood. But the house remained, its windows and long front porch looming plain in that fire glow.

"Now, how are we going to get to those people," Brock fretted, "without them shooting at sight of us?"

"I expect," Lin said, "I better snake my way down till I can holler to 'em. They know my voice."

"They know mine too," Brock answered. "You hold the horses. I'll go down myself."

Lin remained on the bank. Brock made his way cautiously. He stole warily within shouting distance, then called, "Ho, Clay—ho, Clay Stark!"

For a few seconds no answer came, then Clay's voice echoed, "That you, Brock?"

"Yes," Brock called back. "Lin Pickett and me. We saw the fire and rode over. Are you all right? Can we come in?"

Another brief silence. Then old Gene called, "Come on. But keep outa the light."

"Lin's up on the bank," Brock called. "I'll go back and get him. We'll both come to the back of the house."

Clay met them at the back door. "Come in," said he. "The outside air ain't healthy tonight."

The kitchen windows were blanketed. A lamp burned on a table. Dave's wife, Ed's wife, and Wally's with three of the younger children squatted on the floor, their backs against the wall. One small child slept with his head in his mother's lap. Clay and his father and young Gene were the only men visible. The others, Brock surmised, would be on watch at vantage points.

"We saw this blaze from my ranch," Brock explained to the old man, "and started over here to see if we could do anything. Then we heard shooting. And we ran into a parcel of riders, who were quite free with their guns for a few minutes. Any of you get hurt?"

"No. Lucky for us," Eugene Stark frowned. "Nobody got hurt. But we done lost every pound of hay we had up an' all our harness an' stuff in the stable. Damn Injuns anyhow!"

"Indians?" Brock echoed blankly.

"Bucks on a raidin' party, I reckon," Clay nodded. "I raced for the stable when the fire woke me up. They cut loose at me. I spotted one an' I think I downed him. But his partners packed him off. I got his headdress. See?"

Eagle feathers stitched into a buckskin headband. It lay on the table, the white of the feathers stained with fresh blood. Brock and Lin looked at each other.

"Indians," Brock repeated. "Well—maybe they were."

Chapter Twenty-One

INJUNS?

"SO FAR AS WE COULD TELL, they certainly were," Eugene Stark declared. "You reckon otherwise? Who'd you think it might be?"

"The WP," Brock said frankly. "More particularly Tuck Munce and his private collection of thugs. There's a raid on at my ranch. And we know that it's not an Indian raid. Dill Pickles and a bunch of WP men were smoking up the Diamond B to a fare-you-well when Lin and I broke away. I thought—well—we saw this fire and came over."

"Whyn't you stay an' defend your own place if it was bein' attacked?" old Gene asked.

"There were eight men there fixed to stand off as many as the WP could bring, without half trying," Brock said. "We knew it was coming and we were ready. And I didn't know whether you were or not. Hang it all," he ended, "you've got to get rid of that feeling of distrust and suspicion of me. I'm not the WP. They're handing it out to me just as strong as they ever will to you. Right now that fire's burning up square miles of feed that we'll want this winter. Let's get out and fight that instead of standing here giving each other the bad eye."

A faint smile rippled across Clay's face. His father didn't smile.

"We'll need that grass, all right," he said morosely. "But we'd all be marks against that blazing fire. I don't feel like riskin' my boys."

"I'd take a chance, Dad," Clay put in. "Let's half of us go out with Lin and Brock."

"How?" his father demanded. "Every horse in the stable was cooked to a crisp. Every saddle is burned up."

"Uh-uh. Mine and Wally's is laying by the bunkhouse door," Clay said. "There's horses in the pasture. Brock and Lin have mounts. They can bunch the horses for us."

"Better wait till daylight," Eugene Stark counseled.
"Tain't but a couple of hours now."

"Two hours may bring a wind," Clay declared. "Then
the whole darn country's gone up in smoke, as well as our
hay and stable. Tain't like you to be backward, Dad."

"Go ahead then," his father gave in. "Get up them
horses. But watch out for hostiles. Your scalps is worth
more'n any amount of grass."

Clay took Lin's horse and rode with Brock into the pasture. They gathered a bunch of saddle stock within that
pole fence along Big Birch and roped out half a dozen. The
fiery heaps were dulling to a feeble glow. While they
moved warily Brock felt that they were safe enough. The
war wasn't openly on yet. Tuck was cunning. He would
hit and get away. Whether he moved according to Bill
Parsons's orders or in accordance with some scheme of his
own—and Brock even in the face of his father's declaration
could hardly believe Bill Parsons capable of deliberate
arson and murder without the definite excuse of retaliation in kind—Tuck would be foxy. He would harass the
Long S, cripple them without risking much, without re-
vealing his identity, until the Starks in desperation turned
on the WP. Then the forty riders would use their weight.

And this *might* be Indians. Brock doubted it; yet he
had to give the WP the benefit of that doubt. Those blood-
stained eagle feathers were not a cowpuncher's gear. But
there was no doubt about Pickles lying behind a ridge
waiting for dark to close in on the Diamond B. Why that
move? No idle gesture that. Nor a mere bluff. There was
method in it, purpose behind that strike.

He gave over puzzling when Eugene Stark, Clay, Mike,
and Wally loped out with him and Lin Pickett to where
that blazing line crawled like a burning snake, looped in
sinuous fiery folds. Two of the Starks rode bareback. They
were armed with sacks and pieces of old blanket, with dry
rawhide cut in broad strips like a paddle to flail out that
fire.

It lay all west of Big Birch. Unless the wind fanned it to

racing speed and flung blazing wisps across, Little Birch would stop it on the west. Otherwise it would cross, spread the flames to the Diamond B, up to the Block S, make the Bear Paws a smoky ruin. And if it was not checked on its northward march, it would still ravage the hills. It was up to six men to beat out two miles of grass fire between Big Birch and Little Birch.

Dawn found them slapping at the last three hundred yards of little flames licking through scanty grass on a stony hogback. Sunrise saw them in a group rolling a cigarette each, six sooty-faced, tired men on the edge of a black triangle.

Brock stared away toward the Diamond B. Shafts of sunlight stabbed across the rolling foothills. The Bear Paws lifted a score of gold-tipped pinnacles. The green of the pines was like new velvet.

Off on Chase Hill were his men still holding the fort? Had the raiders vanished with the dawn? No column of smoke marred that horizon. No shot could carry that far. He didn't worry. The Diamond B would prove a hard nut to crack, planned and manned as it was.

"Let's get home," old Gene said at last.

"I think Lin and myself better hit the trail." Brock turned to his horse.

"Come on, have breakfast with us before you go," Eugene Stark invited. "You're a Parsons, but by thunder, you're makin' it hard for me to remember that."

Nevertheless, eating hot cakes and fried beef at the same table with the seven Stark sons, their wives and children, Brock felt and knew there was a different attitude toward him than there had been through those months when he was one of them, a Long S rider, accepted for himself. The faintly smoking embers of stable and stacks kept drawing their eyes away. Brock understood that situation. Indians or range raiders (and Brock still had his secret opinion about that) it was too late in the fall to get feed, to cut hay. There was none available because during July and August they had gathered up all that a mower's blade would reach. The Stark men were thinking about that phase when they went out on the porch after breakfast. Four saddled horses and the two Wally and Mike had ridden bareback stood in a row, heads drooping.

"It looks like we'll just have to abandon this ranch for the winter and let the stock look after itself," old Gene muttered. "We can build a stable. But we can't keep up ridin' and workin' stock without feed. Damn redskins anyway. I expect they run off a bunch of our saddle stock too."

"I have five hundred tons of hay stacked," Brock said. "Take as much as you need. You're welcome. I've got plenty to spare—unless it gets burned up too. If you can make out to haul it over here. But if I were you, I would send the women and children to Fort Benton. There may be other Indians jump the reservation."

They looked at him sidelong—all but Clay.

"Or white Injuns from Chip Creek," Clay drawled. "Is that what you mean?"

"The WP has raided me." Brock shrugged his shoulders. "So long as W. J. Parsons holds the idea that he does about me and about the Long S, and Tuck runs the outfit for him, you can expect almost anything from that source. That crowd would spell trouble on any range. It's money in those fellows' pockets to keep the feud going. They're drawing double pay to fight as well as ride. I don't like these raids."

"Let 'em raid," old Gene said sharply. "We ain't sidesteppin' an inch no more. If it was a buck party off'n the reservation, they'll be hunted back where they belong. There's cavalry in this country to tend to that. If it was the WP, they won't raid much more without gettin' raided themselves. I'll buy a hundred ton of hay off you, Brock, if you have it to spare."

"Buy it or borrow it, it's all the same to me," Brock said. "You're welcome."

"We got wagons, but no harness now," the old man ruminated. "We might borrow a few sets from Adam Sutherland. One of you boys take a pack horse an' jog up to the Block S an' see if you can raise enough harness to fit out two four-horse teams."

"I'd better get back and see if I have any ranch or hay left," Brock grinned. "If it does happen that we're cleaned out, I'll send you word. If you don't hear from me, send your teams over whenever you're ready."

"I'd better ride with you," Clay suggested. "What about it, Dad?"

His father pondered a few seconds. "Maybe you better," he agreed. "An' then go on up to Sutherland's an' see about that harness."

Brock headed straight east as nearly as he could recall the way he and Lin had approached the Long S ranch in the night. As he rode he kept a sharp lookout over the ground. Everywhere a thin film of black ash from the burned grass covered the ground. Wherever a horse or man put foot that dark layer broke through to brown sod. A track across that was as plain as a trail in fresh snow. Brock, remembering that group of horsemen who fired and ran, was looking for their trail.

"It must have been about here we ran into them," he said to Lin Pickett. "Spread out a couple of hundred yards apart and see if we can pick up their track in the next mile or so."

Lin Pickett, riding to the north of his fellows, signaled them before long. They loped over. There were tracks. They followed.

On the brink of a coulee they came on a dead horse, a beast that had died with sweat marks of saddle and bridle on him. A typical Texas cow pony, with a bare, bloody patch where a piece of hide had been slashed off one hip.

"They cut off the brand so he couldn't be identified," Lin frowned. "Left hip. That's where the WP is on horses. We nicked one all right, Brock. This horse went a ways before he fell. So much for that. Let's see which way they went from here."

Five plain sets of hoof marks continued west to Little Birch. Across that, in ripe grass, the trail was harder to follow. But three pairs of keen eyes marked it well enough to determine that one horse veered off toward Chip Creek, and the other four turned straight north. They followed the larger trail for a mile. Without a swerve it bore straight for the upper reaches of the Bear Paws, for that jumble of canyons and peaks between Tiger Butte and the head of Eagle Creek.

"No use going farther," Brock pulled up. "No way of proving anything, but I'm willing to bet a Stetson hat against a plugged nickel that Tuck Munce and his pets were hovering around the Long S last night while Pickles took a fall out of us at the Diamond B. If they were Indians that attacked your ranch, Clay, what were these *hombres* doing around there?"

"Search me." Clay shook his head. "I couldn't tell only what I saw. Eagle-feather headdresses and war paint an' ki-yi-in' spelled Injuns to us, until you said your say."

"If I didn't have something else on my mind, I'd trail this bunch to hell," Brock growled. "I'd like to identify this gang that wants to keep under cover so bad they skin the brand off a horse that was shot from under them. However, let's pull for home. I want to know how the scrape went."

It had not gone with any marked success either way, they learned when they walked in.

"They never had a chance to get in close on us," Del Pickett said. "They didn't try no rush. Wish they had. Just stood off an' kept poppin' at us. When one of us fired at a flash they smoked hell outa us for a few minutes. Scandalous waste of powder. We got enough lead in those log walls to sink a ship. About half an hour before daylight they let up. At sunrise me and Reg took a little *pasear* around. It was Pickles and the WP men all right. They come down from layin' behind that ridge like I told you. They rode straight toward the WP. Kind of a damn fool sort of performance. They never had a chance to do us no damage."

"It might not have been such a fool proceeding if we had been caught by surprise," Brock pointed out. "If we hadn't been on the lookout they could have sneaked in and fired the haystacks and potted some of us when we surged out."

"That's the second crack they've taken at us," Del growled. "Every time I think of last spring I remember that other fire an' a dead cook by the Dutch ovens. How long before we step out an' hit back? You got more patience than some of us, Brock. Pretty soon they'll get the idea we're yellow."

"When they start to act on that idea," Brock sneered, "they'll learn different. I have a notion they'll learn a lot they won't like when the time comes. And it may not be so very long."

When Clay, assured that the Diamond B haystacks were intact, rode for the Block S to borrow harness as his father directed, Brock turned to Lin Pickett and Bill Spear.

"They killed Tom Slater because they thought he might have told us something we already knew," said he. "They're not raiding to clean us up, but simply to keep us guessing so hard we'll sit tight on guard here around the ranch. The only real reason for that is to enable them to have a free hand elsewhere. There's definite purpose in that. Tuck and his crowd have been gone from the WP for days. Where are they and what are they doing? I don't believe Indians attacked the Long S last night."

"I have my doubts about that too," Lin said.

"There's a way to find out," Brock declared. "Run in the saddle bunch. I'm going to the WP myself."

"By yourself? You are like fun," Lin Pickett demurred. "Not on your tintype, Brock. You'd last about as long as a snowball in hell."

"My father is there," Brock countered. "Rabid as he is about the Starks and sore as he is at me, I'm his son and none of these hired killers that he has around is going to drop me before his eyes. I've got to talk to him about this. If he is behind this deviltry, I'll find it out, and I'll know what to do. If he's not sanctioning the outfit's sneaking attacks in the night on both myself and the Starks, then he has simply started something that has got away from him. If that's the case, we've got to take the aggressive in self-defense."

"I've been wonderin' how long it would take you to come

to that conclusion," Lin Pickett grinned. "But just the same, you ain't ridin' alone into that Chip Creek ranch, Brock, old boy. I know you're game, and fast with that old white-handled gun. But no man can beat a dozen—if something broke loose."

"We'd better all ride over with you," Bill Spear suggested.

"No," Brock refused. "Tuck Munce nor any of his bunch daren't deliberately pick a row with me on that ranch before his eyes. I don't want anybody. I'd rather go alone."

"Listen," Bill Spear said. "Don't be a darn fool. All you say may be true. Maybe your old man has got everybody around there eatin' out of his hand. He owns the outfit an' pays the wages, an' naturally they're not goin' to do anythin' openly that he wouldn't stand for—like killin' his kinfolk. But just the same you *are* takin' a long chance ridin' into that nest of skunks. Maybe Bill Parsons has went away. Maybe—lots of things could go wrong. Leave me and Lin go with you. I know the layout of the place like a book. Me'n Lin can lay on a little hill within a hundred yards of the door. You can go down an' parley. If your old man ain't there an' Tuck should be, you'll be jumped sure as sin. If we're out in the clear they'll hesitate. Don't be a damn proud fool."

They compromised on that. Brock rode away flanked by Lin and Bill Spear. Del Pickett made a last statement to Brock as they mounted:

"If you three ain't back by sundown, right side up with care, there'll be guts to clean on Chip Creek before mornin'. The Pickett family has just about had its bellyful of takin' it without handin' it back!"

Chapter Twenty-Two

A Showing of Teeth

Brock rode boldly into the WP dooryard. For all that
Lin Pickett and Bill Spear lay on the crest of a little hillock
that topped Chip Creek, with carbines before them in the
grass that partly screened their prone bodies, Brock knew
that his chances of riding safely away from that place were
slim indeed—if his father was absent and Tuck Munce
happened to be there. Tuck would never have a better
opportunity, knowing that whatever he started his crew
would finish for him. Brock gambled on a bold front and
his father's presence.

And he won. Men moving about the stables stopped to
stare, curious but undisturbed by a lone rider. And when
he pulled up by a low porch that ran along the front of a
good-sized L-shaped house of logs roofed with sod, three
men got to their feet at sight of his face, and one was W. J.
Parsons himself. The second was Dill Pickles. The third
man Brock did not know. He had a bandage around his
neck and one arm in a sling.

"What do *you* want here?" Bill Parsons growled.

Brock got off his horse. He came up the two steps to the
porch floor. He had caught a flicker in Pickles's eyes that
made him wish to be at close quarters. Surprise and uneasiness had been reflected for an instant on the man's hard
face, in his cold, agate-gray eyes. And when an individual
of his type and instinct grew uneasy he was doubly dangerous.

Still, Brock considered his position strategically sound
enough to be made stronger by a bluff that after all wasn't
wholly a bluff.

"I want to talk over certain matters with you," he said
calmly, "and just in case any of these gun-toters you have
around might think this is a good time to have at me, I
wish to remark that I have some right smart gunmen on

my own pay roll. Some of the best of them are lying up on that hill where they command this porch. So let's talk peaceably. Where is Tuck Munce? I'd like to have him hear what I've got to say to you."

"He's somewhere out on the range," Bill Parsons answered coldly. "Less you have to say to Tuck the better for both of you."

"Out on the range, eh?" Brock smiled. "I have an idea what he's up to out on the range, too. Which is probably more than you know, Dad. At least I hope it is. Because it isn't any credit to you to turn a bunch of murdering thieves loose on men who are merely attending to their own legitimate business."

"Young feller," Pickles's pale gray eyes got more flat-looking, and his lids fluttered for a second like the wings of a humming bird, "that's pretty strong talk about this outfit. I—"

"Shut up! I'm not talking to you," Brock said insolently. "I was speaking to my father. I'll talk about you and *to* you in a minute. Meantime, keep out of this conversation, you dirty, bushwhacking thug!"

The man's face didn't alter its cold, intent expression. But he seemed imperceptibly to grow more tense, to gather himself together, to hunch forward slowly.

"Don't reach for that gun, Pickles," Brock said with a taunting smile. "If I don't kill you before you get it out, one of the boys on the bank will do the trick with his Winchester. You have no chance to win any fight with me this morning. Better be a good dog, Pickles. It's safer to bark at night—in the dark—from a bush—than to bite in daylight."

As Tuck Munce had done in the bar of the Grand Union, Pickles looked at his employer. For the first time that Brock could recall, his father stared at him doubtfully, puzzled, with a trace of wonder.

"Are you willing that your hired men should kill me?" Brock asked him sharply. "Is it part of your new policy to encourage them to make war on me?"

"You know darn well I got no such idea," Parsons answered stiffly. "You ain't no credit to me. Your mother spoiled you. You got your head so full of highfalutin' ideas there's no room in it for common horse sense. But I bred you, such as you are, an' neither the outfit nor any of my men are after your scalp if you leave 'em alone. You're just a darned stiff-necked fool runnin' round in circles on the wrong side of the fence."

"If that is the case," Brock said, "why did the WP set fire to my grass and kill one of my men? A harmless pot juggler. Why did this killer Pickles lead a bunch of your riders last night to attack my ranch? I was located in this country before you moved in here. What right have these gunmen of yours to try and run me out of the country? I have never lifted a hand against you yet. If you're not sanctioning these moves against me, why are you allowing your men to go after me as if the Diamond B and I were something the WP wanted to eliminate?"

Pickles shoved forward before Bill Parsons could reply. "Do you mean to say *we* ever molested your damn ranch?" he snarled with a fine show of righteous indignation.

"I do say so," Brock replied evenly. "It happens that we all have eyes in our heads, Pickles. Also I've been suspicious enough of the WP crowd to keep tabs on 'em. Two of my riders were watching you when you lay up behind that ridge waiting for dark. That's why you didn't get a chance to fire my buildings or haystacks—like Tuck and his imitation Indians"—Brock took a random shot—"did at the Long S. And perhaps that's where and why this fellow with the bandages got his. Did that fellow gaping out of the window with his head all tied up get nicked when you were smoking us up in the dark? You're a dirty double-crosser, Pickles. My father says the WP is not molesting me. And *you* threw enough lead at us last night to sink a battleship. What's the idea?"

"If you say we did that," Pickles replied very slowly and with a venomous inflection, "if you deny that either some of your crowd or the Stark boys fired on us with no provocation about dusk when we was ridin' home, then I tell you an' I tell your old man that you're a lyin' son of a bitch!"

The epithet was scarcely out of his mouth before Brock knocked him down. That had been in his mind from the first. That was why he stood near enough to Pickles to reach him. He didn't want to kill Pickles then and there. But he knew Pickles would show his teeth, would try somehow to cover the issue with smoke. That conviction came to him as soon as he stepped onto the porch. Pickles craved action. Well, he had got it. And he was harmless, his teeth drawn for the time being. Because Brock landed on him like a tiger as he went down from that blow and snatched the Colt out of holster on the man's belt. He stood up with Pickles's gun in his hand.

"People don't call me names and get away with it, Pickles," he said calmly. "Probably you've been told that I'm nothing but a dude. That I don't know anything. That I can't do anything. That's a slight error. I can be just as fatal as any twenty-minute egg from the Nueces when I want to be. Sit down on that bench until I finish what I have to say to my father. I don't care to have you getting hold of another gun and taking pot shots at me from somewhere about this ranch. Sit down!"

Pickles's thin lips quivered but he seated himself. Perhaps, Brock reflected, he was helped a little to that decision by Bill Parsons's imperative gesture to obey.

"Furthermore," Brock continued, "while you were holding us—or thought you were—penned at the Diamond B, the Stark outfit was being burned out and shot up too. You're playing a strong hand, Pickles, but it's a losing hand."

"Are you here to take up any grievance the Starks have agin me?" Bill Parsons demanded. "Or are you just clamorin' for yourself?"

"I'm talking for myself first and foremost," Brock answered. "I don't know that the Starks would want me to horn in on your feud with them. I don't think they'd let me, if I wanted to. But your outfit is making it hot for me, Dad. What is the object?"

"The WP is not attacking *you*," Bill Parsons declared

stubbornly. "You're mistaken."

"But they *have* attacked me," Brock persisted. "We've been raided and bushwhacked. You mean you're not personally ordering your men to go after me? Is that it? But this crowd you've gathered together is playing its own hand. Do you know that a boy who rode for you a long time, Tom Slater, quit the other day because he couldn't stand the way things were going? He came to my place to talk it over with me. He hadn't been gone an hour's ride before someone who had an interest in shutting his mouth shot him off his horse from ambush. Do you mean to say you don't know anything about what Tuck Munce and his own particular collection of hardcases are doing up in the Bear Paws? If you don't, it's time you did. They'll make the WP a worse stink in Montana than it was in Texas."

"Listen to me, young man," Parsons said harshly. "I've heard you talk before. You always exaggerate. You git queer notions. I'm willin' to concede that you've outgrowed the dude stage. You play your hand better'n I reckoned was in you. But you ought to know that raidin' ranches an' destroyin' other people's property is somethin' I leave to your Stark friends, damn them. I aim to run them out of the Bear Paws like I run 'em outa Texas, if it's the last thing I do on earth. That's what the WP is here for. There ain't room enough in the United States for them an' me. What lays between you an' Tuck Munce is your personal affair. But that don't give you any license to lay raidin' and bushwhackin' at the WP door. We don't have to sneak in the dark. We're goin' to crowd the Long S with cattle till they ain't got room to graze a cow or pasture a horse. If they jump us for that we'll defend ourselves. You can like that or lump it. I never started nothin' in my life I didn't finish. I'll finish that outfit if they ever buckle on their guns an' go for us. I make no bones about that. But it's plumb ridiculous for you to claim the WP is molestin' you. Your outfit ain't a fleabite on this range."

"A fleabite can be very annoying to some people," Brock observed. "I tell you that Tuck Munce and this man Pickles don't make any distinctions between the Long S and the Diamond B."

"Neither will I," Parsons said bluntly, "if you back them up."

"That's plain enough," Brock conceded. "It tells me exactly where I stand. If you're all cocked and primed to raise merry hell around the Bear Paws to satisfy a grudge, I don't suppose you care what happens or who gets hurt. But don't forget that whatever happens you're held responsible for. You know that if you crowd Eugene Stark and his sons, they'll fight. What you don't seem to see is that if you let your gang crowd me I have no choice but to fight also. Does it never strike you that surrounding yourself with a bunch of men like you've got here, giving them a free hand to be lawless, is apt to be disastrous for you, yourself? You can't import a bunch of killers and thieves and turn them loose in unorganized territory, and keep them in hand."

"Killers an' thieves!" Bill Parsons exclaimed. "That's twice you've made that break now. That's darned strong talk about men on my pay roll."

"The killing has already started," Brock flung back. "The thieving will begin as soon as the lid pops off this kettle you're boiling. This thing's got angles you don't know about, or don't care a whoop about. It'll get out of your hands altogether if you let it go much further."

"I know what I'm doin'," Bill Parsons grunted. "I've got a hundred thousand cattle here and there. I didn't get to where I am by usin' kid gloves to handle hard people."

"Then you're going ahead to precipitate another range war with the Starks, regardless?" Brock asked.

"I am," Parsons stated flatly.

"And if I happen to be in the way, you'll tramp me into the ground too?"

"You, or anybody else," his father declared. "Only if you got any sense you won't get in the way."

"You're not God," Brock said somberly. "You can't make a world to suit yourself with complete disregard of other people's rights and feelings. Old Gene Stark told you in

Oxbow, I've heard, that some day you might look at one of your sons lying dead at your feet and your feelings would choke you. If you go ahead and drench this range with blood, I'll be in it—because your hired men will fix it so that I can't keep out. I don't want to fight you. But apparently I'm not going to have any choice."

He picked the cartridges out of Pickles's six-shooter while his father stood looking at him, scowling, anger making the blood redden his normally florid face. Brock threw the empty gun at Pickles's spurred feet.

"I don't want to fight my father," he said. "But I'll go to the mat with people like you anytime, anywhere. I despise your sort. You're like turkey buzzards, you and Tuck Munce, looking for carrion to fill your crops. It will never hurt my conscience to bump off a lowdown bushwhacking skunk like you. You craved action a minute ago. If you want to do anything about it, there's your gun. Ride up on the hill with me and have it out."

Pickles bared his teeth in a sickly grimace. "Your old man," he countered, "has done told you the WP ain't makin' war on you. So I ain't stagin' any personal scraps with you either, not while I'm a WP range boss."

"That," Brock sneered as he turned away to his horse, "is a damned good alibi, Pickles. But it doesn't pull any wool over my eyes."

"Bill," he said when he had rejoined his two men and ridden a mile up Chip Creek, "I didn't get anywhere. The big noise was there, all right. He is not in on what his crew is pulling on us. Didn't believe me when I told him. He has just one fixed idea: to make it hot for the Long S and either run them out of the country, break them, or kill them. That's the reason for gathering all these bad actors together. He's been cock of the walk so long on the Nueces, so used to everybody jumping through his hoop, that it's impossible for him to believe his range bosses and riders could have axes of their own to grind. About all I accomplished was to make another personal enemy."

"How come?" Bill inquired.

"Pickles." Brock described his clash with that gentleman. Lin and Bill chuckled.

"Oh well," Lin drawled, "Pickles is playin' Tuck's game anyhow, whatever it is. If you know a man's agin you it's just as well to let him know you got teeth."

"There's two wounded men there," Brock continued. "Pickles tells how they were jumped and shot at by some party or parties unknown yesterday evening while they rode peacefully homeward. W.J. appears to accept that as gospel. It seems to me he's got to the point where he swallows just what he wants to believe. And Tuck is still abroad somewhere in the land. I have a hunch he's up to something at that mountain hangout. None of us has taken a squint at that for some time. I think I'll take Lin and go to Sutherland's tonight, and take a scout around that box canyon tomorrow. You go back to the Diamond B, Bill, so the rest of the boys will know the Chip Creek visit didn't lose us our scalps."

They parted with that. Brock and Lin drifted north, keeping to high ground. They were in no hurry. They hadn't slept the night before, but that was no great matter to men as hard as nails. Brock kept thinking of Lou Stark at the other end of the trail. She would be glad to see him, but she wouldn't tell him so.

The Bear Paws lifted rugged summits in the autumn haze. Shod hoofs struck little puffs of dust off the dry earth. There was a scantier stand of grass than spring had promised, since those many thousands of WP cattle had come north of the Missouri. Wherever a man looked, the hills and swales were speckled with longhorns, filing in on water or grazing about. Every creek bottom was trampled like a barnyard.

"A stiff-necked, bad-tempered man, aggressively determined on having his own way at any cost," Brock murmured. "That's my worthy sire, the honorable W. J. Parsons of the Nueces River in the State of Texas. And he's so concentrated on the one idea of getting even with the Stark outfit that he can't see anything else."

"Plumb loco on that subject, ain't he," Lin commented. "Funny. Like some of these gunmen, that once started 'll kill as long as they can stand up and pull trigger—shoot regardless of consequences to themselves or anybody else. It don't seem natural."

"It isn't," Brock agreed. "I don't want to fight him. He doesn't really want to fight me. But he's going to start a fight. Even if he didn't, Lin, Munce and Pickles are going to. And if it starts I'll be in it up to my neck. I don't like it."

"You'll have lots of support," Lin prophesied. "The WP hasn't endeared itself to nobody in the Bear Paws. I don't know if Sutherland and the Cross Seven would stand for the high-handed way the WP is goin' on, if they once come out in the open with it. Gosh darn it, it's like any other outlaw startin' to take what he wants wherever he finds it in a community that ain't organized with courts and sheriffs an' such. People just naturally get together an' abate that sort of public nuisance. Us an' the Starks could just about handle that Chip Creek bunch if it come to a showdown. One darn good trouncin' would make the WP sheathe its claws for quite a spell. So far it's all underhand. If they ever run an iron on a hoof of our stuff, or pitch into us so that we really know who's doin' it, why we got to go after 'em. Us an' the Stark boys would make a tough combination, Brock."

And Brock couldn't explain to Lin that what he chiefly desired was to keep the Starks out of an open clash with the WP. Because that meant more killing, and more Stark blood spilled pried him and Lou farther and farther apart. Brock's day antedated the poet who wrote:

Two things greater than all things are,
And one is love and the other is war.
And since we know not how war may prove,
Heart of my heart, let us talk of love.

Yet that was how he felt, what he desired, and his hand that craved to reach for love was being forced slowly but surely by crude passions and mean desires to lay hold of the instruments of war.

They drew up toward the Sutherland ranch near sundown. Brock rode immersed in thought. Lin Pickett, who had little on his mind but his hat, no woman troubling his bosom, no family feud filling him with distasteful sadness, whistled cheerfully, kept his eyes roving, blithely eager for anything. If he marked the frown on Brock's tanned young face, the cloud in his blue eyes, he didn't say so. He didn't talk at all. He turned and scanned the country as they came up into the foothills. Consequently it was Lin who said suddenly, "Well. There's Clay Stark on that black *caballo* of his burnin' the earth, splittin' the atmosphere like the devil was at his tail."

Brock looked. Clay's horse was at a stiff gallop. Brock knew Clay didn't see them. It wasn't like him to ride unwatchful, nor to ride headlong unless he had reason. Brock pulled his gun and shot in the air. Clay pulled his horse to a stop. Brock and Lin waved. He would recognize them and their gear at that distance. He did, turned sharp, came to them on the run. And Brock had a conviction of fresh trouble that made his heart flutter as the black horse closed the gap between and plowed up the earth with stiffened forelegs as Clay set him on his haunches.

"I was headed for your place first," he said without preamble. "Esther an' Lou went ridin' up Eagle Creek this mornin'. They ain't seen hide nor hair of them since."

Chapter Twenty-Three

THE LAST STRAW

CLAY ADDED DETAILS, speaking in a subdued tone, pinched dry of all feeling. Brock knew better. He knew that outward impassivity masked an inner turmoil that would break loose like a volcano of destruction if Clay could come at whoever had done this thing. For it was no accident. Esther Munce and Lou Stark were not simply lost in those pine-clad hills.

Saturday. No school. They had gone for a ride. The mountains had a fascination for both plains-bred girls. High peaks and ribbons of silver water tumbling down through the green, the shaded canyons and the sweet-smelling forests, drew them like a magnet. They had gone up Eagle Creek, saying they would probably be back at noon. The midday meal found them still absent. Shortly after noon a ranch hand from the Block S had to ride around a pasture that ran east along the foothills. He came thundering back in alarm, having, so he said, seen Indians on the edge of the timber. Sutherland and his riders were south of the Missouri, trailing a beef herd to the railroad. That left a ranch foreman, three hands, Sutherland's thirteen-year-old daughter, four married women, and several children besides the Stark youngsters. Indians were always a threat in the Bear Paws. They jumped the reservation sometimes to steal horses, or lift a stray scalp in the immemorial custom of the red brother.

The foreman took no chances. He gathered his charges into the ranch house and set a watch. Not long afterward five mounted Indians appeared on the hillside above the ranch. They sat their horses in the edge of the pines, like painted statues, eagle feathers fluttering in the wind. For five minutes they were in plain view. Then they dropped back into the timber. Once they appeared farther up the slope, riding north in single file.

It might, the ranch foreman considered, be a raiding party on a small scale, or the scouts of a real foray. He had plenty of cause for uneasiness. When those painted devils drew off, he sent a man up the creek to find and warn Esther and Lou.

This ranch hand came back just as Clay arrived. He had found the two Block S saddle horses tied in a thicket about three miles up Eagle Creek. Of the two women there was no sign. Clay rode with him at once to the place. Nosing here and there, Clay found their tracks, interpreted for himself what he saw. Both girls wore riding-boots. Their pointed heels left unmistakable prints. They had walked here and there along the creek. Clay could follow a trail like a hound. He followed to where hoof prints lay in a jumble, marks in the grass and turf that told their own story. He lost that trail on a rocky slope nearly a mile above that.

"I could hunt single-handed a week in those mountains an' never come up with them," Clay said. "So I came out for you an' the boys. The Diamond B is closer than home."

Brock's heart became an aching weight in his breast. One dreadful certainty settled on him with utter conviction, and that certainty stirred him to a murderous anger that made him tremble until he mastered the feeling.

"Those were not Indians," he said, "Any more than they were Indians that swooped down on your ranch last night. Would Indians take women and leave their saddle horses tied in the brush? That isn't Indian style. Scalps and horses mean more to raiding bucks than women, red or white. They're natural plunderers. No, they weren't Blackfeet or Gros Ventres."

"Who then?" Clay breathed. "And why? I thought of Tuck Munce. But he wouldn't kidnap his own sister. He might mine, but not his own."

"I don't know why, either," Brock replied. "Except it's the poisonous nature of the brute to do anything that seems to be a whack at us. And don't forget that the Guadalupe Kid is running with Tuck. Guadalupe was a nuisance to Esther for a year before she left Texas."

"Why didn't you tell *me* that if you knew?" Clay demanded fiercely.

"For the same reason, perhaps, that you didn't tell me that Tuck Munce was showing signs of hanging around Lou," Brock answered.

"She made me promise not to," Clay defended. "She knows you're dynamite. She thought you might go after Tuck red-eyed, an' she was afraid of what might happen. It didn't worry her him comin' around there. It wasn't nothin' to her."

"We've temporized with a mad dog and it has bitten us both." Brock gritted his teeth. "Come on, let's get on to the Block S, get fresh mounts there, and head for the Bear Den. If it happens to be Indians on a raid we can't trail them in the dark. If it was Tuck, we don't have to find a trail. We know it. No time to go out and raise both outfits. Three of us are good enough—and one of Sutherland's men can ride for the Diamond B and your ranch to tell them where we have gone."

Clay nodded. Cooler reflection replaced that tumult in Brock's breast as they saddled fresh horses in the Sutherland corral. A Sutherland man was ready to ride.

"Tell Bill Spear," Brock instructed him. "He knows the way to the Bear Den. Tell him to bring all the boys but two. You don't know where the Stark outfit is located, so you'd better have one of my riders go there and give the alarm. They'll have to join the Diamond B crowd, because the Starks don't know where this box canyon lies. Tell him what you want him to say to your folks, Clay."

Clay wouldn't trust word of mouth. He scribbled a note, advising his father to bring the women up to Sutherland's, join the Diamond B, and ride for the Bear Den, if he and Brock were not out of the mountains with Lou and Esther by the time they were ready to start.

Dark closed on them riding through those silent hills. Ravines lay black as the pit. Pinnacle peaks lifted against a sky luminous with stars. Up and up over ridges clothed with pine, slanting along the shoulders of gaunt hills, they made their way by instinct, by the lay of the land, with the

Big Dipper and the polestar for compass. Once or twice the shrill yapping of coyotes split that hush. And as they drew up to the top of the divide the eerie, sobbing wail of a lobo wolf sent involuntary shivers up each man's spine. A lone wolf raising the hunting cry—calling his mate, or the pack. They drew rein to listen. Farther, fainter, an answering chorus rose, that weird haunting sound which, from a wolf's throat, made primitive man huddle closer within the sheltering circle of his night fire.

"Off north," Lin Pickett remarked. "Funny the lobos are ranging in the north part of the mountains. No stock this high, nor on the north slope. Never has been."

"Might be some strays," Clay said. "We're gettin' pretty close to the Bear Den, Brock, as I recollect the location. You can just make out the tip of Tiger Butte."

"Yes," Brock agreed. "We ought to spot that place pretty soon."

Between two and three in the morning they were in the semi-gloom of a pine forest that ran up to the western lip of that box canyon. They made cautiously for the brink on foot, leaving Lin to hold the horses. There was a perceptible lightening of the eastern sky, a silver glow that tipped the highest peaks. The segment of a waning moon sailed up, turning all those mysterious heights into ebony and silver. Wherever moonlight fell on leaf and bough and grass touched by the autumn frost it sparkled as if fairy hands had sprinkled diamond dust.

Brock and Clay lay on the rim looking down into inky black, into that shrouded chasm.

"They're there," Clay whispered. "Smell the smoke."

The moon glow bathed the upper west wall. Under that band of light it was like staring into a deep well. Out of this gloom came a faint smell of charred wood. They lay and listened. Once a horse cleared his nostrils sharply far below. Once they cocked their ears, thinking to hear a stir farther along the rim where they lay. But that, they decided in whispers, must be some small nocturnal animal. Someone was in that canyon. That was certain. They stole back softly to where Lin waited with their mounts.

"What's the matter with riding down to the lower end," Brock murmured. "We can leave the horses in timber, sneak up afoot, and plant ourselves right on top of them and wait for daylight to see if the girls are there. If they are it's simple. If they aren't—well—we'll have to use our best judgment about what to do."

They snailed their way half a mile north. The Bear Den widened there, beyond its constricted mouth, like the spillway of a great dam opening to flow north. Little flats lay plain in the moon glare. Presently they came to a slope where by slipping and scrambling they reached the bottom. On the edge of the first flat Brock stopped, pointed.

"Why, there's cattle down there," he said. "Where no cattle ought to be."

Dark objects stood out in the moonlight. Far down that widening hollow they could see other clusters. Those nearest were moving off.

"Go easy," Brock said. "We don't want to start these longhorns running or the noise'll carry to that camp. Those fellows may have a watch set. I want to look at those cattle if we can get a stand on a bunch lower down. Cattle don't stray into places like this of their own accord. We have plenty of time. I smell a rat."

Brock's rat bore a numerous family in the next half hour. Approaching the first bunch of wild, shy brutes started them ambling away. The riders followed, not too closely. If they burned with anxiety over Esther Munce and Lou Stark, they did not lose sight of other considerations. Not one of the three had to voice his thoughts, suspicions, as to why Tuck Munce had been at such pains to seek out a hidden place where no cattleman would ordinarily go, and build himself a cabin and corral. So they followed softly and silently those retreating cattle along a meandering trickle of water that would become a creek pouring into the Claywater, flowing to Milk River through the north plains where no white man had as yet located a home.

Those shifting bunches of cattle increased in number, became a slowly moving mass ahead. As they passed the

mouth of sloping draws they could see stragglers turning
aside, climbing to higher ground.

"Hell, this place is lousy with cattle," Lin said.

"The next good-sized bottom we come to," Brock ordered, "you cut in ahead of 'em, Lin. We'll try to check
them against a bank long enough to look them over."

One short sharp dash and Lin turned the lead of the
herd. Clay and Brock stopped them when they surged
back. A high earth wall on one side of the creek made a
barricade. In a few minutes the cattle settled down to
stand staring at the three riders. And they stared back with
a fairly good view of fresh-run ironwork on hip and rib.
All mature cattle. All fresh branded. The burns had
scarcely begun to peel on some: one an 8 with a bar on
each side, the other two joined X's with a dot between
them. Hundreds of them. Horns glistening under the
moon. Eyeballs like pale opals.

"That's plenty," Brock said. "Let 'em go."

As they came abreast, riding back to the narrow mouth
of the Bear Den, Brock murmured:

"There must be several hundred head in here. Every one
of them stolen from the Long S and the Diamond B. I
didn't think Tuck prowled these hills for his health. And
that's why he wants war. If he can keep us and the Stark
family busy and up in the air on the south flats, he can steal
us both blind. That's why Pickles is stirring things up
now. Tuck and his gang are rustling our stock while we're
supposed to be kept sitting tight and uneasy on our
ranches. Good scheme."

"Bar Eight Bar," Clay said softly. "Nice coarse work-
over for the Long S. Lord, how I do love a thief! There's
got to be a house-cleanin'."

"There will be." Brock muttered an oath. "This crowd
has overplayed its hand this time. Now to get up close
enough to that cabin and corral so that we can see the
whites of their eyes when they start to light their breakfast
fire. Remember, both of you, that we can deal with cow
thieves at our pleasure. Our first consideration is to make
sure those girls are in no danger. And leave Tuck Munce

to me."

"An' leave the Guadalupe Kid to me," Clay whispered softly. "If anything has happened to Esther Munce it will be because of that dirty dog. He followed her here from Fort Worth."

"Oh, you knew that, did you?" Brock said.

"I guessed it, but I never was sure," Clay returned. "Anyway, he's my meat."

The dark, closed-in lower end of the canyon loomed before them. They cached their horses in a thicket, tied them securely. They kept in the shadow at the base of the east well, feeling their way, inching near until the vague loom of the cabin and corral in the pines and aspens told them of successful approach.

"I'd give a lot to see inside that cabin," Clay whispered in Brock's ear. "My God, I can't stand this, Brock!"

"If I can, you can," Brock answered savagely. His own heart was beating double-quick with anger, with a consuming passion to destroy, with a dread of what they might be too late to avert. A woman's voice, a cry, a sob, would have touched him off like so much gunpowder. As it was— "We've *got* to wait till we can see."

Measured in actual minutes they had not so long to wait. Measured by the fierce impatience that burned within them it seemed an unending night. But dawn filled the sky at last above that wall-sided gorge. When that pearly light seeped into the canyon bottom, a man emerged from the cabin. He stared up at the rim on the west side, yawned, stretched his arms. Brock's fingers itched. It was Tuck Munce. Another man came out, a young tawny-headed, good-looking man. Brock felt Clay beside him stir involuntarily.

Chapter Twenty-Four

Trapped

"That's the Guadalupe Kid," Lin whispered.

Clay motioned him to silence. The Guadalupe Kid, like Tuck, turned to scan the upper rim of the Bear Den. A frowsy, freckle-faced youth joined them. Then two older men.

They built a fire in front of the cabin, put on a coffee pot, set about frying salt pork. The Guadalupe Kid mixed a batch of biscuits and set them on in a Dutch oven. He squatted on his heels. They talked in brief, surly sentences. A word or two here and there were all Clay, Lin, and Brock could catch.

"We got 'em dead to rights if we want to take 'em," Clay whispered in Brock's ear. "Wonder if they got the girls in that cabin?"

"I don't know. No way of finding out unless they show outside," Brock murmured. "But we've got to stick this bunch up and make them harmless before we can do any more. When it looks right, I'll give the word and we'll rush them and hold them up. I wouldn't shoot a dog from ambush."

"Look out," Clay warned.

Tuck Munce stood up. He stared all about him. For a minute he looked straight where the three lay prone, almost as if he heard or suspected their presence. The Guadalupe Kid looked up at him with a sneer.

"You're as nervous as an old woman," he said distinctly. "You were a damned fool, Tuck, to bite off more'n you could chew. Got to go through with it now though. So don't get jumpy. Nobody's goin' to walk in on us at daylight."

Tuck growled something under his breath. He stooped to pour a cup of coffee. For a few minutes the five gobbled food. Then five pairs of fingers grew busy with brown papers and sacks of Durham.

"Now," Brock said. "All together. If one reaches for a gun when I holler, drop him."

A six-foot crawl left them about thirty feet of open to reach the group around the fire. Tuck Munce and the Guadalupe Kid didn't turn their heads until the three were well in the clear, carbines up, eyes squinting over the sights.

"Hands up!" Brock called.

The grimy fingers of one older man and the frowsy youth reached for the sky at that sharp command. But the other man and the Guadalupe Kid were of different metal. Their hands flashed to six-shooters. The Guadalupe Kid was like a streak of lightning. His gun was out, coming up, when both of them went down under a blast of fire from three .44 carbines.

Tuck Munce half-lifted his hands. In the same motion he seemed to fall headlong toward the cabin end, as if he had been shot. In reality he leaped, as Brock perceived too late. He hadn't shot Tuck because Tuck made that half gesture of surrender and he wanted Tuck Munce alive if possible.

Tuck had outfoxed him. Brock realized that a fraction of a second too late. When he darted past the cabin he found only agitated brush in the thicket where Tuck had plunged out of sight. Brock plunged in after him. Lin Pickett and Clay could deal with the others.

But in that thicket, among pines and quaking aspens, he was lost. The sounds of his own pursuit prevented him from hearing the other man move. He stopped to listen, moved on at a faint crackle ahead, gained the lower end of that grove in time to see Tuck mounted and in full stride down the bottom.

Fortune rode with Tuck. Neither Lin nor Clay commanded his flight from the cabin. The brush cut off their view. Brock threw up his carbine. Shifting for a better foothold, his toe caught in a root, momentarily threw him off his balance. By the time he straightened up he had only time for a snap shot. Then a jutting point of the rock wall shut Tuck off. The sound of his horse's hoofs was like the roll of a snare drum as he raced for the lower end of the canyon.

Behind Brock two or three reports followed that carbine shot of his. Something came tearing through the brush toward him. Somebody yelled. The frowsy-headed youth broke through the aspens. His mouth was open. Terror, desperation, blazed in his eyes as he caught sight of Brock. His gun swung up—a little too late.

Moving toward that quivering body, Brock saw what this member of Tuck's gang was making for. Beside the horse Tuck had made his dash on, two others were standing tied to saplings, saddled and bridled. Brock left them and went back to the cabin.

The Guadalupe Kid sat with his back against the wall, pressing both hands to his breast, staring defiantly at Clay Stark. Ev Sprott lay dead by the fire so close that the coals had burned his shirt. His hard-featured mate was sprawled on his back, sightless eyes staring at the sky.

"You get that kid?" Lin asked.

"Munce got away on a horse," Brock growled. "That other fellow ran into me with his gun up, so I stopped him."

Pow!

Brock felt something like a bee sting in his leg.

"Hell!" Clay snarled. "Inside. Gimme a hand."

He laid hold of the Guadalupe Kid, who struck feebly at him, baring his teeth like an angry dog. Lin Pickett grabbed that arm. Between them they dragged him through the cabin door. Brock slid in after them. The concealed rifleman shot twice as they got under cover. They felt the wind of those bullets.

"Hit you, didn't he," Lin said to Brock. "I saw you flinch. Whereabout?"

"In the leg," Brock told him. "Don't think it's much."

"We got four of 'em," Clay said grimly, "an one's alive enough to talk."

"Talk! Try makin' me talk," the Guadalupe Kid spat at them. "Sure, let's talk. Better make plenty conversation while you have a chance. Because you have dug your own graves as well as mine, you sons of bitches!"

"Yeah?" Clay retorted. "We ain't worryin' about our graves. Where's my sister an' Esther Munce? You tell me that an' we won't worry you with any more questions. That's all we want to know."

"Watch the outside for that gunman on top, Lin," Brock said. "It's Tuck probably."

The Guadalupe Kid drew a sobbing breath. Little flecks of bloody foam showed at the corners of his mouth.

"Watch an' be damned!" he whispered. "Slim Wayne's on that cliff with a Winchester. He'll hold you here till hell freezes over. Before noon Tuck Munce will be back with enough WP boys to snow you under. You'll never see your yellow-haired *dulce* again, Stark."

Brock caught Clay's arm, kept him from lunging with outstretched crooking fingers at that wounded man's throat. "No," he said. "Don't do that, Clay. He's dying anyhow. Let him be."

He pushed Clay back, while the Guadalupe Kid stared up at them both with that defiant grin. The strain of that exertion reminded Brock of his leg.

"I'm bleeding," he said to Clay. "Leave him alone a minute. Help me bandage my leg."

Clay shook himself, grew calmer.

"You wanted me to see red an' finish you, eh?" he said. "Presently you'll talk, or you'll know what pain is. I was raised in a Comanche country, same as you were. I'll show you what that means after a while, for what you said."

He turned away to let that sink in. Brock sat down on a bunk, stripped off his clothes to expose the wound. His underclothing was soaked, his boots full of blood. It wasn't a deep wound, nor dangerous. Not even disabling. But the blood was pouring out of it like water from a hose.

"Have to tear up my shirt for a bandage, I expect," he said to Clay.

"Might be some better cloth around here. Their blankets ain't fit," Clay grumbled. "Pinch that hole tight with your fingers while I look around."

He began to paw over bedding and pack sacks of stuff. He started up with a cry of triumph, of anger, with an Indian headdress, a fringed buckskin shirt, in each hand, a package of tubes of grease paint such as actors use.

"Aha!" he exclaimed. "Your hunch was right, Brock. Here's our Injun fixin's. Oh, but the WP an' Tuck Munce'll pay for this!"

"Tear up my shirt," Brock repeated. "Get this blood stopped. Then we can talk to Guadalupe in language he can understand."

The riven garment about his leg cut off the bleeding. Brock didn't mind the pain. The dull ache in his torn flesh was less than the ache and anxiety in his breast. He could feel no more kindness and mercy toward the man propped against the opposite wall than Clay Stark felt. Murder, arson, theft, outrage against the woman he loved stirred a fury in him that left him cold and pitiless.

"Now, let's see what *he* has to say," he muttered to Clay, and turned to the Guadalupe Kid.

A dew of sweat had broken out on the boy's face. A strange glassy stare was creeping into his eyes. He scarcely seemed to see them, to be aware of them, bending threateningly over him.

"Hell an' damnation!" Clay scowled. "He's dyin' on us, right now."

The Guadalupe Kid's head dropped. His eyelids closed. "I shouldn't 'a' let him talk me into that," he said in a husky whisper—not as if he were addressing them. More like a man unconsciously voicing his thoughts. "I didn't think a man could be such a fool about a woman—only me. I wouldn't do you no harm, Essie. An' I wouldn't let Tuck molest *her*. Uh-uh. I won't stand for that."

They looked at him, listening in silence. The Guadalupe Kid's head twisted from side to side. His hands plucked uneasily at the wound in his breast. "It burns like hell," he said plaintively.

"Want a drink of water?" Brock softened at that agonized tone.

Guadalupe was scarcely more than twenty. Boyish-faced,

blue-eyed. Like Lin Pickett, only younger. The Southwest produced an odd one like him. Killers in their teens. Afraid of neither God, man, nor devil. Courage and dynamic energy turned into the wrong channels.

"Uh-uh," he whispered. "Don't want nothin'. I'm through. Overplayed my hand."

His eyelids drooped. He sighed, and bloody froth seeped out of his half-open mouth. Brock bent over him. He breathed with a thick wheezing sound.

"Where are the girls?" Brock asked gently. "You might tell us that. They didn't do you any harm."

"In the Bear Den," the Guadalupe Kid said thickly. "It was a plumb crazy thing to do."

"We're all in the Bear Den," Brock said gently in his ear. "Whereabouts did you hide them?"

The Guadalupe Kid opened his eyes. He lifted one hand and pointed. "Cliff. Above corral. Little way," he said.

The words seemed to be jerked out of him with a terrible effort. Suddenly he seemed to come out of that daze. He tried to struggle to a sitting posture. He glared at them.

"I ain't no death-bed repenter," he gasped. "You can all go to hell!"

He coughed in a racking spasm, strangled. A scarlet flood gushed out of his mouth.. He shuddered once or twice and collapsed.

"He was a hard pill," Lin Pickett said from his station by the door. "You'd never have pried *that* out of him by force."

"Bear Den. Cliff. Above corral." Brock knitted his brows. "Let's take a look, Clay."

"Be careful," Lin Pickett counseled. "If that's Slim Wayne on the cliff opposite, he is a darn good shot, an' evidently he has the front of this cabin covered. Size up the lay of the land before you go roamin' outside. An' be darn careful about showin' yourselves."

They did use caution. Windows, empty squares in each log wall, gave a look on each side. The rifleman could only cover the door side and the two ends. It was only a few yards to the timber. Clay slid out the south window. Two steps took him behind the cabin. Nevertheless those watchful eyes spotted him. A bullet smashed into the ground. Brock made good his exit also with a close shave. Lin Pickett fired once at a puff of powder smoke. Then the stillness shut down again in that deep cleft.

"He said along the cliff," Brock puzzled when they were in cover. "Lucky there's timber for a ways. We can't go outside that."

They didn't need to. Near the upper end of this timber patch, which covered two acres more or less, scanning closely the face of the eastern wall, they came to a place where stones had lately been piled against the foot of the cliff. Ordinarily they would have passed that up. A pile of stones was merely a pile of stones against a rock wall. But both men had the Guadalupe Kid's dying phrases in mind. The name of that canyon, Brock knew, had been given by a trapper for good reason. And both men knew that bears den up in underground holes, in hollow trees, when winter comes. There was no hole visible here. But that pile of stones had an orderly look, like a bit of rough masonry.

"If there is a hole like a bear den, why should its mouth be blocked?" Clay said. "Let's dig into this, Brock."

The brushy edge of the timber screened them at this work. When they tore away the upper rocks they found it truly a concealing wall. In ten minutes they had a hole through that showed a dark tunnel four feet high. Brock put his face in the opening.

"Lou!" he called. "Are you in there?"

"Brock!" The answering tone made his heart leap.

"You all right, honey?" Brock was scarcely aware he used that endearment. "Esther with you?"

"We're all right. We're away back in here. Who's with you, Brock?"

"Just a few of the best of us," Clay shouted over Brock's shoulder. "We'll have you out of there in ten minutes."

Less time cleared the blockade. The two girls came blinking out into light that dazzled them after that overnight entombment. Esther Munce threw herself sobbing into Clay's arms. Brock and Lou stood staring at each other. Brock's heart was singing. But he envied the other two. They had no inhibitions, no doubts, nothing like a dark shadow over them. If they had, they disregarded it at the dictates of their hearts. And apparently Lou Stark couldn't do that. Nor could Brock, in that moment. So he stifled that impulse to take her in his arms, and smiled.

"How did you find us?" Lou asked.

"We have known about this hideout all summer," Brock said. "And I was quite sure those were not Indians that kidnaped you. So we came straight here and jumped them at daylight."

Clay and Esther turned to them.

"Well," Clay grinned, "I've got Sis out of all kinds of jackpots since we was little kids, but I never figured I'd have to dig her an' my sweetheart out of a bear den. Let's get back to the cabin an' get something to eat. You girls starved? I am."

Tuck Munce and the Guadalupe Kid had given them jerked venison, bread, a jug of water, and matches when they shut them in and stoned up the mouth of the bear den to hold them prisoners. For it was a bear den, once occupied by *ursus horribilis*. It was better to be in there though, Lou said, with a shudder, than to feel eyes gloating over her.

"What in blazes was their idea?" Clay demanded angrily. "Did they just go crazy when they come across you two on Eagle Creek?"

"Yes. Crazy like foxes," Esther said. "Tuck wanted Lou, and Guadalupe has always wanted me. But they had a use for us besides. They had been wondering how they could get one or the other or both of us away from Sutherland's. And we just happened to give them a fine chance yesterday. We were to be bait to draw first Brock and his riders into this canyon and wipe them out. Then the Starks were to be tolled in. Then, as Tuck put it, the WP would have the world by the tail, and he would swing the WP to suit himself. I hope you got Tuck Munce. That brute isn't human. He—he—well, the Guadalupe Kid may be bad, but if it hadn't been for him, I don't know what we'd have had to face."

"The Guadalupe Kid is dead," Clay hold her, "But Tuck Munce got away."

"Then we'd better get out of here as fast as we can," Esther said fearfully, "because he'll be back with a lot more WP men. They have smoke signals arranged with Chip Creek. Smoke in daylight, and a fire code at night from the top of the divide. I heard them talking about that. You'll be trapped in here, Clay."

"We're trapped anyway," Brock said. "There's a WP man posted on the cliff with a rifle. He could pick us all off once we moved out of this timber patch. But we can hold this place until dark against all the men Tuck could bring. And our own crowd will be here before night. Let's get back to the cabin."

Brock limped perceptibly as they walked. His leg was stiffening. Lou took him by the arm.

"You got hit, Brock," she said anxiously. "You're hurt."

"Not badly," he told her. "Pinked in the leg. Bled a lot, but doesn't amount to much."

"It's the beginning of the same thing over again," Lou clung to him so tightly that he stopped. Clay and Esther kept on. "As soon as we get out, Dad and the boys will go after the WP. Nothing could hold them after this. There'll be more killing. Oh, it's terrible. And you'll get mixed up in it too."

"I'm already in it," Brock said. "Yes, I'll be in it up to my neck, after this."

"Why can't they leave us alone?" she cried. Her eyes grew wet and her lips quivered. Brock couldn't stand that. He took her in his arms, kissed her. And her lips clung to his so that his heart seemed to turn over in his breast.

"Oh, I just can't bear to think of it," she whispered. "Killing, killing! It'll kill me in the end. I want you so badly. And it just can't be. We haven't got a chance!"

"We have to make our chances," Brock said tenderly. "Presently, this thing will be settled for keeps. Then we can draw our breath, and live our lives in spite of our handicap. I refuse to be penalized always because I happen to be the son of my father. But this clash can't be avoided now. There's this about it, Lou. I don't believe my father knows how far this thing he has started has gone. It has got away from him. And it has to stop. Neither your people nor myself can sleep safe until there's a showdown. Tuck Munce and his bunch have started to steal from us both. They're working over the Long S and the Diamond B. There's no law in this country except as we make it and enforce it for ourselves. And this is the last straw. We've got to clean them up or be cleaned up ourselves. It's hell, but it can't be stopped. Not now. We'll win, though."

"We'll lose—you and I—no matter how it goes," she sighed.

"Will we?" Brock questioned. "Look. If I come through this alive, will you marry me, Lou, no matter how it goes? I love you. I don't have to tell you that. And you love me."

"You've known that a long time," she said, and her head drooped against his breast. "But I'm not—I don't know. Brock, I just couldn't marry you—not with my father and brothers against it. I'd feel like a renegade. I'd be one."

"And I am one, you sort of think," Brock said bitterly.

"No, no, you know I don't mean that," she cried. "It's different with us, that's all. You've never had affection and loyalty in your family, Brock, or you'd be fighting for the WP, right or wrong. That's the way I feel about us. If you and Dad and my brothers could shake hands and be friends, I'd be the happiest girl in Montana. But they can't forget what your father has done, what he still means to do. You're a Parsons to them. They like you, but you're still the enemy's son. They aren't tame men, Brock. They never forget us crying over Con when they brought his body home from Oxbow, nor Dave with a hole ripped in his side, nor the other boys who were killed simply because they happened to be riding for us. If I married you in the face of their opposition, they'd disown me. And one of them would kill you."

"You make it pretty strong," Brock said soberly. He stood silent for a second. Then he heard Clay call.

"We'd better move on," he suggested. "We're forgetting what we're up against right now."

Clay indeed was calling. They found him and Esther in the edge of the clearing that held cabin and corral.

"That gunner up there will probably take a crack at us," Clay said. "Let's see if we can get on a line that shuts him off."

They succeeded in working into a position where the cabin stood between them and that hidden rifleman. Then they shouted to Lin. One by one they crawled around the cabin end and scrambled through the window.

"Well, we are gathered together again, dearly beloved friends." Clay grew jocular. "We're in, even if we can't get out. So let's rustle somethin' to eat."

They pushed the body of the Guadalupe Kid outside to join his dead mates sprawled by the charred sticks of their breakfast fire, drawing a couple of shots from the cliff as they showed momentarily. Then Clay with a long stick hooked and drew in a grub box that sat there. There was a pail of water inside.

"We may have a fight on our hands, and we may not," Clay said as he munched a piece of salt pork. "Depends on how good a connection Tuck makes with his signals. Now, if that Sutherland man managed to find the Diamond B, them boys might turn up here pretty early. Short of our own crowd turning up, our only chance is to hold everybody off till dark an' then make a sneak for it. Far as the WP's concerned they can't get here before noon nohow, I don't reckon. We've fought fire all one night, rode all the next day an' last night. Suppose Lin stands watch for two hours while you an' me take a sleep, Brock? Then I'll spell him. You got to favor that crippled leg much as you can."

Brock nodded agreement. It was certain death to step outside the shelter of that timber patch in daylight. He was very tired. His leg burned as if a hot needle had been thrust deep into the flesh. Lin was fresher than either Clay or himself.

Clay stretched himself on a bunk. In two minutes he was fast asleep. Esther watched him for a while. Then her yellow head drooped to his outstretched arm, and she too slept.

Brock spread a blanket on the dirt floor. When he closed his eyes, weariness shut down on him like a fog. In that semiconscious state, he felt a small hand snuggle into his and a kiss pressed on his cheek. He fell asleep holding fast to those fingers.

It seemed to Brock that he had no more than closed his eyes before he was being shaken out of his slumber. Esther and Lou were peering out the door.

"I wouldn't 'a' disturbed you yet awhile," Clay said. "But look what's comin'."

Brock looked out. A group of horsemen were trotting up the canyon floor. The heaviness of sleep was still in his eyes. He reached for his carbine.

"Hey, don't get excited," Clay laughed. "That's cavalry. Good old, United States cavalry. For once luck has broken our way."

Chapter Twenty-Five

OVER THE HILLS AND FAR AWAY

THE BRIGHT MORNING SUN struck an army blue, on carbines, on the sword hilt at an officer's belt. In columns of fours, a detail of thirty troopers, they came jingling to the door, a string of pack mules bringing up the rear. A lieutenant with four days' growth of beard on his youthful face stared down at those bodies. He looked at the faces peering out that doorway. Brock cast an eye on the cliff where Slim Wayne lurked with his rifle.

"Lieutenant," he said without emerging, "we're darned glad to see you. But it isn't safe for us to come out. There's a cow thief with a rifle perched on the top of that bank."

The lieutenant edged his horse nearer.

"Ah," said he coolly. "And who might you be? And what has been going on here?"

Brock gave their names, related succinctly what had transpired during the last two days.

"Hm! Interesting! Decidedly," the officer drawled. "We were sort of scouting around for a party of Indians that were reported heading into the Bear Paws, from Belknap. You say there's a fellow up there trying to pot you. I don't imagine he'll undertake to pot the Fourteenth United States cavalry. Still—"

He ordered two men up on each side of the Bear Den. While they rode away he sat chatting as casually as if he had been at ease on a parade ground. In a few minutes the troopers appeared riding the rim on both sides.

"Was somebody up here, sir, but he's gone," one called down.

"I dare say it's all right for you to come out now," the lieutenant said courteously.

His eyes widened a trifle at sight of Lou and Esther. His campaign hat came off.

"If," said Brock, "you will see us out of this canyon to

our horses we'd be mighty obliged. The quicker we get out of here the better it will suit us."

They put Lou and Esther on the saddled WP horses left tied in the grove. Brock was hoisted up behind a trooper. Lin and Clay walked. In fifteen minutes they were astride their own mounts.

"You feel sure you can get safely home?" the lieutenant asked.

"I think so," Brock replied. "We were trapped in the Bear Den. But nobody is going to corner us now we're mounted and loose in the hills. Thanks just the same. Just for curiosity, how did you happen to wander in there?"

"We saw a lot of fresh branded cattle, and we followed hoof marks in to see if Indians had been killing stock. It's a cavalryman's business to poke into odd places when he's hunting the red brother.

"I'd be glad to escort you to the Sutherland ranch," he continued reflectively, "if you make a point of insisting on it. I'd be stretching my orders a lot to do that, though. I'm supposed to report at Fort Assiniboine tonight, and we have quite a march to do so."

Neither Brock nor Clay wanted a cavalry escort. Any place between the Bear Den and the southern foothills his men and the Starks might already have locked horns with the WP contingent under Pickles and Munce. Cavalry couldn't, and normally didn't interfere in civil clashes unless ordered to do so, or in obvious emergency. If there had to be a forthright scrap with WP, it was better, Brock thought, to let nature take its course. So he thanked the officer again and assured him that he could manage to cross the mountains safely.

They parted with that. The troop turned north toward their post. Brock, Clay, Lin Pickett, Esther, and Lou bore south. They were mounted and armed. They had solved a problem and struck one good blow against a band of thieves. The world seemed brighter with the Bear Den a gash in the hills far behind them. Only the three men looking back once into the lower valley as they climbed saw those grazing cattle and frowned.

"We should meet the boys coming up any time," Brock hazarded. "Unless that Block S man failed to find the Diamond B in the dark."

"More likely to meet Tuck and Pickles with their crowd first," Clay said, "if their smoke signals worked. It'll pay us to be darned careful what riders we let see us until we know who they are. When I think of it, it's a miracle that we got into that place and got away with it as well as we did."

"I heard them talking," Esther said. "They didn't think anybody could pick up that trail and follow it before late today. What they really meant to do was to make a grandstand play by sending word to Brock first that a bunch of Indians had us up here in a canyon. Then they were going to lead you in there and surprise you. None of you would have got out of there alive. They thought they were dead safe with one man posted on the cliff last night.

"They would have been, too, if we hadn't known all about that hangout," Brock remarked. "And the only reason Slim didn't spot us last night was that we moved like ghosts. We must have been pretty close to him when we looked into the Bear Den from the top. We ought to be lucky once in a while."

"If our two outfits start up here, and Pickles is on the way with his bunch," Lin Pickett declared, "there might be a pretty hefty scrap come off most anywhere on these slopes. Because that many riders could hardly cross this country without sightin' each other. An' they'd go for each other on sight, now."

"Like as not," Clay agreed. "If there is a ruckus we'll hear it. I hope we do see somethin' or somebody."

Clay's hope gained fulfillment when they dipped over the highest divide and could look away to the southward flats and the far silver sheen of the Missouri river. The rocky crest of Tiger Butte loomed on Big Birch. Westward, Shadow Butte towered over the Sutherland ranch. They rode with eyes and ears alert, keeping to cover wherever possible, seeing no living thing except two deer that bounded away through the pines. They had ridden over the divide and were dipping down through sparse timber when they pulled up to look over an open grassy stretch which they must cross if they held a straight line. And while they looked, five hundred yards below, a group of riders loped into view, skirting the edge of the forest.

Brock carried a pair of field glasses in one saddle pocket. One searching look and he lowered them.

"That's Tuck and Pickles with about twenty men," he said. "You called the turn, Esther. We're lucky to be out of the Bear Den."

"Lemme see." Clay reached for the glasses. With his naked eye Brock followed the horsemen. Presently he saw them stop.

Clay exclaimed, "Now the plot thickens. Slim Wayne—I reckon it must be Slim—just rode out of the brush an' met 'em. They're holdin' a powwow. Man, oh, man, Tuck'll froth when Slim tells him the cavalry wandered in an' escorted us out! Because I'll bet Slim watched, even if he was too scared to shoot any more. I see Tuck wavin' his hands. Now I wonder what they'll do?"

"Turn back, most likely, an' give it up for a bad job," Lin Pickett drawled. "Or start huntin' round to try an' pick up our trail. They might figure on spreadin' out an' cuttin' us off."

The WP men sat in a compact bunch for ten minutes. Then they turned south, doubled back on their tracks into the timber out of which they had come.

"I wish 'em one piece of luck," Clay said. "That they run slap into our boys comin' up an' that our fellows see 'em first. If we didn't have you girls I'd vote to Injun on their trail right now an' give 'em somethin' to speed 'em on their way."

"Don't be foolish, Clay," Lou reproved. "Three men against twenty."

"There's luck in odd numbers," Clay muttered. "Three men agin twenty skunks. Even enough."

Brock looked over that open slope. "We had better make a detour," he said. "It's not wise to show ourselves. If they spread out ahead of us we may have a time of it yet. Let's follow around in the edge of these pines."

They turned slightly westward, bearing more toward upper Eagle Creek, riding through lodgepole pine in endless ranks. Here and there the open forest was patched with groves of thickset scrubby Christmas trees, young jack pine with branchy trunks. Turning one of these thickets they came suddenly face to face with two men leading a packhorse. A man whom Brock recognized as Steve Jessop, one of the oldest trusted riders from the Nueces. The other was W. J. Parsons himself.

Brock, Clay, and Lin had fingers crooked over carbine triggers. But they had no occasion to shoot. Parsons and his man made no hostile move. They sat their horses, gloved hands resting on their saddle horns, staring at the three men and two women. Bill Parsons's brows were knitted.

"Oho," Clay said. "Here's the old he-coon himself."

"Let me do the talking." Brock gestured for silence. Clay shrugged his shoulders.

His father didn't speak. He stared from Brock to Clay, then at the two girls. Esther Munce he knew. Perhaps he wondered what those women did there, mounted on WP horses, escorted by armed men. Brock had to struggle for a second with flaming, bitter phrases that rose to his tongue. He wanted to talk calmly, to state unpleasant things with a dispassionate finality. And his father had the first word.

"You're a Stark, aren't you?" he addressed Clay.

"I am," Clay replied. "You got any idea you want to do anythin' about that?"

"No," Bill Parsons shook his head. "I'm attendin' to my own business right now. You ain't my business."

"By God, you're my business, though!" Clay's temper flared. "You got a gun, Parsons. Go for it. You'll get an even break, which is more than you've ever given any Stark."

"Clay!" Lou shoved her horse in between them. "Please!"

"Will you let me talk a minute before you go any further, Clay?" Brock pleaded. "Haven't we done enough kill-ing for today?"

"There's always room for one new face in hell," Clay said unpleasantly. "I have declared myself. It's up to him, if he has the nerve to do his own fightin' instead of hirin' it done by a lot of riffraff. Go ahead an' talk."

"Tuck Munce has been attending to your business up here, too, I suppose," Brock addressed his father. He pinched all feeling out of his voice. "Is it part of your business to burn ranches, to kidnap women, to steal cattle?"

His father looked at him steadily.

"I don't know what you mean," he said at last.

"Then I'll tell you, so you will know," Brock continued. "I won't go back to the beginning. You know where that began and why. Polk Munce started that Trinity trouble and you backed him up, carried it on where he left off. You won all along the line there. Any decent man would have been satisfied to let it go at that. But you wanted the earth. You wanted to make every man who opposed you crawl, even me who happened to be your son. Out of sheer ugliness you put me in a position where I had to kill or be killed. You damned me for a renegade because I tried to act like a man. You've vented the same unreasonable grudge on me that you have on the Starks. You made your-self hated and feared and eventually despised in the South-west wherever fair-minded men happened to talk about the WP. I'm not proud of being a Parsons any more, even if you are the biggest cattle owner in the country. I had never been ashamed of anything in my life until I had to face people who had been good to me, including a woman I'd learned to love, and tell them I was your son."

Brock slid sideways in his saddle to ease the pain in his wounded leg. The cold bite of anger and contempt crept into those slowly spoken words. And the red welled up into his father's face; a curious frosty gleam came into those hard, watchful old eyes. Yet he didn't utter a word, only stared at Brock as Baalam must have stared in won-der at the ass when it reproved him.

"So you shoved in here," Brock continued, "to work

your damned spite on people who had only tried to protect
themselves against your aggression, who had left Texas to
avoid a bloody clash with you. You warned me to stand
aside or you'd wipe me off the map, too. You surrounded
yourself with cutthroats—and you've got down to their
level at last. Because you *are* the WP. You are responsible
for what your hired men do. You can't dodge that. Your
Tuck Munces and your Dill Pickles and all the rest of the
assorted scum they've gathered to do your dirty work.
They're your men. And with the scope you've given Munce
and Pickles they've set out to do something for themselves.

"This—in case you don't know—is part of what they've
done: Burned me out in the spring and killed one of my
men. Built a hangout away back here in the mountains
and got ready to rustle stock on a large scale. They mur-
dered one of your own men who tried to warn me. Three
days ago Pickles surrounded my ranch and attacked it, to
hold us there while Tuck Munce and his bunch, masquer-
ading in eagle feathers and paint, as Indians, took a crack
at the Stark ranch in the night. Burned their stables and
hay, destroyed horses and harness and riding-gear, started
a prairie fire that might have swept all the south side of the
Bear Paws.

"During the last few days the same gang, Tuck Munce,
the Guadalupe Kid, Ev Sprott, Hip Gross, Brazos Thomp-
son, and Slim Wayne have been busy with their running-
irons up here in a place they call the Bear Den, where they
have a cabin and corral. They have rustled nearly a thousand head of cattle from the Starks and myself. Worked
the Long S into a Bar Eight Bar. Worked the Diamond B
into something that looks like a lattice with a blotch in
the center to cover the B.

"Yesterday this Munce crowd caught these two girls out
riding on Eagle Creek above Sutherland's. They kidnaped
them. Took them up into the Bear Den and shut them in
a stinking hole to be used as bait to draw me, my men,
and the Starks into that box canyon where they could
butcher us safely.

"But for once they lost out. Clay, Lin, and myself, got

in on them early this morning. And there is only Tuck and Slim Wayne left out of that assortment. Pickles and the rest didn't get up here soon enough. Were you riding up to help the good work along?"

"I told you," Bill Parsons said harshly, "that I was attendin' to my own legitimate business up here."

"Your legitimate business," Brock said in sudden fury. "Your business of backing up a bunch of murderers, fire bugs, common thieves. You must feel proud of yourself."

"I don't know as I care to discuss that with you," his father said slowly. "You said your say?"

"All but one thing." Brock measured his words. "You have declared yourself twice to me in the last six months. You warned me to stand aside. I have stood aside. Not one of us, myself, my men, has made a hostile move against you. Now, when it has come to a showdown, I don't stand aside any longer. You and your crowd have brought a dirty war to us. We'll bring it to you on Chip Creek. That's all."

"An' we'll bring it to you likewise, Parsons," Clay put in calmly. "Old man Stark and his seven sons. We'll clean you like we should have cleaned you in Oxbow when you sent out your lawyer with the white flag. There's no courts and legal twists for you to fall back on here. Nothin' but Colonel Colt an' the Winchester jury. There won't be no appeals from their decision. You've come lookin' for it. You'll get it!"

"From the Nueces to the Bear Paws," Bill Parsons said, "the WP has held its own agin all comers. I have fought you Starks. I'll fight you again. I've had a lot of hard things said about me an' my outfit, but no man has ever said I stole from him. I'll make you eat that."

"Your men have," Brock flashed back. "WP men. Men that you pay double wages to carry out your plans. You're responsible. I'm holding you responsible."

"All right," Parsons said. "We'll let it go at that."

He shook up his horse. He and Steve Jessop and the pack animal passed, vanished through the pines, pointing north.

"I wonder," Clay wrinkled his dark brows, "what W.J.

himself is doin' up here in the mountains by himself, when
his riders are all out on a limb? You'd think—I wonder if
he knows where he's at?"

"He thinks he does," Brock said sadly. "That's the devil
of being old and arrogant. But he doesn't really know. He
can't comprehend anybody's point of view but his own.
I don't suppose he can think of anything right now but
that a worthless son has insulted and abused him, and
thrown in with his enemies. Everybody that stands with
him is all right. Everybody who opposes him is all wrong."

"Did you mean that about jumpin' the WP on their
own ground?" Clay asked. "Or were you just throwin' the
harpoon into him to see how he'd take it?"

"It was a promise," Brock answered, "to him and to myself. And a warning. I don't want to fight *him*. I've got to
fight his crowd."

Clay bared white teeth in a grim smile. "Well, we made
a good start this mornin'," he drawled.

They moved on. A long bare slope slanted down from
the crest of the ridge they were on. Up that grassy escarp-
ment five Diamond B men and five Starks loomed under
Brock's field glass. They moved out of timber and waved
to attract them.

Brock watched Lou throw her arms about her father's
neck, kiss each of her brothers in turn. Talk bubbled all
around him. He sat his horse silent, staring south. Even
when he won he lost. That was what saddened him.

Clay caught that weary expression on Brock's face. "Let's
get on down to the Sutherland ranch," he said. "We're
dog-tired—dead for sleep, us three. An' Brock's got a hole
in his leg. We'll make medicine after we've had a rest."

Chapter Twenty-Six

No Armistice

BILL SPEAR'S HAND ON HIS SHOULDER wakened Brock to bright day. He lifted himself on elbow in a room totally unfamiliar until he remembered that he had gone to bed at dusk in Adam Sutherland's house. Then he snapped back to the present.

He heaved himself over the side of the bed. He had slept thirteen hours. His wounded leg gave him a twinge when he put his weight on it. But it carried him. He could walk. And if he could walk, he could ride. He sat down again, looked at Bill Spear expectantly. He knew why Bill was there. Spear and Hardy had gone scouting before daylight that morning, by his orders.

"We looked her over at daybreak," Spear reported. "They're all at the Chip Creek ranch. Barrin' them you-all left for keeps in the Bear Den. I don't know but it was a mistake for us to have passed 'em up yesterday when we had 'em in the hills. But we wanted to get you before they did."

"No, it will be better to go at them on their own ground," Brock declared. "Go and tell old Gene Stark I'd like to see him in here, will you, Bill?"

Brock nursed his chin in his hands and pondered while he waited for Eugene Stark. If his father would just occupy himself in the mountains for another twenty-four hours. Brock banked on Bill Parsons looking into the Bear Den, finding those cattle with brands worked over, satisfying himself that his man Friday had really turned thief. Brock knew his father. He knew that Parsons, for all his contumacy, hated a crook. Hard as iron, stubbornly asserting his own rights and privileges, an arrogant, power-drunk man, nevertheless as became a man of property, he respected property rights, held them as something sacred. And a rustler, a brand worker, was always despicable to a cattle owner. If a brand wasn't sacrosanct, the bottom fell out of everything on the range. Brock knew that his father would find it hard to believe any WP range boss would turn cow thief. Fighting, killing, destruction, a conflict between two outfits whose interests clashed—Parsons could grasp that. He couldn't grasp the psychology of a thief, nor the passion of love, nor the tenderness of pity. He could fathom only cruder moods and impulses and desires.

Brock had tried to touch his father's pride in himself and the WP, to make him feel shame that his own men had tricked him, used his strength for their own ends. He expected that Bill Parsons would comb those hills in search of those cattle, that he would hunt until he found that box canyon hangout, if for no purpose than to prove his son a liar, or at least mistaken. Brock banked on that search keeping his father high in the hills—while he swooped down on the Chip Creek crowd like an avenging fury, and settled once and for all with Tuck Munce and Pickles and those who trained with that pair. He didn't want his father in the vortex of that fight. It would be a fight. Brock had no illusions about the caliber of his enemies.

He and Steve Jessop would have to go straight there, make close connections, he thought to himself. *They would have to ride all night to get to Chip Creek before we will. And I don't think they'd do that. Anyway, the horns and tail have to go with the hide.*

He was getting on his clothes when Eugene Stark came in. Brock could hear women's voices, the burble of children out in the other rooms. The Long S was abandoned for the time being. The Stark women had come up to Sutherland's escorted by Dave and young Gene while the rest rode for the Bear Den, when they got word. The Block S was the only safe place for them. The WP couldn't molest Adam Sutherland's home, a neutral cattleman's stronghold, without rousing every cow outfit in Northern Montana against them. They wouldn't dare. That left every Stark man free. They had touched on that the evening before, when Brock was too weary to think straight.

Eight Starks, mounted, armed, determined. Leaving Zack the cook and Dave Hull to hold down the Diamond B would make eight in his group. Sixteen competent men, out to lay the ghost of terror that had haunted them so long.

But Brock had a feeling that he wanted only his own hands to strike that blow if he could manage it. That was why he wished to talk to Eugene Stark now.

"Last night," he began, "I had nothing much to say because I didn't know if I'd be able to get on a horse this morning. But I'm all right, barring a little soreness. I'm going to take my crew and be on my way."

"Where?" Eugene Stark asked bluntly.

"To the WP."

"We'll go with you," old Gene said.

"I'd rather you didn't," Brock demurred. "I would rather you and your sons stayed out of this, for the present, anyway."

"Why should we stay out?" old Gene grumbled. "It's our fight as much as yours. They have give us all we can stand. They've stole our cattle. God only knows what woulda happened to them girls if you three boys hadn't been right on their heels. No, we can't stay out. We won't. It ain't that I hanker to throw away lives, but none of us is safe any more, nowhere, day or night. Not while that outfit's on this range."

"True enough," Brock admitted. "Just the same I want you to lay off for twenty-four hours. Stay here and get properly organized. Then come to the Diamond B. I want to try one move against the WP. If it fails, then you can go as far as you like and I'll back any sort of play you want to make."

"You can't do nothin' with that crowd," the old man declared angrily, "only kill 'em or run 'em outa the country. There ain't no law to call in. It's a case of usin' our teeth. You're goin' to tackle them, win, lose, or draw."

"I have to," Brock admitted. "With Tuck Munce and Pickles running that show, I've got a sentence of death hanging over me all the time. I have to fight the WP. Yes.

What else can I do?"

"Then let's go together an' do the job right," Stark said. "At that we're outnumbered two to one. Don't make no mistake, Brock. That crowd's mostly Texans. They'll fight."

"There are two good reasons why I don't want you and your sons in this fight," Brock said reluctantly, in a last effort. "You know where I stand with you all, over Lou. You know how she feels about those Trinity and Oxbow killings. I'm selfish. What will it be like between us after we have fought that to a finish on Chip Creek? Some of us will get it. More Parsons spilling of Stark blood. If two or three of your sons go under, and I come out alive, I'll still be Bill Parsons's son, and you'll have more against me than ever. Even if you didn't, she would. That's one thing. There's another. I have already killed one of Esther Munce's brothers. I mean to shoot or hang the other one if can get hold of him. But Clay will strain himself to get to Tuck first because of that kidnaping. I don't want Clay to go back to his girl with her brother's blood on his hands, much as Tuck deserves it. They're both my friends. I don't want them faced with the same thing I'm faced with."

Old Gene shook his head. His eyes narrowed.

"Leave the sweethearts out of this," he growled. "I'll say this: it's white of you to think of them things. I know what's hurtin' you. I kin see your position. You're in a hard fix. But you couldn't keep the Stark boys out of this thing now, Brock. I couldn't hold them boys if I tried. Clay has talked to them. An' your own men are talkin' it over with them. You can't take this job on your own shoulders. They wouldn't let you. I don't like it. You don't like it. But it's a job that's got to be done, an' done by us two outfits, playin' the only kind of hand we hold."

"All right," Brock capitulated. "Let's be at it, then. We have plenty of ammunition. Our horses are fresh. We can be at the WP in two hours."

"The women folks are puttin' on breakfast," old Gene said. "We'll eat an' ride."

That breakfast was a silent meal. The Stark women and

Esther Munce carried hot cakes and fried beef and coffee in to a long table lined with men. The autumn sun came slanting through a window, making a golden shaft full of whirling specks. Just as men were, Brock said to himself, whirling specks blown this way and that by forces they could seldom reckon with. He kept his eyes on his plate. He tried to avoid looking at Lou Stark. He could see the sober, strained faces of Dave's wife and Ed's. Wally's childless woman didn't even come into the dining-room. Once through the kitchen door Brock saw her standing by a table, her eyes red with weeping. They had come two thousand miles to find peace and security. And their men were going out on the same red quest that had brought sorrow to them on the Trinity. Tears and anguish. Brock understood. A man could face his enemies with anger or exultation, according to his nature. A woman could only sit and wait, tortured by her fears.

He roused himself out of this somber reflection. Chairs scraped back. Men trooped to the stable. In ten minutes the yard was full of saddled horses, riders trying their cinches, looking over their guns, sitting at ease in their saddles smoking a cigarette. Brock swung stiffly up onto his own horse. That gouge in the flesh of his leg bothered him, like a steady gnawing toothache. He looked over the riders. They were all there but Clay. He stood on the porch steps talking to Esther Munce. Lou was in the doorway behind them. Clay stooped and kissed Esther. She clung to him a minute, arms about his neck, as if to hold him fast, her yellow head tilted back.

Then Clay flung into his saddle and joined them. Brock didn't look again. He couldn't. If he did he would only carry away an added pang. So he looked straight ahead while they pointed south at a lope, little spurts of dust kicking out from under those thudding hoofs. Clay swung in beside Brock.

"You're a haughty, stiff-necked devil," he said in an undertone. "You never even spoke to Lou this mornin'. What's the matter with you?"

"There just didn't seem to be anything to say," Brock

muttered.

"There's always somethin' to be said in this kind of an argument," Clay retorted. "Although you an' me appear to be on the wrong side of it so far. If our minds weren't on women we'd be in better trim for this job."

"Our minds will be on the job after the first gun pops," Brock said grimly. "What does Esther think about this?"

"She's game as they make 'em," Clay answered proudly. "She said she didn't care what I did or what happened so long as I come back safe."

"You're lucky," Brock answered that. "You can imagine where I'll stand if one or two of old man Stark's sons gets their light put out in this mess."

Clay looked at him soberly.

"I know," he said. "It ain't hardly fair for you'n Lou to be penalized thataway, is it? But it don't seem like it can be helped. Only you don't need to worry about the Stark boys. It's the other feller's light that'll get snuffed."

While they were still at some distance from the WP Brock said to Eugene Stark, "We will ride along the bench to the top of the west bank above that ranch and size up the situation. If they are on the lookout, probably they'll cut loose at sight of us. If they stay under cover, we simply smoke them out with as little risk to ourselves as possible."

"We can tell better how to go at it when we git there," old Gene said. "If you're goin' to kill a snake, no use givin' him a chance to bite you."

Within a mile of the Chip Creek ranch they edged up to the top of that low valley wall. There were four pairs of field glasses in that company.

"I don't see any signs of life at all." Brock lowered his.

"Not a move anywhere," Bill Spear confirmed. "That's funny."

They watched for a while. Nothing stirred. Not a man moved about that place. No smoke issued from chimney or jutting pipe. The corrals were empty. Stable doors swung wide. Horses grazed in a pole pasture along the creek. But not a single saddled beast stood about the yard. Brock looked off toward his own ranch. Chase Hill lay over a grassy ridge. Perhaps the WP was raiding there again, with only the cook and Dave Hull to stand them off.

"It looks deserted but that may be just bait," he said. "Let's get along. We'll ride in plain sight and see what they do."

Scattered out in loose formation, they trotted along the bank until they were abreast of the ranch buildings. There they drew up, sixteen riders abreast, within short rifle-shot of a place that seemed utterly abandoned.

"Ho, there, below!" Brock shouted. "Show yourselves."

No answer for a few seconds. Then a man stepped out on the low porch, came down the two steps to the ground. He looked up at that line of riders standing sharp against the morning sky. Brock put the field glasses on him.

"Why, that's Steve Jessop," he exclaimed.

The man waved his arms.

"Sit here, all of you, and cover me," Brock said. "I'm going down. Something's happened."

"Alone? Not by a damn sight," his riders swore. "We'll all go."

"As you like. But I'm going." Brock spurred his horse down the bank. He had a curious certainty that no bullets would come singing to meet him, that the WP was as deserted as it seemed. Yet why? Steve Jessop was there. And Jessop had been with Bill Parsons high in the Bear Paws. Brock took the flat on the run, and there was a thunder of hoofs beside him, every man with carbine ready and eyes roaming. They came like a troop of charging cavalry up to where Jessop stood.

"Where is all the WP crowd?" Brock demanded.

Jessop pointed south.

"Gone. Vamoosed. Lit out an hour ago," he grunted. "I'm gosh darn glad you come, Brock. There's been hell to pay. Come on inside."

Brock followed him. Clay pressed at his heels. Behind Clay came Lin Pickett and Eugene Stark.

The log room was like a barn for size, bare of comfort or decoration. A row of bunks lined it and one end held a rough stone fireplace. Through a door opening into another room Brock's questing eyes saw a long table with the litter of a meal, dirty tin plates, cups partly filled with coffee, as if those who breakfasted had risen in haste.

But that was only a fleeting glimpse. The bunkroom itself arrested and held his gaze. His father was propped on a bunk, pillows and blankets piled at his back. Stripped to the waist. One powerful hand held a wet towel clamped against his broad, hairy chest. He stared at his son.

Far down the long room a man sprawled face to the floor, silver spurs on his heels, both arms flung wide, a pearl-handled six-shooter just beyond the tips of those slack fingers. Ten feet beyond him another lay flat on his back, glazed eyes turned to the ridge log. That was Tuck Munce, beyond any man's vengeance. Brock heard the sharp intake of Clay's breath. He walked over to his father. Bill Parson's gaze went past his son to rest on Eugene Stark.

"Did you-all ride down to clean up the WP?" he said. "You're too late. She's done cleaned. I cleaned her myself."

"It was time," Eugene Stark said slowly.

"Yes," Parsons agreed. "It was time."

His eyes, pain-stricken, came back to his son.

"Me'n Steve," he murmured, "we found that place an' them thieves you killed. We found them stolen cattle. I've played my own hand all my life but I never played that kind of hand. No man that ever worked for me ever did it. I didn't believe men I trusted would turn thief. But they did. They was double-crossin' me, both Munce an' Pickles. I suspected that before I made that trip into the mountains. I'd talked to a couple of men in the outfit that was gittin' scared the way things was goin'. But I had to see for myself. I saw, all right."

He stopped to get his breath.

"So we rode all night to get back here, me'n Steve. When I jumped them about it they went after me. I got 'em both."

"You're hit yourself," Brock said. "Can I do anything for you?"

"Not much," Parsons said. "I got two slugs through me,

an' I'm a pretty sick man. But I aim to live a while yet. Although, if I blinked out," he addressed Eugene Stark, "I
expect it would please you a heap."

"You are welcome to live as long as you like, far as I'm,
personally concerned. All I ever wanted of you," Stark
said, "was to leave us alone."

"Well, you win," Parsons muttered. "The WP won't
trouble you no more. Not because you whipped me. I
whipped myself. I didn't know a man could do that. But
I ain't too old to learn. Now, remove yourselves. I want to
talk to Brock."

They clanked out. Brock stood looking at his father.
That problem had found its own solution. A wave of relief, almost of gratitude, swept over him.

"You can put me in a wagon with a lot of beddin' piled
in the bottom, an' Steve can drive me to Fort Benton,"
Bill Parsons said. "I got a hundred thousand cattle. I'm
worth a couple of million. I ain't goin' to die here like a
cow in a bog."

But Bill Parsons had miscalculated his powers once
more for the last time in his career. Brock examined the
wounds in his chest and marveled that even so rugged a
man could still live and speak and plan.

He called Steve Jessop and told him what to do. He felt
in his soul that it was useless. But it was a gesture to be
made. Then he came back to that bunk. His father lay very
still, sweat drops gathering on his face, his heavy-lidded
eyes shut, all the color washed out of his florid face. He
opened his eyes after a time, like a man tired, sleep-heavy.

"Your mother was right," he whispered huskily. "She
said to me last winter before she died that you were a better man than me. Why does a man see things different
when he's dyin', Brock? I ain't particular sorry for nothin'.
Only some things seem plumb foolish, right now. Why
couldn't I see 'em that way before?"

"You're not dying," Brock encouraged.

"I dunno. I feel mighty queer."

Through the doorway Brock could hear a jumble of
voices. He could see some of his men, some of the Starks,

squatting on their boot heels beside their horses, chatting, talking. On ground that might well at that moment have been wet with their blood—except for a sudden *volte-face* by the very man who had woven the tangle that brought them armed and angry to that place. Curious, Brock thought. A man wrought evil in one mood, under one driving impulse, and in another mood and impulse risked his life to undo what he had striven to bring about.

"Brock." Eugene Stark appeared in the doorway. "That wagon's ready."

Bill Parsons turned his head. He looked up at Brock. He struggled to speak. And that was the end of him.

Old Gene Stark walked over to the bed. He didn't say anything. They stood together, the son of the dead man and the dead man's enemy, looking at what all men come to at last. And then they went out into the sunlight.

Brock had been walking the one planked street of Fort Benton, to stretch his leg. It was only a little tender now. He lay on his bed in a pleasant room that overlooked the river from the south side of the Grand Union. He had been there two weeks. It was, he reflected, about time he went home. And lying there passively, not thinking too hard, because he had thought so hard and so long to a fruitless end that his brain was weary, he fell asleep.

He looked up at a touch that brought him out of that slumber to find himself staring into Louise Stark's gray eyes, her hand resting on his shoulder. It was incredible to Brock, unreal. He couldn't believe his eyes. Yet the sun shone through his window into a room familiar with two weeks' occupancy. He knew he was awake even though he must be dreaming. But he couldn't quite accept her as a reality until his hand closed on those soft, warm fingers. He didn't speak. Nor did she. Not until he had caught her in the bend of his arm with a curious fierce tenderness and kissed her. Then he said:

"How on earth did you get here?"

Louise laughed.

"Esther and Clay came up here to be married. I came

along to be bridesmaid. We thought you might like to be best man. We knew you were in Fort Benton. When we registered I looked and found you were staying here at the Grand Union, too. I walked along the hall and there was your room door open and you snoozing on the bed. So I came right in."

Brock thrust her off at arm's length and gave her a little shake.

"You wouldn't come back to me so I came to you," Louise smiled.

"For keeps?" Brock demanded. "What about the family feud?"

"Well," she chuckled, "not long ago when Esther and Clay were talking about getting married Esther wondered if the Stark family would have it. And Clay got on the war-path. He said, 'Hell, you're marryin' me, not the family!' So—"

"You're a darling," Brock murmured. "Let's go and find Clay and Esther and tell them this wedding is going to be double."